MOON SUGAR

Also by Angela Meyer

Novels

A Superior Spectre

Shorter works

Joan Smokes

Captives

MOON SUGAR

ANGELA MEYER

transit lounge

MELBOURNE, AUSTRALIA
www.transitlounge.com.au

Copyright © 2022 Angela Meyer
First published 2022
Transit Lounge Publishing

Cover design: Josh Durham/Design by Committee
Author photo: Manda Ford
Typeset in Adobe Garamond Pro by Cannon Typesetting
Printed in Australia by McPherson's Printing Group

A cataloguing entry is available from the
National Library of Australia
ISBN: 978-0-6484140-5-6

The paper this book is printed on is certified against the
Forest Stewardship Council® Standards. McPherson's Printing Group
holds FSC® chain of custody certification SA-COC-005379. FSC®
promotes environmentally responsible, socially beneficial
and economically viable management of the world's forests

And so, if things are splinters
Of the knowledge of the universe,
Let me be my own slivers,
Imprecise and diverse.
Fernando Pessoa

L IGHT POURS INTO the dusty shed, where the astronaut sits among his collection of irradiated samples. Amid blood-orange flakes and light-mustard wafers, he watches his daughter, dappled with tree shade, search out fairy hovels in the garden. An adventurer like him, but delicate in her pastel-blue pinafore dress, dark hair gleaming in sunlight. A cloud takes over the sky, the light leaches away, and his gut twists with grief.

His daughter will grow up without a mother.

He fingers some of the lichen, which arranges itself in circles – mini amphitheatres of saffron. He snaps off a piece of it and lifts it to his mouth. He grinds it down between his teeth, remembering his time floating out in the blackness of space.

He and Rick played cards and chess in between daily tasks on the SS *Avalon*, waiting for the appropriate time to reel the samples into the lock. Being astrobiologists and biophysicists did not stop them from being monkeys. Their rivalry had begun on the ground. In training, they competed to be the strongest, and in the lab, the most innovative.

No doubt it was partly fuelled by the fact they were both attracted to Sally, from ground control. Careful, petite Sally, with that surprisingly deep and confident voice over the radio. And Rick knew who Sally preferred.

Why did he let Rick push him, though? Playing competitive games for so long that they failed to complete their checks. Just on that one day, but it was enough. By the time Houston let them know there were higher than normal radiation levels inside the ship, they had already been exposed to filaments. The samples were sealed back off. On the ground, it was deemed they were safe enough.

A year passed before the surprising effects began to show; he hid them from everyone but Sally, who was by then his wife. It was another year after that before NASA approved his phony research and granted him some of the samples so he could try to find out what had happened.

He wonders if it would have been better to end up like Rick. Last he heard he lived in London, was still single, teaching at Oxford but spending his summers in Europe – exploring, partying. People got a slight glow in their eyes when they talked about him.

The astronaut and Sally bought a house in upstate New York. Time for his quiet research – both legitimate and clandestine. And his daughter. His precious daughter.

He watches her. Space had been nothing compared to the expanse of loss, of the cold knowledge inside him now that his wife is gone.

The lichen at least helped him understand the way Sally, he, his daughter, even Rick were all connected and continuing: atoms and gases, infinite universes opening out from each moment. And yet, he still has to cope with being here, now, without her corporeal form.

He doesn't know if Rick has experienced what he has. What he still experiences, because of the lichen. When the effects first came on, he had just married Sally and the thought of Rick still gave him a bad taste in his mouth. So he decided not to contact him to check. If Rick *is* like him, though, he can understand a bit more the cult-like way people speak about him. Rick would be stupid to make it obvious, though.

Perhaps he should still get in touch.

No, it's Rick who should have reached out, offered his condolences over Sally's death. Fuck him.

The sun peeps out again, and the tall grasses shimmer in a light breeze. His daughter turns and sees him through the window. He smiles, and she waves enthusiastically. She is sweet and beaming with life. He will do anything and everything for her. He will share the secret, but only bit by bit, as she matures and is able to understand why it has to be kept under wraps. Maybe he will begin now. He will go out to the yard and show her a little magic trick.

Now

THREE DAYS. IT'S BEEN three whole days since Mila heard
from Josh. She is training a client, Bob, in the park. Bob
finds the outdoors helpful – the fresh air, the sunlight.
Many clients have been this way in the past year, after so much
time spent indoors. It's winter in Melbourne, and he de-layers with
each sprint back and forth. Mila has not slept well; her stomach
churns and she itches to check her phone again. When it buzzes
in her pocket, adrenaline floods her. She pulls it out to check.
Just another client.

Bob runs past her, puffing, and gives her a pointed look. 'How
many have I done now?'

'Just do one more,' Mila says, forcing an encouraging smile.
She wants him to do ten, fifteen more. She wants his lungs
to scream.

She aches to look at the photos of Josh on her phone. That
smile – cheeky-intelligent – kind and electrifying blue eyes, and
dark hair falling just so across his forehead. That thrill through her
whole body whenever he gave her a seductive look. A look that
made her think: So, this is how men have always felt. And not
just looking at a photograph of a girlfriend, but walking around
in the world. That advertisement, that promo shot of an actress,

the pictures of women you know on Instagram: all looking at you like that. On offer.

Mila took this offer. And took. But has now been cut from the supply. Though it had been confusing, lately, trying to continue to objectify him, since her feelings and their friendship had developed.

The feelings are a betrayal, something that seems to belong to the old Mila.

She wants. She wants a message. She worries. What if he's hurt? In hospital?

'Okay, good one, Bob, bring it in,' she says to her sweating client. He fist-bumps her before doubling over, hands on knees. 'Come on, chin up. We still have some ab work to do.' He groans. She rolls out a mat for him, and he gets to work on the abs and obliques.

Josh had been developing feelings for her, too, hadn't he? He'd been more affectionate. They'd held hands, that last time, after sex. Just slotted them together. And they went through that whole strange experiment together, as mates rather than client and provider.

She'd fantasised about going on his trip to Europe with him, going to galleries and art deco bars. Looking into his blue eyes. Gently pushing aside that strand of hair.

Everyone craved it, after all that time just surviving. Adventure, touch.

This ache is overtaking her, pushing out from her core, swelling to her skin, making each breath laboured.

His phone must have died, like completely broken. And then maybe he went to have a few drinks, thinking: I'll fix it in the morning. And then he took a pill and stayed out all night and is still recovering. Maybe he is with someone. She never asked him whether he'd be continuing to finance his trip through sex work, by sugar-babying over there. She only once asked if he had other clients, but it came out all wheedling and she hated herself as it did, so she immediately took the question back: Never mind. You don't have to tell me.

She absently tells Bob to go into a plank: 'One minute, I know you can do it.' She slides her phone out of her pocket again, goes to Josh's Facebook profile. There's a new message from a friend on there.

Can't believe it. Will miss you mate x

What? She scrolls down.

Messages.

Many messages.

'I'm …' she manages to say to Bob. There's pressure behind her eyes. Something is happening to her face at the same time, a rubbering. *I have to go* is what she wants to say, but she is down on the grass now – Bob's red face and slack mouth above her.

'I'll call an ambulance.'

'No!' she manages to say. 'I just … got some bad news.'

His thick hand is on her wrist, clammy. 'Can I do anything?'

'No.'

'Can I drive you home?'

'No. I'll … Just leave me here.'

'I won't leave you.'

'Leave me,' she says in a kind of growl.

'Okay, okay. I guess we all deal with things differently.' He gets up and gathers his sports bag, then walks across the park towards his car, giving wobbly looks back at her.

Mila sits and scrolls.

We may never understand why but we hope you are at peace xxx

Suicide? No. He would never.

She flips to the news. There it is:

Young Australian man missing, presumed drowned in Berlin.

A photo of Josh. She reads the details, eyes blurring, stomach heaving. He had taken off his shoes and clothes, and emailed a note to his family, and gone into the Spree. She thinks of his parents. His sisters. His friends. His housemate. Herself.

Herself.

The sky has turned sunset pink.

She stands, unsteadily, and looks towards her car on the other side of the park. The distance is vast.

As she walks, she can't imagine what she will do next. Right now, but also tomorrow, the next day. How can she work? How can she put food in her mouth? How can she make sounds from her throat?

No one knew about them, so who can she talk to about this? The only person she'd begun opening up to was him. Was Josh. The secrecy of their relationship allowed a greater unburdening, for her. She hasn't even told her best friend, Kate.

She gets in her silver 2008 Mazda 6 and begins shaking, juddering. She has to wait for it to pass. The sky continues to darken. When the shaking calms, she starts the ignition. She is thankful she doesn't live too far from the park.

She makes it home, to her small southside apartment, and she crawls into bed and sobs, achingly, until she passes out.

It is still dark when Mila wakes. A dream of churning river water sits behind her eyelids. She flips on the lamp and reaches for her laptop. She minimises a browser tab on alarming amounts of methane being released from permafrost and puts on her out-of-office. She blearily examines the day's appointments. Not a heavy day, thank god. She texts the two clients, not giving a fuck if it's early. She lies her head down, awake, spinning. The Ikea print on her wall looks like dried blood.

Josh had told her that his family didn't know about the sex work, yet, though he was building up to telling them. He thought his mum would be cool with it but was a bit more worried about his sisters. They were supportive and accepting of his sexuality in general, but this felt bigger. Close friends knew. It was his special other life.

'What about the extra money?' she'd asked.

He told her he didn't flash it around. He saved most of it, and he had a job in a bar that covered essentials.

Should the police know, in this situation? Could she tell them while respecting his desire to withhold it from his family?

The information could be relevant if, over there, he'd been seeing other sugar mamas. Had been with one on the night. The articles don't say anything about his phone, so they may not have much to go on. If he'd emailed a suicide note, the phone must have then gone into the river with him.

She stares at the awful print and wonders if she should make coffee or chamomile tea. Or pour herself a whisky – she has half a bottle of cheap malt. But it's difficult to move.

She thinks about the experiment. Should the police know about that? Could the substance have had any adverse effects on mood? Should she be worried about herself then, too?

There is no suspicion of foul play, the articles say. But something doesn't feel right about it to her. Josh is the most together, full-of-life person she knows. Knew. He had an unparalleled fondness for life, for every person he met. He was calm, positive and energetic and shared this brightness with those in his orbit: cashiers, strangers on public transport, even the scientists in the experiment.

But how can I claim to know him? she thinks, picking her phone back up. Even after ten years with her ex, Scott, there were moments when she'd realise he was a stranger. It never failed to shock her each time she would comprehend this: how truly separate two well-meaning, partnered human beings can be. It could be why she also has trouble maintaining friendships. She seeks intimacy but somehow attracts surfaces. Her friend Kate is persistent, despite the different paths their lives have taken. Mila is grateful for it, but also feels a sort of obligation.

She opens her banking app, looks at her savings account. $11,785. All the money she has in the world. More than half of it is earnings from the experiment. She is renting, has a run-down car, second-hand furniture. Her parents aren't well, and it may not be that long before she has to look after them, impeding her ability to work, to earn. She has no partner's second income.

But she will fly to Berlin. She will make sure nothing has been missed. Because who's to say Josh didn't have other secrets? They had more than one secret together. Within the walls of that windowless brick building on Liverpool Street, that blood-coloured substance, chalky on the tongue. She still has the dreams that started during that time: orange platelets multiplying in a circular shape, a brain of tiny cups. She wakes from these dreams feeling pleasant and relaxed, like she's just stretched out all her muscles.

She sits up in bed, then stands and removes the Ikea print, turns it around and rests it against the wall. She walks down the dark hall and flicks on the light in the flat's small lounge-dining area. She pulls the bottle of Jameson from the shelf and pours herself a generous dram. Her mind races. Her body feels hollowed out, the way it had before she met him.

The memorial is torture for Kyle. The weirdly casual sort of ceremony, and the tears and snot just pouring out of his face, with nothing to use but the sleeve of his oversized op-shop coat. His glasses getting all fogged and messed up. He thinks about being curled up in a dark casket himself. Not that there's a casket. There's no body. But the thought of a little velvet bed, that's comforting. The thought of not being around all these people – that's good, too. It's not like anyone knows Kyle; he's just the housemate.

That girl Josh tended bar with at Chunky puts her hand on his shoulder as she comes down the aisle. That's good of her. Some old lady next to him, an aunt or something, is not crying at all.

Josh's sisters stand on the stage, choked up. Their mother stands and goes to them, wraps them in her velvet shawl. Its deep purple matches the half-moons beneath their eyes.

'Josh was always there for us,' manages the younger one, Cece. 'I can't believe we weren't there for him.'

And then Maggie, his older sister, talks about their dad. How, in a similar way, she remembers his smiling and kidding around when she was little, and how his death was also a shock that left a hole in their lives. She is hinting at the fact that they were never quite sure if the car accident was an accident. He had been drinking a lot.

Kyle thought Josh had come to peace with his father's death a long time ago. And he'd given no indication that a depression of his own was taking over.

How the fuck can Josh be dead? Did he not know how much we loved him? He must have had so many thoughts Kyle didn't know about.

Kyle is still getting on that plane to London tomorrow, to land in the place where he and Josh were due to meet up. Where Kyle was meant to join Josh on his big Euro adventure. He's already left his job. What the fuck else is he supposed to do?

Jesus, poor Josh. Lying on a cold riverbed in a strange city. What would it have felt like? That whole system shutdown.

In the apartment after the memorial, Kyle puts raw kangaroo mince into a bowl for Sokka, his cat. The floofy boi is getting on a bit. Kyle's gut flips when he thinks about leaving him with the cat-sitter for a month. Over the past few years he's barely been away from him for a night. And Sokka is his closest intimate now.

Maybe he should just stay here with the cat, he thinks, as he scratches that little groove between Sokka's ears and skull. The cat licks his lips. Blep. But all that unplanned time – the sitting and thinking. He'd had enough of that before he moved in with Josh. Working from home and not being able to go outside. Getting in Jeanie's face. Until that blew up.

No, he will go. He will tromp through Europe with a ghost.

But there's somewhere he has to go first.

Before leaving the apartment, he pauses at Josh's door, presses it so it squeaks open. This feels utterly surreal. The room smells as though Josh has just sprayed on deodorant and ducked out for a date or a ciggie. Kyle will contact his parents and deal with cleaning it out when he gets back from Europe. There's just no way he can do it now.

Long-legged Mila crosses her legs and tucks her foot in behind the seat in front every time the flight attendant walks or wheels past. She's had the soy crackers and a few bites of the plastic chicken meal, and now she's sucking on the eucalyptus lollies found only at airports and servos. The muffled sound of the movie comes through her headphones, but she's really just waiting for the pills to kick in.

Her gaze keeps landing on a woman, across and down, who is breastfeeding her baby. The top of the child's head has wisps of hair that look so soft, Mila aches to cup it in her hand. To kiss it, even though the baby is a stranger. The lockdowns were almost helpful in that she was no longer confronted with these scenes in real life. She didn't have to be around Kate's sweet toddler with his tight dark curls and open, trusting face. Around Kate rolling her eyes at his tantrums. She knows it must be hard. She sympathises. But still.

And then her lover was helpful too. In more ways than helping her forget. In helping her find more, find richness beyond what she'd once thought she couldn't live without. She can feel that whatever was left inside her, propelling her from day to day, client to client, to the shopping centre, to stack the glasses in the dishwasher, to answer emails and return calls, has run empty.

'Bit hard to sleep on a plane, hey?' says the man in his fifties next to her.

She pushes her headphones off her ears. And somehow her voice ripples up, almost normal. 'Always.' She digs around in her seat pocket for her eye mask, hoping to dissuade him. Eye mask, face mask, a complete block.

'Going on holiday?'

'Yes,' she says.

'I'm off to the Frankfurt Motor Show …' He gives her the tedious details of the event and the cars involved and his role, and she pulls the eye mask to just above her brows, ready, but nonetheless nods as he speaks, her heart racing with anger and effort. Can't he see she's tired, not interested, just a black hole? Even her ex-partner Scott used to do this. She'd start opening up to him, finally letting a bottled-up emotion free, and he'd jump in telling her how he felt and how he related and how he understood. And then she'd comfort him.

She lets the man gasbag as she sinks back into the seat, hitting the button to request more alcohol. All the bad is seeping in. The distance she is now putting between herself and her parents, prioritising her lover even now.

She thinks about the time that still seems nightmarish a few years ago, the bushfires – thick curls of smoke for weeks outside the glass doors of her parents' lounge room. And then, when that was over, disease. Her mum didn't quite grasp the first lockdown, and both Mila's parents had the bad luck to get infected. For her dad, the resulting pneumonia caused long-term effects, his lungs possibly already weakened from smoke exposure. He suffers from inflammation and chronic fatigue; some days he can't get out of bed. Her mum recovered better but struggles with her world having to revolve around her husband's health. She's become short, stressed, but has never been good at articulating what she needs.

Mila has been travelling to the country once a month to be with them, to help out, and they reassure her they are okay, though they bicker, drink, and do less and less around the house and the yard. Mila doesn't know what else to do. When her dad tries to talk to her the way he always has, she kind of clams up. Her dad is the one she usually has the emotional conversations with; her mum is more reserved and practical. She wishes she had some good news to tell them.

Her gaze again strays to the baby, sleeping in its mother's arms.

The flight attendant arrives, and the Motor Show man thinks they're having a party. He orders two Scotches. He continues talking, and she downs her drink, throwing in a nod here and there. The plane drones. The pills start to kick in and she feels like her face is sliding off.

'I'm sorry,' she butts in. 'I'm tired.' And she pulls her eye mask down.

There's a woundedness in his voice as he tries to wrap up his story. Banging on now about an ex-wife. That tone is familiar, but something she never heard in Josh. Why can't this man be dead instead? she thinks, as sleep finally blooms within her.

⁓

Kyle takes the 96 tram across Melbourne from north to south, to fulfil his final task. He wears his black cotton scarf pulled beneath his mask, knotted at the back of his neck. He feels kinda safe tucked up like this, especially in winter – in black and medical blue, new Melbourne style. Out the window he sees the city still coming back to life: new shopfronts, bars revived, and cafes that clung on through the worst of it by selling milk and bread and hand sanitiser.

He wonders what it will be like overseas. He will have the one trip he took many years ago to compare it to, what it was like then as opposed to now – but it makes him sad to think about that. Who he'd shared it with.

Should he try to get used to loving people only from a distance? A long, long distance in the case of Josh. The memorial had been devoid of religious stuff, but if Kyle can summon it from his childhood for a moment, he can imagine that Josh still exists somewhere, whole and shimmering, perhaps winged – an angel. He can see why people want to believe.

What Kyle has been thinking about more, since the news, is Heisenberg's uncertainty principle. The discovery in physics in the 1920s that didn't just shake up science but also philosophy and culture.

As he steps from the tram into a slight wind off the bay, he looks out at the grey-blue water. What people had thought, in 1927, was that if we can't ever know at the same time both the position of a particle and its momentum, then how can we pin down *anything* in existence? If we know one of these things for certain, we must give up on knowing the other.

It's always given Kyle an intense feeling of anxiety that the small masses of which the world is composed can't be neatly gathered. And he knows that something about this discomfort – or about the desire to *resolve* the uncertainty – is at the core of his flaws as a human being. In his relationship with Jeanie, as he pushed to be certain about what she needed, he lost the ability to see how she was changing, moving forward. Her momentum.

Stretching the principle into a kind of poetry, he thinks about that beam of light aimed at a particle; the higher he turns the beam of light the further away the particle squirms.

Kyle arrives at the apartment block where he had dropped Josh off a couple of times when he was running late. It's the upstairs street-facing flat. The first time, he stayed and waited like a mum until Josh got to his destination, giving Kyle a thumbs up. Then he drove away before Josh knocked on the door, to give the woman some privacy. She is the only former client of Josh's he is dropping in on now, because she seemed closer to Josh than the others: from the way he spoke about her, and because he drew her into that experiment and spent that time with her outside paid hours. Kyle isn't supposed to know anything about the experiment, but Josh trusted he wouldn't tell anyone (or didn't have any closer friends to tell).

He climbs the open-air concrete stairs to the second floor and knocks on the apartment door. Nothing. He knocks again. No answer. It's okay, he has his contingency plan. It's not the nicest way to receive news, but he's leaving soon and he doesn't have her number so it will have to do. He crouches before he opens his notebook, leans it against his knee. He writes her as kind a note as possible, then hesitates before signing off with 'I hope this finds you in the best possible health and I'm so sorry to have to be delivering this terrible, strange and sad news' and a little 'x'. He folds the note and props it behind the screen door. He knocks one more time, in case she has been in the shower or something … and nothing. He leaves. His mouth feels dry and foul, and his heart beats in weird flutters. He hasn't eaten yet today and he can't tell if he feels hungry or sick. He can't put off the packing any longer.

On the tram, he opens the notebook to the oft-visited page where he'd recorded a Snapchat message from Josh. At the time, Kyle didn't want to look pathetic and screenshot it, since Josh would know he had, so he wrote it down.

I can't wait to share this big trip with you – mate, you mean so much to me x

It is hot in Berlin. The streets are crowded with people amid the mishmash of old and new buildings and crumbled, painted sections of Wall. For the first two nights Mila is in a hotel. The navy blue and white room is starched and clean. She sits in air-conditioned comfort, high above the sunblock and onion, asphalt and bratwurst smell of a street festival.

She will go to where Josh stayed, but she can't handle it yet. She needs to try to sleep a little bit. The jet lag combined with the emptiness is turning to sharpness and paranoia. Shapes in the corner of her eye. She needs to build up to a semblance of clear thought, and the ability to appear normal, so she can ask questions, gain some understanding.

As she puts her phone on the bedside table, she sees notifications. The top one is a Facebook message from a potential client querying whether she'd received their email a week ago. A spitting heat comes over her. How can people's lives be so unoccupied that they want to chase her across the internet? And yet this compulsion to answer it politely, even in her exhaustion and rage.

Then there's a message from Kate. Mila replies: *I'm in Europe!* ☺

Immediately Kate calls her. She almost doesn't answer, but it would seem weird since she just texted. 'Hey, hey,' she says, trying to keep the void out of her tone.

'What the fuck?'

Mila can hear little Ty chattering in the background.

'I dunno, I just needed to get away.'

'Why not Queensland?'

Mila laughs.

'I feel like I haven't seen you in forever, and now you're on the other side of the world!'

Mila feels even worse now. Kate has been a solid presence since high school, through everything. The break-up, her parents, all of it.

'I'm sorry, K.'

'No, don't say sorry. It's just, it's not like you at all.'

'Hm, true,' Mila says.

'Like, remember how you booked our accommodation in Bali six months beforehand, and then when we arrived the place was being renovated —'

'And we were literally the only room booked and they had to work around us, yeah.' Mila laughs. 'Oh god.'

'Hon, are you okay? What is going on?'

'No, I'm okay, really. I just need a break from work, and … everything.'

Kate takes a deep breath. Ty starts to cry in the background. 'Look, I gotta go, babe, but let's talk soon, yeah?'

'Yeah.' Mila wishes she could call her friend 'babe' or 'hon' so easily; those words don't quite come off her tongue. She hangs up.

The hotel is near the Wall. Near where Josh stayed in a hostel around the corner, near where David Bowie stayed in the 1980s, when this was the West. Mila leans out her window to look down at the beer-swilling festival punters and thinks about the lovers in the Bowie song 'Heroes'. The division of the Cold War. How these streets would have looked then and how they would have looked even just a year or two ago. How quickly we collectively move on.

But the next disaster wasn't far away, she thought, squinting through sausage-fat smoke haze at the sun.

She wants to sleep, but can't. There's an acid of guilt on top of the emptiness: a young man has just disappeared off the face of the earth, and she is thinking of her own reserves. What about his mother? His sisters? She barely even knew him.

And yet she did. She knew of the comfortable sexuality within him; she knew his sense of humour and his curiosity and generosity of thought. He never said a bad word about anyone. She knew the way he slept, spread like a star, and she knew that one of his fondest memories was climbing the oak tree in his grandparents' backyard and talking to the invisible boy next door. She knew he loved Mexican food, and beer, and he only smoked after three drinks. She knew he hadn't loved school but enjoyed history. She knew he was making his way through the young man canon, Kerouac, Dostoevsky, Bukowski and so on, while also reading Janet Frame and Muriel Spark. He'd watched *True Detective* S1 about four times. He liked EDM, trap and some bassy R & B.

She pulls on black jeans, puts on a bra under her t-shirt. She hesitates before leaving the room, her hand on the cold metal doorhandle. She has her swipe key and her phone with its digital money. But also that feeling of having forgotten something.

Another dizzying plummet of grief.

She opens the door. The corridor hums with quiet. No one in the elevator.

In the foyer, she watches tropical fish swimming around in a giant cylindrical tank. She takes a seat in the bar, from which she can continue to watch. Loneliness swims in behind the grief.

She should call her dad.

After three beers, she goes outside for a cigarette, just as Josh would have done.

⌒

Mila has pushed through the crowds to the hostel by Checkpoint Charlie. There are bicycles lined up outside its vibrant orange façade. She remembers the selfie Josh took in Tiergarten while riding one: he wore a close-fitting t-shirt as bright as the bike, showing his lean, honed biceps. She bends over and wraps her fingers around the handlebar of the last bike in the row, before walking up two steps and through a sliding glass door. She pauses to sanitise her hands. Ahead of her there's a reception desk, and to the right is a common area with some beanbags, a TV, a bookshelf with worn bestsellers and Vintage Classics, and a couple of plugged-in old Macs. Two young people, slack-jawed with headphones in, are curled in beanbags.

A guy around Mila's age, with a shaved head and street look –
white T, hoodie despite the heat outside – stands from the desk and
greets her. 'Checking in?' German accent.

'No, thank you, I just …' A rush of adrenaline brings sick to her
throat. 'I don't know what I'm doing here exactly, but …' His brow
furrows. 'Well, I knew the young Australian man, Josh Field, who
was staying here …'

'Oh,' he says, putting his head down, sadly.

'You met him?' she asks.

'Yes. Are you a relative?'

She hadn't considered how to approach this. 'Yes … his aunt.'

'I'm very sorry.' The guy twitches like he needs to get on with
a task. He fiddles with the pendant on a chain around his neck,
an esoteric gold cross with rounded edges and etchings that Mila
can't make out.

They stand there awkwardly for a moment.

'He was very tired,' the guy says.

'He was?'

'The first time he arrived, I mean. He had just come from
travelling to get here.'

Mila pictures Josh, rumpled, standing where she is now. She
is very tired, too. She closes her eyes and gets a flash of that flaky
starburst corona she dreams about. She takes a deliberate deep
breath. The muscles of her face are straining.

'What do you want to know?' He tilts his head.

'I'm not sure. I guess, who he was spending time with?'

'All the young people here – they mix, you know?' He keeps
playing with his necklace. 'One day it's with a guy from South
Korea, next day a girl from Canada. I don't really pay a lot of notice
unless they are breaking hostel rules.'

'Like?'

'Like to have sex here.'

'I see.' She is not sure why he is bringing this up.

'They drink a lot and it is shared spaces and we are not prude, you know? But we are mindful of people taking advantage and so it is safer to say no.'

'Like non-consensual?'

'Yes, and it can be non-consensual of course to do it in front of a person in the other bed. But I do not remember any problem with Josh.' He seems to notice he's been fidgeting and drops the necklace to his chest, smoothing it down. 'In fact sometimes his bed looked not very slept in.'

A dredging, nervous churn in her abdomen.

'Probably out dancing,' the guy adds. 'We have famous clubs here.'

'I know,' she says, a bit defensively. Does she not look cool enough to know that? Maybe vegan leather jackets are a bit passé now. 'Is there anyone else still staying here who may have spent time with him?'

The guy looks down at the iPad in front of him, pauses – perhaps reluctant to give out information – sighs, and opens it. 'Not from last week, really. They stay three days, you know, Europe tour? Except one woman, Belle, who was here for both his visits. She is looking for a place to live and for work. I don't know if they crossed paths much, but she is here a lot.'

'Is she here now?' Mila notes the edge in her voice and tries to smooth it out. 'Or I could come back. No rush.'

'What do you want to know?'

'I, uh … I guess how he was before …' She struggles to finish, swallows. She really doesn't know what she is doing here, except that something doesn't feel right. Or maybe, she thinks gloomily, she just doesn't know how to accept or process endings. She is going to go around bothering people on an impossible quest.

'It is very hard to lose someone,' he says, poignantly. 'I will have a look.' He walks away from the desk and up a stairwell to the left. She hears a knock, some voices, a door closing, and him coming back down. 'They are not sure where Belle is, but they think she has a trial at this bar, Die Lampe.'

'Okay, that's helpful. Thank you.' Mila turns to go.

'Good luck,' he says.

At enough of a distance from the hostel, she leans into a wall, legs shaking. It does not feel natural to go around asking questions about Josh. Will she get anything more from the girl? Maybe she should go straight to the police and tell them it's possible he was seeing people through SugarMeetMe. That one of his clients might know something about what led to him going into the river. The cops don't have his phone, as far as she knows, and he was using a travel sim so she's not sure how easily they could look at what sites and apps he'd been on. But how can she get away with walking into the police station, saying she's his aunt, then telling them all of this?

Maybe she can find out more on her own and bring it to them – if there's a reason for his disappearance to be thought of as suspicious, they might look into it. Yes, she can gather information, and if there's any chance he was killed or foul play was involved, she will go to them. She won't turn up on a whim with hot air.

Or, she could come to terms with why she is really here and not bother the police at all.

Either way, she has to know what Josh was like in those days before.

She is badly craving a drink, so she'll head to the bar straight away. She gets out her phone to consult the map, and as she's walking off, she glances back at the hostel. The employee she spoke to is standing in the front window, watching her, frowning. She catches the look before he darts back, out of the light.

London is compact, Kyle thinks, peering out the window of the hostel in Oxford Circus. Contained. But not ordered. Maybe it's the jet lag, but he feels completely overloaded just from catching the Heathrow Express and the packed tube. Everyone seemed to know where they were going and had no room for anyone who did not. Certainly not someone with a backpack.

In the minuscule hostel room, he looks across at the empty bed that is meant to be Josh's. Kyle is going to be moving from place to place with spaces beside him: a seat on the train to Paris, a bed in another hostel, another seat on another train. Josh paid for them, and Kyle doesn't have the emotional energy to look into cancelling them.

It's mid-afternoon but the jet lag is keeping Kyle horizontal, his mind foggy. Or maybe it's grief. He's all puffed up from crying under a blanket on the plane.

He wonders about the messages that must be going between members of Josh's family and friends – his sisters, those guys who would come around and drink with him while Kyle would go up to his room and play *Call of Duty* or watch something on Binge. No one has Kyle's number, but he's received a couple of DMs from people who remembered he exists, like Josh's older sister Maggie from Brisbane. That was kind of her.

Kyle never really felt like he could claim to be Josh's friend. He thought he'd been more like a fill-in until someone more interesting came along, or a comfy blanket Josh would pull across his toes when he came in after a wild night. Kyle liked being around him and had looked forward to being around him on this trip – speaking a little French for them both in Paris, to order the nicer beer; carrying their tickets, which he'd printed and slipped into a travel wallet;

and reminding Josh to pack up his bag each night before moving on. And Josh would, in return, force him past his claustrophobia down into the catacombs and make him taste the breath of skulls; make him stay out later than he wanted to and end up having some unexpected deep conversation with a pretty physics student; and help him feel less guilty about ordering McDonald's in the former Eastern Bloc.

Now, alone, Kyle can only honour him by trying to push outside his comfort zone.

People come into the room and he makes polite conversation before explaining the jet lag and turning to the wall. He scrolls on his phone.

There's a post from Josh's younger sister Cece.

She has made the strange choice to share Josh's emailed suicide note on social media. Maybe it is not a strange choice – maybe she thinks the note will help some people to feel a sense of closure. Kyle had been to a funeral in high school where the dead girl's parents had photocopied her suicide note onto paper of different rainbow colours so her friends could each take one home. Kyle found that, even though he hadn't known the girl well and felt a sense of horror about her death, he wanted to both read and keep the note. And he still has it somewhere.

Of course he has been curious to know what Josh shared with his family before making such an extreme decision. He reads the sparse black text against a white background:

I'm so sorry. I just couldn't take it anymore. I love you all.

Cece's accompanying message shows bafflement, but she also talks about their dad again and how maybe a genetic light switch flicked on. She says they'll be talking to the embassy in Berlin about next steps, but that without a body and with a suicide note, the police investigation is stalled.

Kyle stares at the note. It is suspiciously unlike Josh. He would write something long, expressive, full of dashes. No one else on Facebook seems to have considered that the note was likely not written by Josh.

Mila walks into Die Lampe. No windows, cheap chandeliers on exposed brick, a bluish light, and a young woman behind the bar with a bob and dark eyeliner. Her crystal earrings match the chandeliers. It's mid-afternoon and not busy, with just a few people on the mismatched paisley lounges in the corner. The air is cooler in here than outside, to Mila's relief; she started to sweat on the half-hour walk here. In English, she orders a gin on ice with lemon. The young woman doesn't smile or nod but makes the drink swiftly and then points at the machine for Mila to tap her card.

When the emptiness is this large Mila knows she shouldn't drink, but it's when she craves it the most. She takes a sip – tart and silvery smooth, a hint of spice.

'Are you Belle?' she asks.

The young woman frowns. 'I am.'

'Did you know … Josh?'

'Who are you?'

'His aunt.'

Belle smirks. 'Sure.' She wipes the bar in front of her, a vintage-style rose tattoo twitching on her bicep.

Her response throws Mila off. She feels a spike of rage, or is it jealousy? Heat in the forehead. 'You knew him.' A statement.

'Look, not well. We hung out a couple of times.' Belle picks up a straw and starts chewing on it, looks Mila in the eye. 'Just in bars – here, other ones.'

'Before he disappeared?'

'A few nights before.' The chewing and the staring and the short sentences are arrogant, judgemental.

Mila burns. She stares past Belle at a display above the bar of carbon-neutral spirits. 'Well, was there anyone —'

'Look, it happens. It's fucking sad. But it is what it is. He was pretty wild.'

'What do you mean?'

'He just liked to party, you know? He was probably out of it. Flipped.' Belle shrugs.

Mila thinks about him lying in bed with her back in Melbourne, snoozing and safe and perfectly comfortable. He was off drugs when they were together, at least that's what he told her. Except pot. Clean of the hard stuff. Taking a break. This was recommended during the experiment, and he said it was a good excuse. To have a clear head for a while.

Now she feels she is missing something huge. Maybe he was totally different when he went on a bender; maybe that's why he was avoiding it all back home – earning money, keeping his head down. Can't this woman go into detail? Reveal a bit more? Mila can tell, though – is old enough to tell – that Belle is the kind of person who clams up as soon as you push more, who feels pressured by the questions and has more power in denying than answering them. Mila will try one more question for now, but she might have to come back another day, sit here, drink, wait until Belle opens up more on her own terms.

Mila sips her gin. 'I just want to know if there was anyone, I don't know how to put it ... influencing him?'

'He wrote a suicide note, yes?'

'He did.'

'I don't really think so? But he did travel to Budapest with this woman, you know, that none of us met.'

'He did?'

Mila is remembering the snaps he sent her, the messages, and no word of this woman.

'She was older, like you.' That smirk again. Belle leans in towards Mila. She has big, gappy teeth. 'I think she was paying him.'

Mila stays silent, gut churning, face hot.

'He called her Leana.'

She takes a few more sips. He called her that to you? she wonders. To your other friends? And why did you think Leana was paying him? Was it just because she was older?

Mila sets down her empty glass. Belle takes it. 'Leana is in Budapest,' she says.

'Was she here when it happened?'

'I'm not sure. Like I said, we didn't meet her. Good luck.' The words are definitive, and she turns towards a customer who has just come in.

Leana. Probably not even her real name.

After Mila leaves the bar she walks several blocks, directionless. She has to calm down, slow down, and think of the next step. If Leana spent the most time with him, and if Belle didn't see him in the few days before he disappeared, then Leana is probably the one to try to talk to – to find out more about what happened in the lead-up.

Mila doesn't want to go back to the hotel. If she stops, she will have to think about why Josh didn't tell her about Leana. Belle she can understand – he often said he was going to bars with people he'd met. But when he was snapping and Instagramming from the train to Budapest, from Buda Castle, from the Danube, all that time Leana could have been with him. An older woman, no doubt a sugar mama. Like herself.

She could go to another bar, keep on with the gin. Just stretch out that black hole wider: why not? She starts walking. People look too happy, too sunny, to her. And then she sees the white spires of a church. She's always a bit curious but usually too shy to peer in, not really knowing the rules. But she watches some people who look like tourists going up the steps, and with the buzz of the gin in her blood she decides to follow.

This is what some people do in a crisis, isn't it? Instead of going to another bar?

Once through the shadowed doorway, in the heavy, hushed interior, the street sounds fall away. Tourists wander and point at frescoes and stained glass. Other people kneel or sit in the pews and pray. How do they know what to do? she thinks. How are they not self-conscious? She thinks of how her dad became a science teacher and staunch atheist after his Catholic upbringing, though he never discouraged her from asking questions, even let her go with a friend to Sunday school. She wonders what he would think of her now, walking through a church, and she knows she has to call him soon. Check in on him and Mum. She sighs. Walks towards a statue of the Virgin Mary. She does not think there would be a traditional place for her in all this: an unmarried, childless woman of indeterminate sexuality. Maybe her shame has a place here, though. Catholicism likes that, does it not?

What she wants to feel is the transcendence. The lifting and the light. The comfort of confiding and being held. She shuts her eyes for a moment and yes, there is some hum behind the cloistered quiet. It could be coming from the air itself. Or, perhaps, it is coming from inside her.

The thought is incomprehensible to Kyle. That someone would do this to Josh. Kyle doesn't know what time it is. He has surely missed the hostel breakfast. He can't move. This loop of thought – the idea of someone emailing that note and then, what? Pushing him in? Did they drug him? Or the note, the shoes – are they a ruse? Does Kyle dare to hope he could be alive?

It's convenient that the device that would have recorded his movements up until that moment was missing. But convenient for whom?

How can Kyle possibly go on sightseeing, holidaying, with that empty seat beside him, knowing the police got it wrong? And that Josh's family are swayed by the official story? Perhaps Kyle could claim to be Josh's closest person after all. The one Josh showed his notebooks to: his scrawl about politics, his terrible poems, thoughts about the experiment. Kyle is certain Josh rarely, if ever, revealed these writings to anyone else. But Kyle is just that kind of person people open up to: a comfy pillow man, a bland white pal.

And so Kyle knows about the women helping to finance Josh's European trip, at least some of them. His sugar mamas. He knows those women took some of the photographs and videos in Josh's Oglr feed that aren't selfies. Perhaps he should look at the feed and track the places Josh was in, rather than go where they'd planned to go together once he got here.

This kind of reorganisation of an itinerary, of Kyle's thoughts, is difficult. He lies there as though paralysed, his heart racing, his hand still holding the phone. The sound of someone laughing in the hall stabs his eardrums. He doesn't know where to start, and once he starts, it'll be dominoes.

It's a shame they communicated mainly over Snapchat – Josh sent him some of the names of these women along with their photos, but of course those messages disappear once you look at them. That information probably wouldn't have been enough anyway, especially since the names might have been fake, and the women were in big cities. There was an Ivona in Prague. A Reina … where had she been? Leana was one. She and Josh went from Berlin to Budapest, and she stayed on there, but did she meet him back in Berlin? Kyle doesn't remember any names mentioned from back in Berlin. From the end.

It's too overwhelming. He tries to let the thoughts go. He is in London. He should leave the hostel, walk, see the city. He forces himself upright, gathers toiletries from his bag and heads for the showers. In the stall, tears come again. He feels faint and turns the hot water right down. Streams cold water across his face. Shivering, he dries himself with a rough hired towel. Josh's whole complicated, often secret life – who can Kyle talk to about it?

He should at least alert the police about his suspicions regarding the note. He should do that immediately. His mission decided, he gets dressed and heads out to buy a local sim card.

Kyle finds a central number for the police in Berlin and dials. He is walking – who knows where – and trying not to be in anybody's way.

'Berliner Polizei,' comes fast and flat.

'Uh, so sorry, but am I able to speak English with someone?' He swallows.

'Eine Minute.'

He waits.

'How can I help?' comes a feminine voice.

'Hello, I'm not sure who to talk to. My friend recently went missing in Berlin – his clothes were found by the river, and it was deemed a suicide, but I have some information I'd like to make available? Perhaps I need to speak to whatever … unit was assigned the case, if that's the right term?'

'When was this and what was your friend's name?' she says.

He gives the information.

'Hold, please.'

He is on hold for some time. He looks up at the grey clouds pressing down on the crowded streets. Chain clothing stores, sandwich shops, money exchanges, phone repair outlets, pubs.

She comes back on the line. 'I'm afraid that unit is busy, but I can get someone to call you back. What is your number?'

He panics. 'I'm sorry, one moment, I just got this sim.' He drops his bag on the ground and digs around for the information that came with it, parting a stream of people. 'Uh … here it is.' He reads off the number. 'Do you know when they might call?'

'I'm not sure,' she says.

'My name is Kyle.'

'Okay,' she says, then hangs up abruptly.

He feels like it's a step forward. He has done the right thing. He will tell them about the writing style, and they will look into it further. He must trust it to the police.

He keeps walking. He will walk towards the Thames – there is surely something he can do down there. And walking is feeling good. He turns a corner and there is Trafalgar Square, with its majestic lions. He feels nothing. He tries to remember what is on his list – their list. Maybe he should go to the Tate Modern. Or the V&A. He doesn't think he can stir up interest in Tower Bridge or something mouldy like that; he needs a blast of art and darkness. The BFI was on the list. Maybe there'll be some long arthouse film showing, and he can just go sit in the flickering light. He feels guilty for this thought – he can watch films at home. But he was meant to be here with a friend, and it's all different.

He consults his phone, then crosses Hungerford Bridge towards the film museum. The 1926 film *Faust*, directed by F.W. Murnau, is starting soon. German expressionism is not something he's super knowledgeable about, but he thinks the mood will be right. All those distorted shadows.

He sits in the dark as the alchemist Faust becomes bound to the demon Mephisto, for power, for pleasure, for youth. Kyle remembers something in Josh's notebook about this film, or maybe Goethe's novel. Josh was writing about the experiment he had participated in, how the powerful always wish to find the secrets to 'advancing' humanity, and how, no matter how well-meaning, it's always about their own curiosity, their own entitlement, their own power. Kyle took these words in because he liked to try to be on Josh's level, intellectually; to have these conversations with him.

The screen is crisp. There is such order in the contrasts: black and white, good and evil, young and old. The gleam of teeth. The glisten of tears. It is too beautiful. The whole row he is in is empty. The row behind and the row in front. Somewhere, another lone person munches popcorn. His chest is on fire with sadness, with being alone.

⸺◦⸺

Mila is sore on her way to Budapest by train. Her muscles aren't used to being this inactive. She rolls her shoulders and looks out the window as the entrails of the city start to give way to fields and freeways.

Her phone loads Facebook slowly, like the unravelling of an ancient scroll. She reads the confusing note again. Doesn't know why she keeps coming back to it. She re-reads the comments.

There's a restrained one from Kyle, Josh's housemate, to Josh's sister Cece: *Hope you're doing okay – as okay as can be, that is.* She can't help clicking on his profile.

It's darkening outside, so she turns on the reading light above. Kyle's profile loads, but then stops loading. The wi-fi symbol has disappeared from the top of the screen. *Oh, fuck off.* She tries to read a book instead. She jiggles her foot, picks up her phone, tries again with the wi-fi. Kyle's profile loads quickly now. She sees that he's checked in at a London hostel. So he's still gone on the trip, she thinks. Josh told her he and Kyle were going to meet up and travel together. Her finger hovers over the message button.

Hello Kyle, I know we don't know each other, but we both knew Josh. And it looks like we're on the same side of the world. What did you think of the note?

The reply dots spring up immediately. Minutes later, a novel of a message comes through. He explains that he thinks the note is a fake and is amazed that she is also in Europe.

I'm here for him, she writes.

We could meet up, Kyle responds. *We could try to find out what happened together.*

That is, if you want. I don't want to impose.

Mila writes back, relieved to have some help and maybe just the chance to talk to someone who knew Josh. Who knows about her, too. The darkness inside brightens ever so slightly as the sky goes from grey to black outside.

They message back and forth and come to the name they've both heard: Leana. Kyle will come meet Mila in Budapest.

Holding her phone in her lap, she wonders if she's held off long enough for a glass of wine.

The phone starts buzzing repeatedly, then her dad's face is on the screen. She pops her headphones in and answers the video call.

'Hi Dad,' she says, guilt flooding her at how it should have been her calling him, checking in.

'Hi sweetheart.' He has his iPad on the coffee table, and she is looking up over his round belly and polo shirt to his warm face, longish whiskers covering chin and neck.

'Everything okay?' she asks.

'Yeah, yeah, your mum's here.' Her mum waves hello from the kitchen in the background. 'Yeah, we're alright – just worried about you over there.'

I'm forty years old, she thinks, exasperated.

'I'm fine, Dad. On my way to Budapest.' In the smaller rectangle she can see her face: angular, with thick curved brows, short unruly hair, eye bags.

'Oh yeah, your mum's got some ancestry – not sure where exactly, right, Theresa?'

Mila knows this, was frustrated a bit when younger that her mum wasn't ever really that interested in figuring it all out. Other people knew their backgrounds going back a few hundred years – Kate had a proud Greek heritage, for example. It seemed pretty important to your identity. 'Didn't your mum tell you?' Kate would ask, incredulous. One of Theresa's grandmothers had come over as a child; Slovak or Polish, was all Mila could get. Her mum would say, 'I'm Australian, doesn't matter,' and shrug. And yet she had given her the name of that grandmother: Ludmila. 'We just liked how the name sounded,' was how she explained it.

Theresa shrugs now, says, 'Czechoslovakian or something.'

Mila's dad, whose parents were run-of-the-mill ten-pound Poms, rolls his eyes a little – Mila doesn't like her father berating her mother, who has a lot on her plate with him being sick, but at the same time treasures the way he makes her feel that their connection is unique and intimate.

And then the train wi-fi gives out on her and her dad's face disappears from the screen. She feels an instant yawning inside her, like she is going to cry. Is suddenly aware of the extreme distance between them. Her mind conjures her first sleepover, when she tried to call her parents from a fax phone that kept beeping in her ear and cutting her off, and the overwhelming sense of loss and anxiety that had provoked. The strange other house, alien adults, carrots in the spag bol, and no choice but to bear this long night away from home.

For Christ's sake, you're forty years old, she thinks.

She tries to get a message through to let her parents know that the signal is patchy on her end.

She looks back out the window.

She might be travelling over land her ancestors were from. Do the people here look like her? She glances around the carriage. Probably all tourists anyway. She googles, not for the first time, 'Slavic immigration to Australia'. Pages take an eon to load. Russian Jews fled the pogroms after Tsar Alexander II's assassination. A later wave of immigrants after the Russo-Japanese War. There were minimal settlers from Bohemia and Moravia, and then the renamed Czechoslovakia, before World War II.

The internet drops out again.

Thoughts of her ex, Scott, creep in. They travelled together, when he was well enough, or when she dragged him out of the funk of their tiny apartment and into the world – to Europe and Asia, and New Zealand. Then there was that time he had an episode just before they left on a big trip. He never remembered calling her home from work, and what if he hadn't managed to call her? It still turns her stomach to think about what she found when she arrived. She had never seen someone she loved mid-dissociative episode before. When the person you love is muddled and barely recognises you and says to you, over and over again, 'I want to die I want to die I want to die.' And what choice do you have but to be the solid one, to hold the door closed and drag a tissue across his streaming nose, which he lets you do as though he is a child. 'I don't know what's happening,' he kept saying, and it was the first time she'd witnessed such terror in someone's eyes.

She tries again to read. She thought she'd only want something plot-based and easy. But does she really just want to be *propelled*? Maybe even in crisis she has room for a story that wallows or expands or sits beautifully like a painting. Or that embraces open spaces and mysteries, rather than folding into neat shapes. Those kinds of narratives are a break, too. A break from a life that is already full propulsion – to work to feed to strive to buy to fill to be. To find. Perhaps what she needs right now is a narrative that sits somewhere in between.

She sits the book back in her lap, fingers the rough edge of the pages. She wonders if Kyle will be anything like Josh.

Mila wakes with sun on her face, as it peeks through the thin vertical blinds on the window. For a moment she forgets, and is calm. Waking up in Europe in summer. A simple budget room in white and grey, with a tiled floor. The feeling that someone is coming to see her today. When the full knowledge hits, there is nothing to do but curl over and press her hands against her stomach. Again, she is surprised by the physicality of the emotion.

There are several Facebook messages on her phone. One is from Sara, a regular client. Did Mila forget to tell her? What day of the week is it? She is tempted to delete the app, but it's how she's keeping in touch with both Kyle and her parents. She looks at the

ANGELA MEYER

preview on her home screen. Sara is expressing concern for Mila. What has she let slip? She sees the time and realises she has to duck into the shower. Kyle was catching the red-eye.

When she comes out of the shower she glances at her phone again. Kyle is early, is already in the foyer. 'Down in ten,' she writes, flustered, and throws on jeans and a singlet, tones and moisturises, and puts a little product in her hair so it might have a chance of drying the right way. About to leave the room, she pauses and goes back for mascara.

When she steps out of the elevator she sees a young white man, thin but soft, curled over his phone. He has thick ash-blond hair and black glasses. She recognises him from his profile photo.

'Kyle?' she says, her arms across herself.

'Oh!' he says, looking up, then standing, sliding his phone into a jean pocket. 'Um, hello.' He opens his arms for a hug, with a questioning look on his face, and she unclasps to let him in. He maintains a distance between their bodies, and she catches the smell of toothpaste. When he stands back she sees his eyes are hazel, and there's a grizzly, babyish stubble across his chin and cheeks. His eyes well up, and he puts a hand to his mouth as though he is about to vomit.

'Hey,' she says, 'maybe come up to my room and sort yourself out, and then we can check if there's a vacant room or ...'

He lets out a sob. She moves back in and puts her arms around him, and he tucks his head into her chest. As she feels the wetness of his tears, some mixture of fatigue and anxiety comes over her. She's not sure she remembers how to do this, or if her body will let her. 'Hey, it's okay,' she tries, in a cooing tone.

I want to die I want to die.

'Let's just get upstairs, can you do that?'

'Oh god, I'm so sorry.' He sounds a bit like he is choking.

Rein it in, she thinks. The concierge is by her side, subtly handing her a tissue. She nods her thanks. She pushes it into Kyle's hand. 'Here you go.' When he puts it to his face, she breaks their bodies apart and goes to his backpack. She picks it up.

'Oh, I can ...' he protests through the tissue, but she just walks towards the elevator. He follows.

The elevator is small and awkwardly quiet. He trembles a little across his chest and shoulders, watching the door, sniffing but not crying afresh.

She opens the door to her room. 'It's not very big, but there's a chair.'

'Thank you so much,' he says, all run together. He moves the chair to a spot by the window. 'Mind if I open it?'

'Yeah, no worries.'

He sits, half-facing into the room but with the sun and breeze against his cheek.

She grabs the small white jug and fills it in the bathroom sink, flips it on, and sits on the bed.

'I'm really sorry about that,' he says.

'Don't apologise.' She barely recognises this tone in her voice anymore. Placating. She notices the light crankiness beneath.

'I can't imagine what you are feeling,' he says.

The crankiness dissipates. 'Well, I barely know what I'm feeling.' She realises that expressing this is very intimate. He has one of those faces, easy to open up to. 'I didn't think anybody really knew about me, either.'

'I don't think anybody else did.'

'I guess you were his best friend, then?'

'I don't know.' Kyle's face twists up in a way she can't interpret.

'He mentioned you, I think – well, as his housemate. He mentioned his housemate, like when we were chatting, and that you would be home that night, or you would be watching something or playing a video game in the other room.'

He smiles warmly at that, but tears threaten again. He licks his lips and sniffs, clearly trying to hold back. She waits while he gathers himself; she stands and rights two mugs, adds tea bags and a sachet of sugar to each.

'A cup of tea with sugar is restorative,' she says, knowing it sounds naff. She adds the water and uses up all the little plastic tubs of long-life milk. She hands it to him.

'Thankyousomuch,' he says again. There's a great deal she wants to ask, but they have to get the order of things first – find him a room, work out what they will do.

'Have the Berlin police called you back?' she asks.

'No,' he says. 'I don't know how long to give them.'

'We'll try again.' She peers through the open blinds. 'I don't know. I don't know what to do.'

'Me neither, really.' He sips the tea. 'Do you think we should find these women he was seeing through SugarMeetMe and suss them out or find out if they know anything?'

'I guess so, but I wonder … if they were involved, would they tell us anything?'

'I'm not sure.'

'Was it only women?' she asks.

'Oh, on that site, yeah. He has – had, I don't know what to say – phases. At least with the paid work.' He wipes the tissue at his eyes.

'I think you need some rest,' she says. 'We'll think of a way tomorrow.'

'Yeah, I'msosorry.'

'Don't apologise,' she says, weary. 'I'll go down and see about your room.'

'Thank you, I really appreciate that, Mila.'

She stands, stops at the door. 'I thought that we had a special connection.' She pauses. But now I wonder if he was just very good at making people feel like that. I don't know … I still want to think we did.' She hates that she is digging; she can't help it. To meet someone who was so close to him. There's a lot to know.

'He did talk about you,' Kyle says, nodding emphatically.

'And other people, too?'

He winces a little. Well, at least she's going to get honesty. 'Not as much as you. Truly. Especially with like the trial you were on and everything.'

'Ha. We weren't supposed to talk to anyone about that.'

'He didn't like share any details or whatever,' he says a bit too quickly.

'Okay.' She smiles reassuringly. 'I'm going down now.'

She closes the door and gets in the elevator, but when she gets downstairs she doesn't go to the desk. She walks out front and stands in the sun, letting her own tears come.

⌒

Mila and Kyle sit in a cafe that purports to sell real coffee. Mila's is more like a milkshake, and Kyle's is watery.

'We are so spoiled in Melbourne,' Mila says, spooning froth off the top onto her saucer.

Kyle takes out a spiral notebook and opens it on the table, sits a black gel-ink pen beside it. Mila can see dot points and neat writing on the right-hand page.

'So, I will call the police again today,' he says, pressing his palm against the spine of the notebook. 'And then, I thought, Leana definitely took some of the photos and videos on his Oglr, so maybe we could go over those – if you don't mind, if it's not too painful – and it might give us an idea of where they stayed, where they spent time. Maybe we could find her that way.'

His Oglr? Mila frowns.

'Or,' says Kyle, animatedly, 'maybe she was one of the people who left comments there, and if we can work that out we could contact her.' He sips at his watery coffee and stares out onto the street, flicking a pen against the open notebook.

'What kind of photos are they?'

Kyle stops flicking his pen and looks at Mila, concern on his face. 'I thought you knew. I thought you took some of the photos.'

'No, I've never seen it.'

'He mentioned you – well, in code. I just assumed.' Kyle blushes. She waits.

'It's pornographic. Like, a twink Oglr, I guess you'd call it.'

Mila holds the shock inside her body. For some reason, the amount in her bank account plays across her eyelids as she blinks: $8762. Dwindling – that's the word. Knowledge, money, what she can cope with.

'Show me.'

Kyle's hands shake a little as he brings up his phone. 'I … I'm sorry you didn't know.' He hands it to her.

The very first – the very last – photograph, is one Josh also sent her privately. In a hotel room mirror, fully naked, full-length, so you can even see his lovely, hairy feet, his long toes. 'Monkey toes,' he'd joke, wiggling them in the bed beside hers.

She scrolls. Pictures, videos. Some she has seen because he sent them to her, many she hasn't; in some there is another body, always faceless, pressed against his. One she pauses on, where his face sits on someone's stomach, and he looks like there is a weight inside him, but he is home, here, nearest someone's most private spaces. The body of a stranger – to her, anyway, but maybe to him as well.

It's a selfie, and she wonders if the person was sleeping, if they knew. It wouldn't be like him not to gain consent. The skin is quite like her own, but the surroundings are not somewhere they were together. Still, she won't scroll further, for now, because she's not sure how it would feel to see herself or *not* see herself among these other bodies, among this proliferation of posts.

'I …' She hands the phone back to Kyle, who still looks concerned, and embarrassed at the same time. 'He showed you?'

'I helped him set it up,' Kyle says, 'but I don't usually look at it, I just thought it might be helpful …'

She nods.

'Well … he did often show me. I guess that's a bit strange. I don't know. We were close.'

'He showed you the pictures of himself naked?' Mila can't think of a friend – now or at any time in the past – with whom she would share something so intimate.

Kyle nods, looking puzzled like he hasn't really thought this through before. 'With consent, of course. He was just very open, like, about his sexuality, his body.'

'In different ways to different people, perhaps.' She says this more sharply than she means to. She can feel the hurt, definitely a kind of jealousy, but she doesn't want to feel it. Jealous of Kyle or envious of Josh? Of his ability to be open. She needs to tuck this inside until she is alone. 'Did he ever make a move on you?'

Again, Kyle looks puzzled. 'I'm straight. Which he knew.'

Mila stares at him, realising just how young he is, in this moment. Young and self-conscious and perhaps oblivious. But then, there's also the fact that she didn't often let in the thought that Josh slept with men. Or was attracted to them, or perhaps loved them. She supposes she didn't want to think about him sleeping with, or even thinking about, anyone else. And, she reasons, her not wanting to think about those things was justifiable – in the package of the fantasy she had purchased: where in the moments with him only *she* mattered, where he was to be fully present for her.

Now that she knows Kyle knew him differently, she is so hungry. She needs to know if she was at least approximate to the truth of him. She feels she was. Kyle did not know him bodily, and there were many things Josh opened up to her about. Maybe only her.

She will be cautious and slow, let Kyle share with her. Cooperate with his methods, be trusted.

'Okay,' she says, 'I think it's a good idea, to have a look at the Oglr to find Leana. But would it be okay if you did it? I just don't know how much I can look at it right now.'

'Yes, yes, of course.' Kyle closes the notebook decisively, even smiles. 'It's good to have a plan.'

'I should probably do some emails today, too,' Mila says. She needs to be alone.

'No worries, I'll get started on these tasks and maybe we can meet back up for dinner?'

'Sounds good. Thank you, Kyle.'

He nods and stands, notebook, pen and phone tucked between hand and hip.

Once he is gone, she gets out her phone, ignoring another Facebook message, and puts in the Oglr address. She stares at the first photo for a long time, and the caption, and the comments. She walks out of the cafe and goes back to the hotel, and up to her room. She lies on the bed. She scrolls through images of flesh, and past a picture of a lush painting of ripe fruit, to a video of Josh, cum leaping out of his cock in a softly lit room. His bedroom, she recognises from their correspondence. And Kyle probably in the next room – would he have heard? She is so aroused she feels nauseated. She keeps the video on loop as she lifts her skirt and tucks her hand into her underpants, moving her fingers, circling, slow, then fast, until she comes.

⁓

They are to meet her in a bar in the hole – a literal hole, Leana had explained to Kyle – caused by the abandoned construction of a car park. Because Leana used her real full name when commenting on Josh's Oglr, Kyle managed to track her down on Facebook. The weather is sweltering as he and Mila walk across the Danube, on a spectacular bridge guarded by lions. Mila is quiet and gaunt-looking today, like she's been emptied of something. She's wearing black jeans and a grey t-shirt, and with that haircut weirdly she looks a bit like Josh from the back.

Kyle is bursting to talk and share, to think out loud about the history of Europe, about ethnic ancestry and religious and cultural, aspects passed down and things that get lost, but he doesn't know Mila's background and doesn't want to trigger anything. Ludmila, he knows from Josh, is her full first name. It seems Eastern European. He is a mutt – such a mix of settler and immigrant cultures it is hard to feel connected to any in particular, though he often craves to.

He does ask her a bit about her work, as they walk, which seems easy enough for her to talk about. And she asks him, and he tries to explain his role as a sustainable systems analyst without being mansplainy, and how really it is good or bad depending on the sustainability manager you work under and how committed the company is to the cause, and it can be satisfying and it pays well. Especially not being that far out of uni. He quit work completely for the trip, knowing he'll be able to slot back in somewhere when he gets back. 'Employable young white dude,' he jokes.

They get to the hole. It's mid-afternoon but the outdoor tables are packed with relaxed craft-beer drinkers.

'I need one of those,' says Mila, nodding to a pint. He can see the tension drawing in her Pilates-sculpted shoulders.

'There she is.' He points out a woman in her forties with light brown skin, cascading tight curls and a heart-shaped face. A shiny designer bag sits on the table in front of her.

Mila takes an audible, steadying breath. 'Okay.'

They walk to the table, and Leana stands to shake each of their hands, her face teetering between solemn and friendly. 'It is very nice to meet you. I still cannot believe …'

'I know,' says Kyle, shaking his head, then feeling a jolt of anxiety when he remembers he is supposed to be on alert for signs she knows something. He doesn't know how to interview someone for information. He knows he assumes too much that everyone is lovely (if damaged) and doing their best. How would he ever spot a killer, an accomplice, a liar?

'I'll get some drinks,' says Mila.

'You are sweet like him,' Leana says to Kyle, with a touch of sultriness.

His face gets hot. So she's an outrageous flirt, perhaps easy money for Josh. Though Kyle feels bad to think that way.

Could she push a grown man into a river?

Mila comes back, and Kyle notices she's already knocked the top off her beer.

'And you are so stunning,' says Leana.

'Thank you,' says Mila coldly, sipping. 'You're pretty too,' she mumbles into her drink.

'So,' Kyle and Mila start at the same time. Kyle should let Mila take the lead if she wants to. He gestures for her to do so.

'Sorry,' Mila says. 'Leana, we were both close to Josh, and we are just sort of gathering ideas of what he was up to.'

'It may sound morbid,' says Kyle, 'but we want some closure on, you know, his final days and such, if that's okay.'

'Is there anything you can tell us?' asks Mila. Kyle can see her hands, tight in her lap between sips. Is she desperate for answers, or jealous?

What would Josh have thought of these two beautiful women meeting? There's a strange, sick feeling as part of this grief, like a mind-trick, where in the moment when Kyle wonders this, a part of his brain is slow to remind him that it's possible Josh can't think or feel anything anymore. This takes only one second to remember, but it's a genuine shock to the body. Kyle has to make himself focus back in on the present moment. This hot weather helps a bit, the physicality of the sun on his neck.

Leana is talking about how she and Josh met in Berlin, via the SugarMeetMe site. She paid him a daily rate to travel with him to Budapest. She is from Amsterdam; she is travelling around during summer. A 'sexy holiday', she calls it. She was in Berlin for a while because of the 'scene' – the sex parties, clubs. But she wanted someone to herself for a bit. She uses the website regularly but never sees the men for more than a week because, she says, they can get attached.

'That's probably a good idea,' says Mila.

Kyle is surprised by the wryness in her tone. She's finished her pint – it might have something to do with that.

'I'll get us some more,' he says, even though his is still half full. He's even slightly tipsy on that.

On the way to the bar he notices a big guy in the corner with a cap pulled low, glancing in Mila and Leana's direction. Some kind of perv? *Gross.*

When he gets back with the three drinks they both look grateful.

'And so he moved on to Prague and back to Berlin and that was that?' Mila says.

'Pretty much, though we did stay in touch a little bit.' Leana looks down at her glass, taps it with her finger. 'I have to admit he was special.'

Mila nods. 'He really was.'

And Kyle knows from their tone that they are talking about a quality in Josh he was not privy to, something intimate.

He has to bring it back to the mission. 'Was there anything he mentioned, you know, in the days leading up to … his death, that was unusual?'

'No, nothing at all. We had fairly esoteric conversations anyway. He maybe seemed a little manic?'

Mila looks puzzled. 'What do you mean?' she says.

'He was talking more than usual about …' Leana gestures broadly, 'expansion … light, the universe, how we are all connected – things like that.' She smiles, then seems to remember to be sad, and looks down. 'And he was excited after learning that story of Praha – Prague – about it being founded by a witch queen, Libussa. He was reading a book about it.'

Kyle doesn't think this is unusual. Josh was always curious about, fascinated by, and wanting to draw connections between people, places, and the stories and myths within them.

'Did he mention any of the other people he spent time with?' Kyle asks.

She frowns thoughtfully. 'I think he went to Prague because he was going to meet someone.'

'No one back in Berlin, near the end?'

'I don't remember, I'm sorry, I don't think so.'

Kyle bites his lip. Yes, Josh had mentioned people in Prague to him, but he doesn't know if they were friends or lovers, and it was all over Snapchat so the messages are gone. Maybe there will be more clues on the Oglr, in the photos and messages around that time. But should they trace Josh in this way or just go back to Berlin, to where it happened? Kyle's sense of completion and order means he feels they should tick off Prague before going back to Berlin, just in case. It makes logical sense in his mind to follow the trail. But he will call the Berlin police again first.

He's hungry. They are drinking more slowly, and a gloominess has set in.

'I have to go now,' says Leana. 'I have a date.' Her smile is cheeky and cute, and she doesn't actually look very old, Kyle thinks, though she may be close to fifty.

'Well, let us know if there's anything else you want to share,' says Kyle, putting it in a way that doesn't sound suss. He and Mila each give Leana a hug.

He glimpses that creep in the cap still looking over, probably jealous of him getting to touch these women.

They sit back down so Mila can finish her drink.

'She's pretty,' Mila says.

'Josh had good taste.' He holds back a burp, hand over his mouth.

'People age differently when they have money,' Mila says, pushing around the condensation on her glass.

'Or when they don't have children,' Kyle says. 'Like you – you look younger than your age.'

She frowns at him then skols the rest of her beer.

'I'm sorry, I …' He has definitely said something wrong. She stands up. For some reason, words keep tumbling from his mouth. 'Do you consider yourself middle class?'

She picks up her bag. 'I suppose so. Or at least culturally privileged. I'm white, I'm educated, I obviously have enough money to travel. But I have no assets, and a career I'll age out of. I'm alone ...'

He wants to say something corny like, We're all alone. But he just nods, follows her from the bar.

'I guess I'm middle class,' he says.

'I think so,' she says.

'My dad has a boat.'

She looks back at him, cracks a smile.

As soon as they are in the crowd he realises he is drunk, very drunk, and thoughts of Josh now rush in and he wants to sit down on the ground and cry. They walk, and the sunlight smears through his soft tears; he tries not to sniffle too loud and walks a bit behind Mila, but at some point she turns back and just rubs his shoulder a couple of times, and he feels bad she has to be the one to comfort him. He will try to do better.

⌒

In the late afternoon, while Kyle is napping off his beers, Mila slips out to go to the baths. Josh had been here. He had taken off his clothes and put them in a locker and felt the damp, steamy tiles under his toes. They never bathed or swam together, and she wonders what colour and length of shorts he wore. She imagines shorter, a neutral colour like navy-blue, sitting low on his slim hips. She feels awkward being here alone – with people in clusters and lots of couples pinned around the edges of the small and large indoor pools. This closeness of bodies is still a novelty.

She places her bottle of water on a bench and wades into a pool with a little room. They're all different temperatures and this is a hot one, almost too hot, but she keeps going and wedges herself into a corner, and all her limbs want to float to the surface. She has come here to try to force from her head the silly, hopeful idea that the experiment worked. That Josh is just lost and navigating a new power. That he did encounter the witch queen, Libussa, in Bohemia – perhaps at the bottom of a bottle of absinthe. Or that the ghost of Marlene Dietrich smuggled him from a Berlin street down to the old air-raid shelters, and further subterranean.

Mila's muscles can't resist what the temperature and property of the water does, and despite herself she relaxes, her mind smoothing out like melted butter. Her shoulders spread away from the spine like wings. Her lower belly unclenches. And she lifts her fingers out of the water to smooth warm drops across her brow.

People do not talk. She looks around at steamy skin – young, old, pale, dusky. Contrasted thighs of couples, walking past; a man in a nearby pool being helped from his crutches; a young woman tugging at her bikini bottom; and soft, serene smiles on faces. And where are they to look but each other? There are no phones, no books.

This feeling is not unlike that in the church.

In her pool, immediately across from her, a young woman floats, her breasts curved above the water, head back towards a young man. He holds her gently up, seated behind her. Beside them, a rotund man in dark shades. Because it is bright through the windows? Or is it so he can stare openly at the bodies? He, like Mila, is by himself.

Was Josh by himself here, too? In some ways he seemed very solitary, independent. But he was also young and enjoyed sharing experiences with friends, lovers.

In contemplation – slow, floating thoughts – Mila accidentally locks eyes with the young man whose companion floats before him.

He is handsome in a leonine way, and his eyes are collegial. Was she looking at the woman's breasts too long? Or has this couple come here to pick up? Is that something that happens here? Had Josh locked eyes with someone and followed them into the bathroom for a gentle, relaxed tug? Her jealousy spikes to arousal, and under the water she feels it throughout her groin, liquidly expanded nerves. She could come here with sunglasses, like the big man, and spend all day drinking in bodies.

The floating woman drags her head out of the water, dark hair streaming across her shoulders, slicked back at her smooth forehead. Her collarbones pop as she turns towards the young man, giving that same serene smile: the code of the baths. They hold hands beneath the water, and his gaze again flicks towards Mila – something knowing, but is it inviting as well? And they walk past her to the steps of the bath, and she doesn't know whether to follow with her eyes or not.

If she is being honest with herself, she wants to. She wants to go with them and watch them and touch them. She thinks of the stories some of her gay male friends have told her: once, walking home from work, locking eyes with a tradie, and the next thing they're in a park sucking each other off. How do men know? she thinks. What is the exact look? She knows when a man speaks if he wants to fuck her, that's not too hard. But these silent exchanges and the consent that is given through the eyes – she has not been trained in it.

Would Josh have known? Would he have given that look?

She can feel that the man with the dark glasses is looking at her now. Her lips slightly parted, pinkened no doubt by blood. He is probably expert in picking arousal, looks for it. She does not feel alarmed or disgusted by him. There is no leering to it, more curiosity. She submerges herself to just under her lips. There is no need for thought in here. One can just be a body, and a gaze, both spreading out.

The next morning, Mila wakes and fans her arms across the bed – a starfish – remembering jokes with Scott about being able to do that when one of them was away, rarely for more than a few nights. She used to miss him so much when they were apart that she would never plan trips without him. She'd visit her parents for three days max; she'd get tearful as soon as she closed her car door, and he'd be waiting on the front step for her when she got back.

Stretching across the bed now she remembers how she and Scott didn't cuddle all night but she'd touch his calf with a toe, or their hands would meet and squeeze at some sleepy interval. But then there were the long nights of his insomnia, and the way it extended to her, and then only panic would embrace her. What was he thinking, staring at the ceiling like that? And how could she possibly comfort him? How could you stop someone from thinking of their own death? Her anxiety spiked at 4 a.m. when she would wake from dreams of tidal waves bearing down, or planes falling out of the sky. A few mornings, nightmare extended beyond liminality and she was convinced the tidal wave was coming. Her heart raced sickly; she clutched at him; he was not so good with words of comfort, but he did hold her. And slowly, rationality returned. It frightened her that even she – who was not so close to the edge as he seemed to be – could tip over into unreality, even if just for a few long minutes. But she could. So how could she look after him? And couldn't he see that it was hard for her and that she was suffering, too? No, his cloak was too heavy, too dark.

He would see a tram going past and think of his own mangled body beneath it; she would see a tram going past and her fingers would tingle with the desire to grip him, because she saw him seeing his mangled body beneath it. She would see his head smashed on stairs; she would see him slipping over a balcony. The images plagued her, sent adrenaline shooting through her body. And she wondered why she wanted to have children so badly if this was the way it was when you cared so much about someone. Whenever he snored, her annoyance would pass because she would say to herself: At least you can hear him breathing.

What's strange is how much she did not fall apart when it ended. She remembers reading *The Days of Abandonment* by Elena Ferrante some six months later, about a woman shattered by loss after her husband leaves her – a relentless, tumbling read. No sparing the reader in terms of the woman's anger, depression and numbness; the effect on her children and the dog. Maybe, because Mila did not have the children and the dog, there was nothing to fully reflect her state back to her.

Around this time she really dived into her work, too: took on more gyms, more shifts, started putting together some YouTube output. And she was seeing friends like Kate a bit less. Maybe I successfully distracted myself, she thinks, and hid that yawning crater deep within, but here it is, opening out in the face of this new grief.

She's always had this fantasy, this desire, when she is busy and stressed and overburdened. It has the label of 'lost weekend' in her mind. She sees lights and loud music and a luxe environment – like a hotel room of marble and gold – and there are bodies and a glass of champagne in her manicured hands (they are normally short, unpolished, practical) and she sees herself snorting cocaine off a man's lean stomach. And that man kisses another man, but he looks at her the whole time. This fantasy never lingers, but when it comes on it takes over her senses for a few moments.

After the break-up this desire was strong and frequent, and yet she never did it. She never allowed herself. She wondered who all these people were who could *let go.*

The closest she has come to the sensation of the lost weekend was sex with Josh.

Kyle gives a faint knock. She stands, aware she is in a singlet and underwear, doesn't care, opens the door. Her hair must be wild about her head.

'Sorry ...' he says. 'We were going to get the 10 a.m. train?'

'Isn't it like seven now?'

'Yes, I just thought with breakfast and getting there ...'

She feels both annoyed and wrecked. She is not used to someone else doing the organising, the rounding up. She has been on her own for a few years.

'I need coffee before I can talk,' she says.

'Uh, I can probably get you one.'

She stares at him, puzzling. Her auto-response being something like, No, it's okay, I can get it. Her weary mind fights that, thinking, Let the man get you a coffee. The first thought kicks back through. The second again. She says nothing. She frowns.

'I'll go get you one,' he says. He gently closes the door. She stares at the door. She sits back down on the bed: tired, guilty, tired.

⁓

Kyle and Mila sit face to face over a table seat on the train. Mila wets a tissue with her water bottle and rubs at a previous passenger's coffee-cup stain. Kyle has just tried the Berlin police again and spoken to an unimpressed cop, a different one to last time.

They seemed to find the information about the note flimsy, and they maintained that it's an open-and-shut situation. The cop also said they're in touch with Josh's family through official channels, presumably the embassy, and seemed a bit annoyed about this sideways approach.

'But,' Kyle says to Mila, spinning his laptop towards her, 'look at this.' He found the article last night as he sat up googling and thinking, sipping tea for his mild hangover. 'A year ago a young guy went missing pretty much in the same way, and in the same place – similar things left on the riverbank: clothes, shoes, and a handwritten note. But his body was actually recovered not long after.'

Kyle watches Mila's face – fatigued, confounded. She still rubs at the stain.

'There's a Facebook page about it, too. Like, that they don't think it was a suicide.'

'You sound almost excited,' she says to him, looking up over the laptop, pushing the dirty tissue to the edge of the table.

He flushes with shame. 'No, I just … It's more to go on, you know? Sorry.'

'Don't apologise, it's fine.' She squeezes her eyes shut and rubs a hand across her chin and mouth. She has shadowed cheekbones, a slim neck, thin pale lips. Her hair is a little greasy and flat today, and she pushes it back from her forehead, opening her eyes again. She stands. 'I'll be back.'

Perhaps he shouldn't have told her yet. He has to learn her moods, be sensitive as to when to time things. But he is energised by this difficult information; to know that what they are doing isn't fruitless, it almost pushes aside the tragedy, gives purpose.

He supposes it also isn't time yet to tell her about his idea. If the police are going to be useless, he and Mila really have to do more themselves. He could barely sleep, thinking about it. He switched on the lamp and wrote copious words in his notebook just to get it out of his head. He wants to fall on his sword for Josh. But he doesn't know if it will work.

Mila comes back with a bottle of white wine and two glasses. She now has a blank, reserved look on her face. She sits her cargo on the table between them, unscrews the lid, and pours out two glasses without asking Kyle if he wants any. It is 10.30 a.m. 'What are we going to do?' she asks.

He follows her gaze to the window. Outer suburbs, uniform high-rises and concrete industrial areas tapering out into country houses with roofs of perfect triangular overhang. Shutters or arches on doors and windows. Creams and browns.

The idea is pressing at him. But the same loops go through his mind as those from last night. It probably won't work anyway. He is nowhere near as attractive, as charming, as Josh. And he might have to sleep with the women, so he can be intimate enough to ask questions, and what if the anxiety means he can't perform? Well, that would be a disaster. But the only times that really happened to him were when Jeanie couldn't get off or seemed to be going through the motions, and he supposes if these women are keen, he will be okay. That's his jam. He's not one to care overly what they look like. He feels shameful about that, too – isn't that a very tox masc thing? To *not* be discerning? To see a woman as a warm body? The shame over indiscriminate lust is probably what's kept him from sleeping with anyone since the separation. Women don't deserve to be treated like that.

Not to mention, he might get murdered.

Yeah, it's a bad plan. He sips the wine. He was expecting something cheap, but it's very good.

Mila half smiles at him. 'If you're going to drink in the morning, it may as well be something nice.'

'Indeed.'

'So, Prague,' she says. 'And the Oglr?'

He does have other, related news. 'Last night I figured out the password for his SugarMeetMe profile.'

'Oh yeah?'

'Yeah, Josh pretty much used the same password, or variations of, for everything – a habit I tried to get him out of, but I guess it's useful now …'

'Sadly,' Mila says.

'There are two women through that he met in Prague.'

'What about Berlin?'

'Nothing.'

'Fuck.' She drinks. 'Okay, show me this Facebook page, about the other … victim.'

He flips his laptop back towards himself, brings up the page 'Find Matthew's Killer', hands it back.

She scrolls. 'He died around a year ago?'

'Seems so.'

'I wonder if he was on SugarMeetMe.'

'You met Josh through the site, yes?'

She nods.

'You could search, since your profile would be set to look for sugar babies. Unless they take down inactive profiles after a time.'

She sips. 'I hid my profile. I didn't want to meet anyone else once I'd met Josh.'

'But you can access it again easily enough, yeah?'

She nods, seeming reluctant. 'Okay. Should we contact her, too? The sister, Eloise?' She points at the laptop.

'We should. I can do that.'

Kyle gets out his notebook and writes dot points:
Mila to check if Matthew is on SMM site
Kyle to contact Eloise
Mila, topping up her glass, smirks at him.
'What?'
'I used to be like that.'
'Like what?'
'Lists and notes.'
He waits.
'As much as you try, the world does not come to order,' she says.
He knows that. Intellectually. Of course. But the notebook still makes him feel better. Depositing thoughts, forming plans, creating a cocoon around each situation. He had a lockdown notebook during the eternal Melbourne lockdowns. He had a different notebook for his separation from Jeanie, the moving out, the divorce: all of the splitting of their meagre assets accumulated in a rented apartment. All those kind wedding gifts. People had been so in love with their love, and amused by their youth. But they had trusted it – that it would work, that they would stay there in the suburbs where they grew up. He was all in. He knows all the things he did wrong. He knows why she started spending more time on Zoom, Discord, Skype, even making new friends in a time when you couldn't physically meet them. Partly youth, partly his clasping.
If there's ever a next time, he'll do better.
'I've been to Prague before,' he says.
'You never said.'
'For my honeymoon.'
Mila sets her glass down. 'But you're ...'
'Twenty-four, yeah. High school sweethearts.' Kyle blushes. 'We don't have to talk about it.'
'How many years?' she asks.

'Six, all up.'

She stares at him. 'You proposed when you were how old?'

'Twenty.'

She stares at him. Then she smiles. 'That's really sweet.'

'Nah.'

She looks out the window. 'I was with someone for ten years. He didn't believe in marriage.' She clears her throat, looks at Kyle. 'Are you hungry? I am.'

He is curious – of course he is. But he'll do his best to let her tell him in her own time. You have learned not to be *clasping*, he tells himself. He better not have any more of the wine.

'Sure, I could go some chips or something.'

She nods, stands up and leaves again.

—⁓—

It would be cheaper if she and Kyle shared a room, but Mila needs space for her thoughts. She is so high on adrenaline that every mouth noise, every knuckle crack, she knows, would make her grind her teeth. This is the benefit of being forty. To understand your needs and know what will tip you over. She idly plucks her eyebrows in the tiny bathroom. She presses her chin against her neck – softness, already. She has noticed this effect before. All it took were four or so days without doing crunches, which didn't just keep her abdomen tight but also the skin on her neck. She remembers a sign in her regular gym: 'Doing weights is like a facelift for the body.' She turns around and looks at the carpet, thinking she should at least do some planks, some squats ... She sits on the floor. The carpet is scratchy. She imagines tiny bugs crawling across her skin. She leans over to the bed and lifts the sheets and blanket, checking for bed bugs. Soon she has checked all the way around, and inside the pillowcases. Nothing. Her phone buzzes on the bedside table, and more adrenaline flashes through her. A sign above the bin says: *Do Not Bring in Outside Food*. Rats, there must be rats. Bug-clawed rats. She returns to the mirror, plucks more hair from beneath, above, between her brows.

She has reactivated her SugarMeetMe profile and looked for the dead guy. He is not on there, or he isn't anymore. So there is no lead to follow.

How can the cops ignore two such similar deaths? Maybe it is just a coincidence.

Maybe she could find some drugs, in Prague. But she is heightened already, even beyond her usual anxiety, and the taste of the blood-orange substance from the trial strangely seems to be on her tongue. Probably because she is thinking of Josh. She should just make a cup of tea. She finds the kettle in the cupboard, begins to uncoil the cord. No – the idea of the tea in these dusty packets. Plastic milk. Nothing seems palatable.

Like Kyle, she has been to Prague before. But in winter. In fact, that was the longest time she was apart from Scott during their relationship; the trip had been planned before they got together. She doesn't like to think about how hard it was, the distance of those phone calls, and how, when she returned, she realised where his head had been. That was when she first learned about what he carried inside him. So was it not wanting to be apart from him that made her rarely travel after that, or was it worry for his life?

She remembers a blue-cold, unpopulated Prague. None of this squash of rowdy beer drinkers and giant tourist groups following protruding flags – even with virus variants still raging. None of this noise. She can hear the hum of it from here, though the crowds are mainly across the Vltava River, in the Old Town, not where she and Kyle are staying in Malá Strana.

The worst of the terror is when she lets in thoughts of how many people there are, pressing down on the earth. A tidal wave of bodies, with their hunger and waste and stench. Being pressed in, eventually trampled. Even in a room with the window open and air all about her, the clamour of people. Her breaths come shorter and shorter.

No.

You know what this is.

She sits up, moves down onto the floor. There are no bugs, she tells herself. She pushes up onto her hands and toes in a plank. She feels the strong, taut line of her body, on this upper floor, flying above the people on the streets. For a moment she is so light; it's as though she might actually lift from the floor. It makes her dizzy.

She hears Kyle's door open and then a knock on her own door. She stands, tries to take an even breath, opens it. He looks rumpled, as though he has napped, his hair flat on one side. The sight of him relaxes her. 'Hey,' she says.

He returns the smile.

She motions him in. 'You had a nap?'

'Sort of,' he says. He sits on the bed. 'I have an idea, but I don't know if it's silly.'

She crawls onto the bed too, presses up against the wall and crosses her legs, hugging a pillow in front of her, between them. 'Tell.'

'Okay. It's silly. But I was thinking about how, if we meet up with these women, they're not really going to tell us anything, if they know anything.'

'I guess.'

'I mean, *if* they're suss.'

'Yeah.' She has never seen him looking so twisty and self-conscious before. 'Spit it out,' she says.

'Well … maybe if I try to meet up with them, as a sugar baby …'

She considers him: sleepy and boyish. Needing a haircut. Eyebrows a bit wild. Eyes shrunk slightly by his glasses. But cute – not Josh-level sexy, but softly appealing, and perhaps the same women would be interested.

'But … if one of them is dangerous?' Mila says. 'It could be dangerous, Kyle.'

His lips tilt. Well. This is a side of him she hasn't paid attention to. But he is a man, a cis dude, after all. The heroic narrative heavily embedded. A chance to rise above his sensitive stamp.

'I would be really careful, Mila.' He speaks now with greater confidence. Is it because he's getting more familiar with her, or did he practise this in the mirror? 'Josh wasn't aware of possible danger, but I will be.'

'Will you?' She is sceptical. 'And what about the sex?'

'I mean I'm not going to be flippant about it, but I think I can go with it if I have to.'

She rolls her eyes.

'Yeah, I know,' he says. He looks chastened.

'It's so fucking easy for men.'

'I'm sorry.'

'Did you know, even if I am really, really, attracted to someone – like, completely aroused – I hardly ever come the first time I sleep with them?'

He stays silent – is hunched over like a question mark. She feels unreasonably furious. Just all the years – dissatisfaction, effort. And he can meet a stranger and get a hard-on and go for it.

'What about the women?' she asks.

'I imagine the idea is that it'll be all about them. I don't need to … you know, get off.'

She scoffs.

'I don't understand why you're so mad,' he says.

She is fatigued; more waves of adrenaline crash through her. She is clutching the pillow. 'Can you just leave me alone for a bit, to think about it?'

'Yeah, of course.' He gathers up the wounded look on his face, hunches to the door and lets himself out.

She stares at the salmon-pink façade of the building across the street.

Josh didn't come, sometimes, when they were hooking up. He wanted it to be all about her, he'd said. But she found it difficult, when he left without coming. It made her jealous, the idea he didn't need her to take care of it. And this was even after she'd been feeling a bit better, was a bit more in touch with herself and knew, psychologically, what was going on. She knew, but the misplaced jealous feeling still arose. Every man, every boy, from when she was fourteen. Finishing him off – that was the goal of the sex. That was how she knew he was satisfied, that he liked her. That early boyfriend who got off three times a day to porn but couldn't come during intercourse; she'd had to jerk him off, every time, for two years. With Scott, when his orgasms tapered off, when the depression made him uninterested, that was when she started going to the gym more, paying attention to calories, carbs. He still got her off, like a chore. She was a chore. Her orgasms were a chore.

And she loved to get them off. Whether learned or not, that was a genuine feeling. Pleasure at their pleasure.

Josh loved to get her off, it seemed. But it was confusing. And she was paying him. She wished she could have fully embraced it, the idea that her pleasure was more important than his, in that specific scenario. But she always felt better if he came, too.

She could never explain all this to Kyle. He wouldn't understand the complexity – the years and layers of emotion. He would just have to deal with her becoming strangely angry. She's spent too much time apologising to men for it; she's done with that.

She realises she is still hugging the pillow. She relaxes her grip.

Kyle's plan is actually okay. But dangerous, for sure.

She sighs. She gets up and goes into the hall and knocks on his door. When he opens it he is still a bit cowed, as though she is going to punch him. She hates this most of all – the way men fear being chastised. As though she is his mother, giving him a little smack. But she is mindful that she is heightened. And so, with much effort, she puts on her softest face. 'Can I come in?'

'Of course!'

She sits on his bed, now, mirroring him. 'The plan is good, Kyle,' she says. 'But I will be worried about you.' If he wants to act like a chastised child then perhaps to mother him and show warmth is the way to be kind.

'I promise I'll be really careful,' he says.

She nods. 'You'll have to keep your phone on you. Or perhaps we could get something inconspicuous. Do beepers still exist?'

'What's a beeper?'

'Never mind.'

'I have a smart watch,' he says, waving it in her face.

'Oh good,' she says. 'So who's first?'

He grabs his notebook, which was sitting square to the edges of the desk. 'That little bar downstairs. Shall we go?'

She is still feeling the crush, the noise of the crowd in her blood as it pumps through her temples. But the bar hadn't looked too populated – a bit run down, really. Friendly. Perhaps they could sit up the back. She knows Kyle is accommodating her – her increase in alcohol intake. And maybe trying to help get her out of her head. He is generous. She can see why Josh loved him.

'Sounds like a plan. I'll just put on a bra. And maybe shoes.'
She laughs.

Kyle knocks on a beautiful peach-coloured door. His palms sweat, and he swallows and swallows. He tells himself the things he always did when he had to give a presentation at work: It's just an hour, it's just a day, you are a speck, no one cares, it'll be over, everything will be over. That got him through the event, and then later he would allow himself the going over and over of what happened and the things he said and did wrong.

This time, it will depend on whether he survives the event in the first place.

A slim woman in her late forties opens the door, smiling: Ivona. Dressed cleanly in linen and cotton, with greying hair pulled back. 'Come in, come in!' she says, heavily Czech-accented.

He follows her down a hall – more peach – to a small lounge room where sunlight from a well-placed courtyard shines through a large glass door and bounces off the furniture.

Not many gaps in which to conceal weapons.

'So many Australians around lately,' she says, gesturing to the lounge.

'Oh yeah?' he says as he sits down.

She pours him fizzy water, sits across from him. Her face is warm and open. 'Do you want to know anything?'

'Um … only if you want to tell me. And please … if you want to know anything, let me know.' Halfway through saying this, Kyle realises he has defaulted to 'nice guy' and perhaps already ruined his chance to get some details. 'I mean … I might need to know just what you like and so on, if that's okay. What you normally do.'

'Well, it depends,' she says.

That's helpful.

'I'm actually not someone who has a specific kink, if that's what you mean, other than the fact I just like men, young men, to be intimate with.'

He has forgotten the list. The lines of questioning he could take – it had all been thought through, written in his notebook, memorised. But in the moment, he can't get past feeling rude and intrusive, even with the possibility of danger. She seems so warm.

'That's good,' he says blankly.

She comes over to sit beside him. She doesn't seem muscular enough to overpower him. He wonders if grilling her afterwards would be the best time, when her guard is down – that's how they do it in movies, right? The femme fatale uses her sex-charms to disarm the suspect, and then he'll tell her anything.

Ivona seems to be waiting, her eyes crinkled up at the sides. She has spent her life smiling, he thinks. A killer wouldn't have those laugh lines. He kisses her. She tastes of mints, of thoughtfulness. He tries to be subtle as he wipes his palms on the couch before touching her. He removes her light jacket, waits for her to lift his shirt before lifting hers. Her kisses become hungrier. He has never been with someone so old – the thought flits in. But kisses and hunger work upon him. She is keen, and so he is hard. They move to the bedroom. She guides him more with her hands than her words. He follows her lead. His hands upon her breasts, and then between her legs. She likes to keep looking at his face. She stays reclined. She puts the condom on and guides his cock in. Presses a hand to his lower back to slow him down. When it is appropriate, once she is satisfied – her eyelids scrunching and a sound similar to pain – he comes easily.

The guilt swims inside him, afterwards, as he lies on the clean white sheets. Did he pull her hair? Grip her wrists too hard? He has to force down the self-reprobation, for now. Has to remain alert. This is it. His chance. For Josh.

'Do you like to hang out a little afterwards, or …?' he asks.

'If you don't mind, yes. Nice to have a warm body in the bed.' He aches at this. But no, it's good to be useful to someone. 'Did you know that once, in Bohemia, women were the rulers?' she says.

'Uh, yes.' He stretches his mind back to the conversation in the hole in Budapest – a witch queen was mentioned. 'I know something about it.' His brain throws up confusing images of Wonder Woman.

'In the golden age, Libussa ruled and her warriors – also female – had their own castle and chose to sleep with whomever they wanted.' She rests her head on one hand.

'That's very cool.' Was this where Josh learned about Libussa, too? Kyle has to get back on track. 'Would you mind if I ask: do you like to see someone a bit, form an intimacy? Or do you prefer the one-offs?' Lines of enquiry.

'I have only ever been with a paid companion once each,' she says firmly.

It is not likely, then, he thinks. Also, the laugh lines.

'Although,' she says. 'There was one young man. I probably shouldn't be telling you. I saw him once more, maybe would have even again, but he went to Berlin.'

'Do you spend much time in Berlin?' Kyle tries to sound casual.

'No, too big for me. I haven't been for years.'

He looks at her, soft light on a face that is already more familiar, and therefore more beautiful, to him.

'Do you read much?' she says.

'I try to.'

'I like to offer a parting gift to my young men.' She reaches to the bedside table and then hands him a copy of a thick novel, a Vintage Classic – Iris Murdoch's *The Sea, The Sea*. 'It's one of my favourite books. About romantic obsession. The ways we delude ourselves.' Ivona laughs. 'And seclusion, too. How we try to move away, take stock, but can't really escape our pasts, our losses.'

He thanks her profusely. 'You really don't have to.'

'Young men often prefer Goethe or Dostoevsky, or Bret Easton Ellis, god forbid; they don't realise how much else there is to discover.' She pats the book. Funny that she's mentioned Goethe, after he recently viewed that adaptation of *Faust*.

'Thank you so much,' he says again.

She shrugs, turns away. A signal for him to get up and get dressed. He's actually feeling a little sick, and so he does. He knows he can't trust his instincts about her, really, because his instincts are too trustful. But he really doesn't think she could have anything to do with Josh going into the river.

Once dressed, he takes the book and the cash, kisses her on the cheek, and wishes her all the best.

———

Mila waits for Kyle in a cafe down the street from Ivona's house. They'd decided she should stay close, in case of danger. She sips a black coffee and checks her bank account. Again. Her email. Ignores the missed call from Kate. To get through the pandemic, she'd put up more Pilates videos on YouTube and held online classes for her regulars. The videos still offer a trickle of income, and she's just received her monthly instalment, which goes straight to rent. The numbers in her account continue to go down.

Her coffee tastes bitter.

All those years with Scott. She'd believed. She'd held. She'd known what she wanted, and she thought they would do it together. She was just waiting for him to feel better.

He didn't believe in marriage. He said that pretty early on. He believed in grunge, in guns in mouths, in death leaving behind art, not a 'piece of paper' saying until death we are locked in. She didn't think marriage had to be like that, a piece of paper. She thought it could be like having an anchor in each other. Finding projects that joined their skills and made each of them happy. Taking turns to be down and out with the other giving backrubs. She was never able to fully express why she wanted it. The fact he didn't want it made her feel foolish.

And the subject of kids? Well, don't you know the world is ending? Of course, she would think. He is right. It would be selfish to have them.

She remembers conversations with Kate, his words coming out of her mouth:

'We love each other, that's all that matters.'

And Kate would say, 'That matters a great deal, yes. But you've always wanted kids.'

Mila couldn't repeat Scott's words about overpopulation. At that time, Kate and her husband were trying for a baby. They owned a house in Cranbourne. They complained about the long commute to work in the city.

Mila would return from visiting them to the apartment she shared with Scott. Posters on the wall like in a teenage bedroom.

It would be selfish to have a small creature at your breast, calling you mother. Someone who would have no choice but to accept the love you have to give.

Is there some in-between? she would think.

She was thirty-seven when he ended it. They are still friends. They are connected. They still care about each other. She doesn't like to feel the hot rage that is coursing through her now. The fiery heat in her neck, her hands. She remembers reading something about alchemy, how the element of fire symbolises passion. Rage and desire are passions so close to one another.

Kyle enters the cafe, flushed, arms wrapped around himself. He sits heavily across from her.

'How did it go?'

'Nothing. I didn't …' He looks pale, almost green.

'Are you okay?'

'I'm so sorry,' he says, 'I think I'm actually coming down with something.'

'Oh … okay.' She scrapes her chair back. 'I'll just pay.' Has he made himself sick with nerves?

While she's paying, Kyle's chair scrapes back too, and he runs to the cafe's bathroom. He emerges eventually, one pale arm placed dramatically across his stomach. She hustles him out onto the street, avoiding the proprietor's eye.

'We'll have to delay our plans,' Kyle says, his lips like sun-dried worms. 'I've already texted Reina, the other woman we need to suss out. To change the meeting.'

'Let's just get you back,' Mila says, ordering an Uber. 'Put on your mask.'

At the motel she settles Kyle under the polyester sheets. 'Can I get anything for you?' she asks. But the words are stones in her throat, forced out. He looks pitiful. She wants to smooth his hair down. She wants to walk away.

'Um, only if you're going out. Just electrolytes or something. Thank you so much. I gotta stay vertical.' He gives a weak smile and flops his head down on the pillow. The rapid test on his bedside table is negative. They suspect gastro or food poisoning. She shuts the door and goes back to her room.

Mila is stuck. Frustrated. She'll have to wait to ask more about the woman, but it all seems like dead ends. She doesn't want to sit in her room and think about death, murder, the ghosts of relationships past. The ghosts of past wants. The spacious lives of others. And about her poor sick parents who will never have a grandchild to play with.

She tries to breathe through the heat rising again on her neck. One foot in front of the next.

Eloise, the sister of the other victim, has not yet replied to them.

The police – a different person on the end of the phone each time – don't believe that anything needs to be done.

His family, according to Facebook, are tied up with the embassy and don't have any other answers.

How Josh had stood at the end of the bed and stretched, biceps by blue eyes, a tickle of hair from his belly button to his cock. The most beautiful, slim thighs she had ever seen. The way their hips fit together. The way he knew the exact moment to slip his finger in.

She is a vibration of skin, a hollow instrument. She grabs her handbag and hesitates – the safety of the cocoon – but then opens the door and goes down the narrow stairs and out into the street. She walks towards the river and a bridge to the Old Town. She will go to where Franz Kafka used to meet with his friend Max Brod. To have a champion like Max Brod. Better than a lover. Well, perhaps. There was Kafka's last love, Dora Diamant, with whom he finally went to Berlin, escaping the tensions around his family relationships in Prague, and with whom he laughed. He would read to her from his sickbed. She did everything she could to make him comfortable and happy as he got sicker and sicker. They were each other's worlds. Dora thought of Franz as 'the substance we call life', and believed there was an 'ancient consciousness in him, ancient things and ancient fear'. Mila remembers these sentiments because of how she, too, sought this kind of insight and intimacy in a partner when she was young, and how she thought she had found it in Scott. Franz and Dora only had a year together. Just one year, before he died. But it shaped the rest of Dora's life.

Mila tries to block out the sounds of beer-scoffing Brits spilling from pubs; she keeps pushing through, pushing through, not thinking about the crush, just thinking about the author on a cold afternoon, greeted by the warm smile of a devoted friend. She finds the Haus Minuta, one of Kafka's childhood homes, with help from her phone. She looks at the little balcony where the writer's father once left him locked out in his nightgown – an incident recalled in the scathing letter Kafka wrote to his father at age thirty-six. She always imagined that if she had a child, it would be a little boy. She would never leave him in the cold.

Mila has always read about people's lives and loves. When she was in her twenties and taking various arts degrees and getting into debt, of course she didn't just want to connect with someone of depth and mystery like Kafka, she wanted to *be* Kafka, the brilliant one. In her thirties she realised it was perhaps better to accept she was Max Brod – to recognise and foster potential in others. She wonders now if she is neither; if she is more like one of Kafka's flailing characters: hungry, misrepresenting herself, running up against walls. The memory comes again of calling her parents on that fax machine when she was a child. The distant crackled voices and then the loud beeping.

She scrolls through her last messages with Josh – the last ones that were saved, anyway, since those on Snapchat were ephemeral. She wonders what the last thing was he heard. Was it muffled, distorted through water? She stops at the final text messages she sent, that remained unanswered. *What the hell?*

They are now marked as 'read'.

People rush around her in the square, as her heart pumps.

She texts Kyle: *My last messages to Josh have been 'read'!*

He doesn't reply; he must be asleep. She starts walking back. Thinks about it some more. Josh's phone was never found, as far as they know.

I suppose it could just be that whoever took his phone has finally figured out the code, she texts.

The person responsible for his death or disappearance? Or just a random horrible person who sifted through his belongings by the river?

As she's arriving back at the motel, a message comes through from Kyle.

There'll be no way to know. But it is definitely weird ☹ *Could it be possible …*

She replies: *He would have contacted us!*

True ☹

Mila's gut rumbles oddly. A hungry but bilious churn.

⁓

The following day, Kyle is finally feeling better. He opens the curtains and then lies back down, flexing his hands, easing out the cramps in his calves. His stomach growls. He craves hot chips with chicken salt. It feels incredible, to be so well! His brain, on form, throws at him an image of Josh lying on river silt. No, Kyle thinks. Not yet. He grabs the room service menu. Okay, the chips won't have chicken salt, but they'll be close enough. He texts Mila: *Feeling better!*

As he's waiting for the chips, a reply comes though: *Yeah, my turn* ☹

Ah, shit, he thinks. *Just grabbing some food then I'll come check on you* ☹

Don't come in smelling of food!

K – what can I bring?

Dunno. Nothing. Don't worry about it.

He looks at the text for a long time. Okay, she doesn't want to be disturbed. She does seem to have this solitary way of coping with things. He can respect that.

The chips arrive and though they burn his tongue he wolfs down handfuls of salty potato. He may never have tasted chips this good. He should get out and about, and leave the window open and hopefully return to a clean room, devoid of sick smells.

He goes to leave the building. Halfway across the foyer, he spins back to the reception desk and asks the concierge to let the housekeeping staff know his friend is sick and may not want to be disturbed. He texts Mila to let her know, adding, *Hope that was the right thing to do.*

Do you want me to compliment you? she writes back.

Harsh. Maybe fair. His temptation is to send a longwinded message about how he is doing his best, but he puts his phone in his pocket. Fresh air. Prague in summer.

He and Josh had wanted to go see the Astronomical Clock. He makes his way across the bridge, excuses himself through the crowds, and gets there just in time.

His pocket buzzes. *Sorry – just sick grumpiness!*

Don't even worry about it ☺

He watches the clock. On the hour, the two small windows open above the dial and the Twelve Apostles appear, once Death has rung his bell. Vanity, Greed and Lust shake their heads, unwilling to go with the skeleton. People film on their phones, clustered together in the square. Kyle is overcome by contrasts: the figure of Death, installed in 1410, soon after the Black Death, and centuries before their own pandemic. And yet here we all are, gathered again, close and breathing on one another.

He looks at the other details on the clock, as the hourly show concludes: the astrolabe, the background with its zodiacal ring, and icons of the sun and moon. Below the clock is an ancient calendar and the names of 365 saints. Take your pick! he thinks. Beside the calendar are figures: the archangel Michael, plus an astronomer, a chronicler and a philosopher. An interdisciplinary clock.

He wishes he were sharing this with Josh. Josh sent him a snap, he remembers, saying that he'd taken a look but hadn't stayed for the show; that he would wait until he and Kyle were back there together.

Kyle's eye is drawn to the archangel, also known as Saint Michael: the healer and protector, is what he was taught in his childhood. Someone to call upon in the battle against evil. And this was particularly encouraged in the case of facing evil within yourself. But Michael is also associated with death – carrying the souls? Weighing them?

Kyle can't help imagining what a soul might look like, a wisp upon the scale.

Something twists in Kyle, an understanding of some yearning, even though he considers himself an atheist. He thinks it is connected to his Sundays in church as a child – a comforting weekly ritual; time spent together. Michael exists in the Hebrew Bible too, and the Qur'an, though Kyle doesn't know much about the differences.

This lingering or implanted spirituality, from childhood, gives a quiet emphasis to the world, to what he sees, hears, smells, tastes that is not entirely able to be expressed by words, language.

He watches the Astronomical Clock, standing among others and where others stood yesterday, where his friend briefly stood, and people one hundred years ago, four hundred, six hundred. And their breath still in the air somehow. The dead left inside us.

The feeling that none of it ever really went away, just compounded. And that somehow he's always been able to hold that thought with a kind of love, a pleasure.

He is feeling well, so well. But has given enough time to this.

On the way back, he sends a message to Reina to confirm the new meet-up. And then he goes into a small grocery mart and gets a couple of electrolyte drinks and some dry crackers. He walks across Charles Bridge, plastic bag swinging. Maybe Mila wants to be alone, or maybe she just doesn't know how to ask for help. He hopes he won't be overstepping.

He knocks on her door. 'It's me.'

She opens it, frowning.

'I got you some stuff.'

'Oh, thanks.' She walks back to the bed and lies down. She's wearing a grey singlet and boxer shorts with bottlebrush flowers on them. He feels a tiny starburst in his chest. Again, it's striking that she looks a bit like Josh. Without make-up, and with that short hair. Broad shoulders. But brown eyes instead of blue.

Kyle opens the minibar fridge and removes a couple of cans of beer in order to fit the electrolyte drinks. He brings one over to her and sits it very gently by her head on the bedside table.

'Thanks,' she mutters.

He puts the crackers on the desk so she can see them if she gets hungry.

And now – should he leave?

He sits down beside her, and pulls the comic he is reading out of his bag. Some space adventure thing. He loves it. He doesn't want her to feel any pressure, just to know he's there if she wants company. She doesn't protest.

He's getting into the story when he notices she is shaking a little bit. Ah – he had this fever, too. He puts the book down and pulls the blanket up, starts rubbing her shoulder. He reaches for the air-con remote and turns it off. He keeps rubbing her shoulder. She doesn't say anything or turn to look at him. When the shivers subside, he puts the air con back on, picks up his book again. Soon, her breathing grows heavier; she has fallen asleep. He puts his book down, takes in the quiet of the room. The sick smell is there but it doesn't bother him. He reclines, making sure to leave enough space on the bed if she wants to roll over, and he closes his eyes. He should get some rest and then, later, plan again the lines of enquiry for this next woman.

Kyle arrives at the home of the suspect. He has to use this word in his mind to force purpose. Just because the last woman was so pleasant, it doesn't mean this one will be too. She could know something. Could be a killer.

Reina is actually quite young to be on SugarMeetMe, maybe late thirties. There are four other people in the lounge room, around the same age and a mix of genders, as she and Kyle enter together. Sipping red wine, smoking weed. She sits Kyle on an armchair and admires him like a decoration. There are proud little brass pillboxes on the table, and colourful line drawings on paper smudged with ash. All the furniture is old, but her sportswear looks luxe, with breathable fabric and shimmering labels. Brand-new sneakers. So what she spends her money on is specific: her body – fitness, drugs, sex.

He's picking up on something from his experiences so far on this trip: that once women know what they want, they take it. But that's the thing – *once they know* what they want. He thinks of his mum and her contained, routine life; all her clothes from Millers, Rivers – or Suzanne Grae for something a bit fancier. His dad has a sports car, a boat. What if someone told Cheryl she could have more, be more? What if he did? He knows she'd say something about life not consisting of an abundance of possessions. And she would say he was sweet and that she had everything she wanted. Even though she spent a lot of time talking about how nice the things were in the magazines she kept on the coffee table. The thought of his mother's stifled aspirations leaves him a little queasy. Makes him want to get on a plane home and show up with a bottle of recognisably labelled decent champagne, like Veuve Clicquot or Moët, which she would appreciate more than anybody he's ever known.

So he can understand women wanting to take, wanting to openly want, and yet it still feels strange when this woman takes him into her bedroom, cluttered with plants and ceramic figures and drug ephemera, and straddles him, aggressively. When she tells him exactly what to do. When she clutches him hard enough to bruise. He starts to feel afraid. There are two phones on the bedside table – why?

'Are you okay?' she says, in a monotone.

His distraction has led to him slipping out. He could go down on her, but that would leave his head vulnerable. She's not big, though. He could hold her down easily. Josh could have held her down easily. The others in the lounge room – accomplices?

The phones are an iPhone and a Samsung. Josh had an older iPhone. Full and slow. Not this one.

Kyle goes down on her. She grunts when she comes. No other sound. She doesn't worry about him.

'Thanks,' she says.

He nervously starts to make his lines of enquiry. There's a war within him as he wonders if she is more capable of murder than Ivona, because she does not have the smile lines, because she is forceful, because she takes. And because of the drugs, perhaps?

Reina is monosyllabic and clearly not interested in his presence anymore. She taps out some coke. Yes, she goes to Berlin often. Yes, she has seen people more than once. So what? He feels bad. Bad about himself. Bad about not knowing anything. Bad about the fact he's a terrible, terrible sleuth, and that his plan is shit. He pulls his pants on, grabs his jacket as she throws back a line. She clutches his sleeve as he turns to go.

His heart rate skyrockets.

'Your money?' she says.

'Oh.'

When she hands it over it feels greasy in his palm.

⌒

Eloise, the sister of the other dead young man, has written back. Mila has only just felt up to looking at her phone and there it is: a long, desperate message. Mila is still tired, worn out from the bug, and seeing those red coronas on her eyelids as she often does when she is carrying sleep around with her. She will get up and have a cup of tea and wait for Kyle to return. Actually, she could probably manage a wine. The thirst has turned quickly to a craving. And she thinks they will both need it.

She's not sure how long Kyle has been gone for. Should she be worried?

Skimming the details of Eloise's message makes her worried.

She calls Kyle. No answer.

Well, he may be mid-fuck, she thinks.

She reads the message properly, her heart fluttering with nerves and weakness.

Matthew was from the States, Midwest. He had been living in Berlin. Before he went missing, he was seen at a club in the city's Winterfeldtplatz district with some friends. They were all officially questioned, and one of them said to the police that Matthew had seemed a bit down. He had high levels of GHB in his system. His friends confirmed he liked to take drugs when they went out, but they did not always know what.

What would Kyle do? He would write a list. She can get it started. She grabs the hotel notepad.

Commonalities:
Into the river
Note found
Young male
Dark hair
Clubbing?
Drugs?

Not much to go on. She hears the beep of Kyle's key in the door of his room. She picks up the notepad, her phone and her own key, and jumps up, not worrying about what she must look like.

'Kyle!' she says, knocking.

'Oh hey,' he says, opening the door.

'Eloise wrote back.'

'Oh fuck.'

Close to his face in the doorway, she can smell weed and sweat. 'Are you okay?'

'Yeah ... yeah. Come in.'

'I've made a list.'

'Oh good.'

He cracks the lid on a plastic bottle of water and drinks deeply, closing puffy eyelids. His checked shirt is misbuttoned.

'Was she ...?' Mila leaves some space.

He looks distressed. 'Um, I'm still thinking about it. Very different from Leana and Ivona. I don't really know how to think about someone as a potential murderer, you know? She does go often to Berlin.'

Mila's mind is racing. She's been in the dizzy space of sickness, and now, all this information. Where do they start? What do they do with it?

'Okay,' she says, 'well, here's the message.'

She waits for him to read it. He's still standing, with the bottle of water in one hand, scrolling.

'Sit down,' she says.

'What?'

'Get comfy.'

'Oh.' He's really spaced. He sits and puts the water down in front of the mirror, finishes reading.

'Here's the list I've started,' she says.

'Good, good.' He glances at it, but his eyes are welling up. He looks at her like a scared, trapped animal.

She sighs. 'I know.'

She can sense him aching for a hug, some comfort, so she stands up and gets a tissue from the other side of the bed. The box sits on a couple of books – on top, Iris Murdoch's *The Sea, The Sea*, Vintage Classics edition. Where did Mila see that recently? It was one of

Scott's favourite books. She read it when she was with him and wanted to love it but was too frustrated by the character's solitary leanings. She thinks she might like it more now.

'Didn't know this book would be up your alley,' she says to Kyle.

'Ivona gave it to me, actually. She said she likes to offer gifts to her young men.' He sniffs, takes the tissue from her hand.

'But you didn't find her creepy?'

'No. She was warm.'

'Psychopaths can fake emotions really well.'

'I don't know … The woman tonight, she felt more distant.'

'She might just be more self-protective.'

'I did consider that.'

She notices his tone. Right. 'It's just that men often think a woman *should* be warm, sweet, nurturing, and if she isn't then she's not … normal.'

'I know that. What do you want me to look out for, then? A notebook with drawings inked in blood? A clipping of hair?' He sounds truly angry.

'I'm just saying —'

'Well you don't have to say it to *me*. Not all men —'

'Here we go.'

'Yeah, well, I'm tired, okay?' He wipes his eyes again.

'*I'm* fucking tired.' A lifetime of tired more than you, she thinks. The air-conditioner hums.

Kyle goes to say something else, closes his mouth, shakes his head a little.

'What?' she says.

He exhales audibly. 'I know you're tired.' He gets up, opens the tiny fridge and pulls out two cheap Czech beers. He offers them up with a crooked smile on his crumpled, reddened face.

Mila takes one.

'Glad you're feeling better,' he says earnestly, but not looking at her.

She cracks the can, has a fizzy sip. It's taking her mind a moment to recalibrate. With Scott, she would have needed to keep making her point, hoping he'd hear it at least once before he shut himself off, went into the bedroom and put his headphones in.

'Okay,' she says eventually. 'So what do we write back to Eloise?'

'Let's figure it out on the way back to Berlin.'

Mila crunches from a packet of chips under the large, bright arch on the train platform as Kyle scrolls on his phone beside her. There is just enough mildness in the weather today for her light bomber jacket. She's starting to get self-conscious about her arms, her fading muscles, the looseness. And yet she is eating chips. It's not like you can find snow peas to snack on everywhere, and she's still craving salt after being ill.

She peers over Kyle's shoulder. They scroll through the Oglr, seeing what they can find – what the SugarMeetMe clients may not be revealing.

'I mean, it's mostly him,' she says, 'but when you catch a glimpse of another person you can't really tell …'

'The sex … of the body.'

'Yeah.'

'I think that must have been deliberate,' Kyle says.

'What do you mean?'

'Josh was really passionate about loving all bodies, all kinds of people.' Kyle smiles fondly. 'And so by not highlighting the sex, he showed his welcoming bisexuality, or pansexuality – I think he used both terms.'

'He didn't really go on about that with me,' says Mila. And I feel foolish, she thinks. 'Well, maybe once.' She remembers now. It was her who diverted the conversation, her difficult, unresolved thoughts about her own sexuality making it uncomfortable.

And of course she was paying Josh to make her feel she was at the centre of his world – at least, in the moment.

Kyle starts shaking his head. 'We've missed something.'

'What do you mean?'

'My plan, to tick off the women he was seeing on SugarMeetMe, ignores the other people he could have been seeing casually.'

Mila frowns. 'Oh.'

'I mean, look at this photo.'

Josh's sleepy face, white sheets, just the whorl of an ear and short blond hair by his shoulder.

'This is possibly still in Prague,' Kyle says, 'and that person is not one of the women I just met.'

Mila nods, starting to understand. 'Fuck.'

'Tinder … Grindr …'

'Of course. He loved sex. He wasn't just doing it for money.' She can't breathe for a moment. Her vision blackens a little at its edges.

Kyle has already taken out the notebook, but he holds it closed, staring at the cover. 'We can't do this all on our own,' he says blankly. 'The police need to do something.'

Mila tries to locate a breath. The chip salt on her fingers, food smells from the nearby station vendor, cigarette smoke – everything is pungent on the inhale. The skin on her neck, chest and cheeks grows hot, as though she still has the fever. Is she actually going to throw up? She puts her head closer to the ground, through her knees, looking away from Kyle.

The train pulls into the station, and Kyle gently taps her upper arm. She stands and wheels her bag to the carriage. They find their seats, this time both facing forward. As the train moves out from the station, Kyle puts the food tray down, opens the notebook and starts scratching at it with his pen. They have to write back to Eloise on Facebook, too; Mila clenches her fists, wondering how she will find the energy.

The whole train journey to Berlin, Kyle alternates between the notebook and sighing and huffing as he fails to guess Josh's Tinder and Grindr passwords. He tries obsessively. 'If I could just …' 'But he always used …'

Mila puts in her headphones and listens to Bauhaus. Eyelid-drooping music; scratchy smoky music, as low and repetitive as bad thoughts. The image and sense of Josh is potent after her look at the Oglr. She has avoided scrolling through it since that day in Budapest. She thinks of his nipples, his underarms – her head nestled there after sex. That little kiss he planted, affectionately. She looks across at Kyle's face, frowning over the phone. She stands to go to the toilet, seeing spots, running her hand along the wall. She locks herself in and sobs until she vomits into the silver bowl.

⌒

Kyle and Mila walk past the line of police cars and press a red button for the door with *Polizei* marked above. They'd dropped off their bags and come straight here. Kyle can't bear to wait. They need help. It's all too much for them to try to figure out on their own, and they have to get the police to listen. They tried calling the embassy as well, but the staff said they'd only talk to family. When the speaker crackles Kyle looks down at his page, which he has ready and open, and reads the words in German as best he can:

'I'm sorry, I cannot speak German. We would like to speak to a senior police officer about our friend who is missing, presumed dead, in Berlin.'

The door buzzes open.

They walk into a brightly lit, high-ceilinged reception area. It is noisy and full of people – mostly uniformed – going from here to there with folders, cups of coffee; speaking with each other and on mobile phones; one leading a dishevelled man out past the tall front desk to a bustling area beyond. Kyle has to breathe, stay calm. Beside him, Mila has her arms crossed over her chest. She smells a bit too much like alcohol for this environment. It makes him angry, an emotion that is surprising to him. The way it makes his neck muscles ache with holding back.

A young male officer eventually comes up to them, black buzz cut, clean-shaven. 'I speak English,' he says. 'Is there an emergency?' He looks Mila up and down, as though she might be injured.

'No,' says Kyle, 'thank you. We have called and been put through to various departments, and we thought it might be easier to come in.'

The officer waits.

Kyle clears his throat. 'Our friend went missing here in Berlin …'

'Almost three weeks ago,' Mila says.

'His body hasn't been found. His stuff was by the river, and there was a note so it was ruled a probable suicide.' The officer's face shows concern. 'But, well, not only do we think it wasn't, but there was a similar death around a year ago … Um, they could be linked.'

'Okay, okay.' The officer gestures for him to slow down. 'You have already registered this with which department?'

'I think the Criminal Investigations Unit.'

'In uh, voice? Or in writing?'

'Just over the phone.'

'Okay. This is not my area to look into – a case that sounds like it is closed, or indefinite until a body is found – but I can help you to register a written request to look into this case, and I can get it to the right department.'

Kyle wants to reach up to the man's neat collar, grab it, pull him in and hiss into his face: My. Friend. Is. Gone.

'Thankyousomuch,' he says.

'Follow me.'

As they follow the officer through the busy entrance hall into a room with rows of desks and chairs both behind and in front, Mila adds, 'It's the writing, too, on the supposed suicide note – it wasn't how Josh expressed himself. We can show you other things he wrote – for an expert to look at …'

'Absolutely. You just have to write this all down.' The officer flicks his hand at the wrist, then sits behind a desk and indicates to the chairs in front. 'Please, sit.'

'And once we do, how long will it take for the department to look into it?' Mila says.

'Hmm, I'm sorry that I cannot give you an exact time. It will depend how many cases they have open and how many other enquiries they are looking at.'

A phone rings loud on the desk. The officer glances at it.

'But what if …' Kyle says, sensing there's an edge to his voice, 'this person kills again?'

The officer is repressing a smirk as he picks up the phone and replies to something in German, then places it down. 'A serial killer?' he says.

'Just, you know, some sick person …'

The officer gestures emphatically. 'Okay, okay, I will do my best, I promise, to escalate this for you. Let me just find …' He digs around in his drawers. 'Ah … The form is in German. Will you be okay to use your phone to translate the questions?'

'Yes, thanks,' Kyle says, looking down at the green-and-white form.

'I will come back.' The officer stands and leaves them to it.

Kyle looks down, then at Mila. 'It's something,' he says.

'Eloise went through all this.'

'But maybe when we draw the link between them …'

'Yeah,' she says, 'at least we'll have something more to say when we write back to her now.' But Mila doesn't look hopeful. And she has become more softly spoken, as though conserving energy.

He continues nodding to her, trying to hold her gaze.

She looks away. 'What if nothing happens?'

'We …' He looks down at the form. They would go home, he supposes. Start a Facebook page: 'Justice for Josh.' Or would they? That would mean revealing to Josh's family their suspicion that there was foul play involved, which would upset them if Kyle and Mila are wrong. It would also mean questioning whether he's still alive, which may get his family's hopes up unnecessarily. Is this something Kyle and Mila should just carry alone? And should they come back year after year and keep trying?

He takes a deep breath and gets out his phone to translate the document.

⌒

Mila enters a heavily forested area of Tiergarten where dealers congregate, according to old friends of hers who live in London and come to Berlin in summer for the club experience. There is another park where it's much easier to buy drugs, but the friends have said it's best avoided – bad vibes.

She is thinking about the longwinded text she's just had from Scott. He said he's been thinking about her. He sent her a link to a new song he's written. Funny, in the past couple of years she would have opened it instantly, sent him something encouraging back. It's good that he now has the confidence to express and share like this. But this time, she didn't think she could bear hearing his voice. Instead, the lost weekend fantasy came in, crowding her thoughts.

Now she sits down on a park bench, and soon a clean-cut guy sits next to her and says 'hallo'. She says 'hello' in English, and he switches seamlessly and asks her if she's in Berlin to party.

'I am,' she says, surprised that it is so easy.

Cocaine will be best, she thinks. It's better suited to grief. She doesn't want pure euphoria and empathy for strangers; she wants to be arrogant and sharp. But she wants to cover all bases of potential desire, so she asks for MDMA and speed as well. She could stay up for days in another world – not eating or sleeping while wrenching herself out with music and sweat, pushing the nothingness out of her and into the air. Isn't that what Josh did over here? But with less of a dark impetus.

The clean-cut guy asks her to walk with him, and as they do he rearranges things within his jacket pockets, gathering the elements into a package for her. They get to a tree and he tells her how much it will cost and that she can duck behind the trunk to count it out. He lights a cigarette, looking casual in a way only someone practised could.

Leaning against the tree Mila experiences a natural rush – her heart speeds up and she can hear her blood pumping through her body. The leaves and the blades of grass become clearer, almost as though she can see the veins within them. How odd, she thinks; the anticipation of drugs produces some pre-effect, like she's peeking into another realm.

The sensation dissipates enough for her to finish getting her money together.

Once the exchange is done, the man gives her a warm smile. 'Have fun.'

The song, Scott has texted, is about that moment he was alone and first confronting his suicidal impulse. When she was first in Prague. She can't listen to it, because she knows he will sing about how no one was there. Physically, no one was there, yes. But mentally she had been with him, stretched across oceans.

They persisted for a long time in wanting to think they were inextricably intertwined. Maybe they were, and still are. Soul-twisted. But desires apart, and a physical disconnect.

Josh had understood something about her body, and helped her to understand it about herself – how it was one and the same with the rest of her. How her heart was in her fingertips, her mind in her cunt. And he made that feel okay, and made her feel that she could be whole.

As she takes the little baggies – white powders and pinkish brown crystals – out of her handbag and puts them on the desk in the hotel room, she thinks there could be an option here where she acknowledges, intellectually, what is happening. Of the progress she made previously, the healing and coming into herself, that has been unravelled by this tragedy with Josh. But the drugs – the possibility of them – are like bug-out bags she has packed for disaster that have been sitting, ready, by the door. They contain everything she needs. They are guns and torches and fleece.

But this bomb has not hit her alone.

She knocks on Kyle's door. He doesn't answer.

She goes back to her room. He must be out. Perhaps she should just test something – the cocaine would be best; it wears off quicker. She shakes a little out onto the back of her plastic phone case, cleans up the line with her Visa card. This is going to be stronger than it is in Australia, she thinks. She should probably go easy. She stares at the line. She rolls up a note and sticks it in her right nostril.

When Kyle gets back with his mie goreng he hears dance music playing in the next room. He knocks on the door. Mila opens it quickly, eyes and mouth wide open.

'I have noodles,' he says.

'Oh! I'm not too hungry. I could definitely go a drink, though. Something really smooth, like a nice vodka, or maybe gin – no, not gin, although with lemon …' She is speaking quickly and darting about, picking things up and moving them.

He comes into the room and sits on the bed.

'Is it bright in here?' she says. 'Maybe a bit, yeah?' She turns on the lamp by the bed, turns off the main lamp, frowns, turns on the other bed lamp. 'There,' she says. 'I uh … I'm a little high.'

There's a swooping in his gut. Alcohol he kind of understands – the effects, how to be around her. But he's always been nervous about illegal drugs – too unpredictable. He couldn't even guess what she's had.

'Did you get into Josh's accounts?' she asks.

'Not yet.'

'You might not. I mean, we have to think of more ways …'

'I have been trying.'

The music sounds terrible to him. His mood lately has only been for scratchy old folksy stuff about long-distance longing, about homes and forgiveness.

'Are you okay, my sweet?' she asks. 'I'm sorry about that term of endearment, you know I feel these things and can't say them.

I guess that's what being high can help with. Let that rush come through you. Which is a relief. Such a relief. I mean I still feel all of it – the grief. But it just lights a spark. You should have some. Can I give you a little?'

'I don't want to.' He says it more grumpily than he intends to. He still has the mie goreng in a plastic bag slung over his wrist. He apprehends distance and doom.

'You gonna leave me out here all alone on this island?' she says. 'I mean, of course, you have to do what you're comfortable with. I just hate that this does tap a little bit into my anxiety. You know, that slight edge of paranoia. And then if I have the MD as well I can get that a bit more – sometimes a fixation on something negative, despite the love I am feeling too … But that's —'

'Did you have a lot, of …'

'Cocaine. Well, not really, but it's strong. I can feel it in my throat now. Numbing. It's very nice you know. Am I different? I need to be different. Or more myself. I don't know. I'm not going to apologise for it. Maybe you need a drink.' She goes over to the mini fridge. She pulls out a beer and cracks the top. 'I think I need to go out,' she says. Handing it to him.

'I thought we'd just settle in … We need to think.'

'You don't like doing anything off the plan. Live a little, Kyle. Ugh, what a cliché. I'm talking in clichés. But seriously, don't stop me. We could go and dance, or we could go to a burlesque club – would you like that?' There is some barb in the way she says that.

'No.'

'I've never seen you so angry.'

'I'm … frustrated.'

'You need to go let off some steam.'

He doesn't know how to tell her that he can't because he'd be having to look after her. He sips his beer. 'I don't like clubs.'

'On drugs you would.' She paces, pours a shot of vodka, throws it back.

'You're a bit … controlling on cocaine.'

'It makes you see things clearly. Okay, okay – how about this? We go to where Josh would go. We find out – I can find out, if I go back to this bar where there's a girl who knows him. If she's not there maybe someone else will be who knew him. We investigate. We sleuth. *He did this.* He had drugs and went out. We can find out what might have happened.'

Kyle takes in her unburdened expression. The retreat of her anxiety and even her age: lineless.

'I'm going to put my make-up on,' she says, heading to the bathroom. 'C'mon! Spruce moose!'

⁓

They arrive at Mesmer, after Kyle managed to charm Belle, the bartender at Die Lampe, to find out where Josh would go following their bar hangouts. Mila was too high to be self-conscious about Belle's barbs over her being Josh's 'aunt' this time.

Standing in line at the club, Mila pumps her shoulders, wrists – her smile cracking her underused cheeks. She cannot wait to be inside, to be subsumed by music. Instead of the drug covering up or distracting from the black hole there's this effect where the emptiness is incorporated in her mood – it's less isolated, more expansive and profound. She has a sense of the clothing, hair and skin around her: the strands, the seams, the points, the beads. Each hard bead requesting to be fingertipped and fondled. Each button and zip obscenely superficial but also among the great deteriorating material of earth.

She looks at Kyle, the good sport Kyle, with his frown and shrug, only two beers down, refusing to look back at her. She admires the frown because of the calculations it speaks of. She can feed him ideas and he will then separate out, and connect, all that is relevant. And his mind won't stop working until he achieves this. She remembers that not so long ago that was her, how she operated. The satisfaction of creating perfect 30- and 45-minute workouts that used every muscle group. Spreadsheets of work balance and projected earnings. He, too, could lose the ability. And one day he may want to.

'I can see how your brain works, Kyle,' she says.

He nods, noncommittal to conversing. She knows he thinks she is out of her mind, that he doesn't know which words to take notice of.

'I'm not a baby, you know,' she says.

'I know,' he says. 'But you are vulnerable right now.'

So I can see his mind and perhaps he can see my black hole, she thinks. And this sets off a fresh euphoric rush. With the coke she doesn't have the usual secondary thoughts – the negative overlay, where doubt is added to what she has just thought or felt.

'What?' he says. She is staring at him.

'You're great.'

'You're high.'

When they go through the doors, the music sets goosebumps on her skin. Her nipples go hard under her slippery teal singlet. And, as though her openness has a smell, heads turn towards and linger on her.

She wants more letting go.

'Meet you at the bar?' she says. 'I'm going to the loo.'

Kyle looks flustered, but nods.

In the stall, she opens her powder case to extract one of the MDMA bombs she constructed back in the room – one point wrapped in cigarette paper. She swallows it. She thinks, This will dredge up what I know. Grief and anxiety have made the feelings shy.

She lingers at the mirror, plays with her hair. It's a little bit like when Josh's was growing longer. Starting to curl at her ears. Her jeans, her boots, are like something he would have worn, too. But not this slippery, shimmery top. All of it moves with her, is comfortable. Her muscles feel good to be in motion. She will shock them awake, back into shape, tonight.

A girl is talking to Kyle at the bar. She wears a pink bodycon shift and white sneakers. She sips at a bottle of water. She leans in close to his ear, so he can hear her. Mila sees from his body language that he is both wary and interested. He touches his hair a lot, nods profusely. He catches Mila's eye as she is almost at the bar, just as the girl takes his hand in an attempt to drag him towards the dancefloor. Mila nods to him. He shrugs. Is gone. She hopes he can go with it, but she expects he'll come up to her in an hour and ask to leave.

She thinks of Josh and Kyle's friendship, of them travelling together. Would Kyle have come with Josh to clubs? To parties? To sex bars in Amsterdam? He would have, she thinks, because he loved his friend, but he would always have been torn. In his heart preferring the comfort of Netflix on the laptop and a nice local craft beer on the bedside table. He is both curious and comfortable, she thinks. A young man and an old man in one.

He dances with the girl, who is doing druggy arm circles and swinging her head. He's shifting from foot to foot.

I better take him a drink, Mila thinks. She orders two vodka sodas.

'Do you know a guy called Josh?' Kyle yells over the music to the cute girl in the pink dress. Mila places a drink in his fist and starts dancing – skilfully, with shoulders and neck and hips – beside them. Of course she can dance.

The girl, Anya, slicks her gaze to Mila. 'Is that your girlfriend?'

'We're friends,' Kyle calls back.

The girl sips her drink.

'So have you met anyone here with that name?' he asks again, the irritation tightening the skin across his face.

'No,' she says. 'Sorry.'

I could ask everyone on the dancefloor, he thinks. But it's ridiculous: every single person in this room could be here for the first time. These clubs are a tourist destination. And even if these people were here every week, Josh was hardly here, and amid a swarm. And the staff? They might recognise his face, but … Kyle looks at the bar. A crush of people moving in and out. How many people would they serve a night? There would be no reason to notice who those people were with.

He seems to have finished his drink.

Anya gestures to him – a winding up, a 'get into it!' motion – and he knows he is half-arsing the dancing, thinking too much. But if he doesn't, who else will do the thinking? God, he wishes he could figure out the Tinder and Grindr logins.

Maybe he will talk to the bar staff. He has to do something.

'No, no, no,' they say – 'never seen him.' 'He's cute, though.' Then one – 'Oh, that's the guy who disappeared, yeah? I saw him, but not that night.'

'Oh yeah?' Kyle's heart races. 'Do you remember who he was with?'

'Um,' the bartender's face strains as he thinks, 'no … Sorry. He came up to the bar by himself, as far as I recall.'

Kyle has finished his drink again.

'You his friend?' the bartender asks, sympathetically.

'Yeah,' Kyle says.

'So sorry.'

'Do you know anyone who saw him the last night he was here before he disappeared?'

'Uh, yeah, Tania – she's not on tonight, though.'

'When does she work?'

'I can check, but you have to buy another drink.' He winks.

'Okay, another one of whatever this was,' says Kyle. Once he has the information, his frustration dissipates a little. Or maybe it's all the alcohol.

He looks for Mila and spots her dancing among strangers, moving her head perfectly in time to the beat, and he feels a momentary sense of wellbeing. This song is familiar. Where does he know it from?

She catches his eye, walks towards him determinedly, clutches his arm. 'I'm coming up,' she says. 'I need sugar.'

'Oh, ah …' He turns back around and orders a lemonade.

She smiles, grateful. 'I … need air,' she says, desperation on her face. Her pupils are massive. She looks at the ground. 'Jesus.'

'Okay, take my arm.' She does, and he walks her towards the stairs up to the open-air courtyard. They take them slowly. He can feel her steadying her breath.

Outside, people are draped across lounges, petting each other, smoking. Small groups move in time with the beat downstairs.

'Oh phew,' she says. 'This is good.'

She looks at him as they find a wall, her hand going on it to lean. Her pupils look alien.

'You are beautiful, Kyle.'

'Yeah, yeah,' he says.

She strokes his hair. He lets her but he wants to get away, too. There are hours of this ahead. Having to listen to her drug talk.

'Sorry,' she says.

So, perceptive enough, still.

'You're only scared, you know,' she says.

No, he thinks, I am angry. He won't tell her what he has learned yet. She's obviously not in the right mindset.

She finishes the lemonade. 'I'm ready to go back down.'

Maybe envious, too, he thinks later, when she is dancing still, and then moving her hands through strangers' hair, across their cheeks, looking like a delighted child. Envious that she can let it go.

⁓

Kyle has left her. It is 3 a.m. She doesn't blame him. They always do. Even if they don't want to admit, even to themselves, that they think she shouldn't act the way she does.

But Josh would be here now, wouldn't he? On the dancefloor, pumping gum in his mouth and feeling the music in the hairs on his arms. Would Kyle have left him here too?

She dances with Anya, whose rubbery pink dress keeps riding up her thighs. She sees Mila looking and she reaches for her hand. Mila lets her. She has soft, manicured hands. She moves in closer to Mila and her hand moves to her waist. Up close when the light strobes, Mila can see her glittery pink lips. Mila is not shy anymore, at this stage of the night, at this stage of peaking, at this stage of grief, and she moves her lips to the glitter. Their breasts press together as they continue moving to the beat. Anya's lips part. She tastes of salt and tequila. Mila runs a hand through her long, soft, tangerine-scented hair. She touches her hips, her waist, her bare shoulder blades. The two women part and dance, keeping eyes locked, and then kiss again. They hold hands and go to the bar. They smile at each other. Sweat has run lines through Anya's make-up. She looks glorious. They go back to dance again. Mila can barely feel her own feet. She is all up-top – in the hands and face and the throat.

A guy on the dancefloor beside Mila takes out his phone and shoots off a message.

And then she has a thought.

DMs.

She excuses herself from Anya, pecking her on her soft cheek. In the bathroom, she struggles to text Kyle. She is too high – her pupils can't focus on the small screen. But she has to tell him, has to remember to look into this. She calls. He doesn't answer. Probably already in bed. She leaves a voice message.

Kyle wakes at dawn with a jolt of anxiety. He grabs for his phone, bleary-eyed. A missed call and a voice message from Mila from several hours ago. He presses play but rests his head back on the pillow, nauseated. His skull is still a vice of anger, frustration – blood pumping at his temples.

Her voice comes through with a faint beat behind it. 'Oglr!' she says excitedly in the message. 'Oglr allows instant messaging. Didn't you help him set it up? Can't you log in?'

Oh my god, Kyle thinks. Of course. With SugarMeetMe, and Tinder and Grindr, all messages are private, hence the need to log into Josh's accounts. But Oglr is more like a blogging site, and so they'd trawled the photos for clues and were able to see who followed and interacted with Josh, and those people's profiles, but neither of them had thought about its possible private messaging function.

The comments they've seen on the photos – flirtatious, beckoning, often knowing, often inviting – are from recurring handles. He sits up straight, the vice grip around his head lessening, the fog clearing. But his hands shake slightly with adrenaline as he opens the Oglr app and tries one of Josh's regular passwords.

Nope.

He tries a variation.

It works.

He puts the phone down. He should be doing this with Mila. He would like to be doing it with her.

He shifts his legs over the bed, looks around for his jeans. He pulls them on and throws a shirt over his head and goes next door to her room. The sun is just coming up but maybe she will be back, and awake.

She is. She lets him in wearing just her underwear and a t-shirt, her hair wild, her face clean. She has earbuds in and is nodding lightly. She raises her eyebrows at him, then gets straight back under the covers. She has surrounded herself with pillows, like a throne. 'I get auditory hallucinations on the comedown,' she says, a little too loud. 'I'm trying to drown them out with Bowie.'

She pats the bed beside her, and he sits. She smells sweaty, but not unpleasantly so. When she closes her eyes, he can't help his gaze moving to her lips, down to her nipples standing up in her shirt. He was half-erect on waking and his dick hardens fully now. He shifts to hide it, feeling shame, feeling inappropriate.

She opens her eyes. 'So what do you think?'

He holds up his phone to show her the logged-in back end of Josh's Oglr account.

She gasps, pulls her headphones from her ears. 'What's there? What do we do?'

'I haven't looked yet. I wanted to look with you.'

She gives him a kind, grateful look. And he feels terrible. How mad he was at her last night, how much he wanted to shake her – tell her she wasn't thinking hard enough about the fucking mystery they had to solve. How much he felt it was a burden all on him.

'You're very good,' she says.

'No I'm not,' he says.

She looks annoyed. 'I hate it when men do that,' she says. And she grabs the phone from his hand, scrolls. 'There are definitely messages here. It's a bit hard for me to take in right now, while I hear something like … tropical music playing faintly, as if in a stadium one suburb over.'

'Tropical music?' He frowns – the song that seemed familiar last night. 'Hang on, pause one sec.' He holds out his hand to take the phone back, then goes to his videos and clicks one near the top. For some reason Josh didn't send this one on Snapchat.

Kyle plays the short clip with Josh yelling happily over a deep house beat with tropical melodies – marimba, steel drums – a contrast of bass and summer.

'What's he saying?' she says.

'He's saying sweet things about me,' Kyle says. 'But then he apologises and says the MDMA makes him lovey-dovey.'

Mila looks off into the distance.

'It's like you had the same impulses,' Kyle says. 'Are you okay?'

'Yes, it's just weird that what I'm hearing in my head is that same music – or maybe not. They must have had the same DJ last night. I do always get these hallucinations if I have a fair bit of MDMA. It's kind of spooky, but also fascinating, to hear something that is not there.'

'Is it always music?'

'Often it is. Sometimes it's voices. Like having a laugh and a chat in the other room.'

'Sounds sinister.'

'Not sinister. Spooky.'

It's quiet for a moment, and her face falls. 'Very spooky. I ... just heard Josh laughing. Mostly I don't recognise the voices.' She stands up and turns on the speaker on the desk, connects her phone. 'I need to drown it out, and try to sleep.' She looks distressed.

'Can I do anything?'

'You want to just stay here and snooze with me? And when I wake up and feel close to normal again, we can have a proper look at the Oglr on the laptop?'

'Sure.' Kyle tries not to look at the softness of her upper thighs, her taut abdomen above the line of lace on her underwear. He doesn't think he will be able to snooze. But he does like Bowie. She's playing the later stuff – *The Next Day*. His fingers itch. To check the Oglr. To touch skin. He'll find a game or something to play.

She lies down next to him, facing away. 'When did he send that video to you?' she asks.

'I think it was two or three days before ...'

Her body shudders.

He watches her until she falls asleep.

⁓

Mila sits by the window, sipping strong coffee that Kyle has brought back for her. She hasn't quite been ready to face the world. The drugs seem to be lingering. Strange effects of light, colour, sound. Her surroundings seem more ... crisp than usual.

The laptop is on the desk nearby. She found the private messages on the Oglr confronting, and she's not sure why they were more so than the photos of Josh with other people. Perhaps because the language is similar to what he used with her – not purely sexual, but sensual, sweet, open. He was not an actor. He was always unapologetically himself, genuine in lust and affection.

There are three people he was in touch with in the last weeks, seemingly in Berlin. Though with one (username: _Moon_) there is no indication of a location in the messages, and her account is only semi-nudes taken indoors, in a room with blank walls, so it doesn't really provide any more clues. One of the others (username: C@llMeByYr) was definitely meeting up with Josh four or five days before the river; C@llMeByYr's account is reposted pictures, screenshots from queer cinema, German captions. The final one (username: Soldeer7) indicated that he and Josh had met in person, but there were no arrangements made through this messaging system – they could have run into each other again at the club? His account has no public posts. Both C@llMeByYr and Soldeer7 sent dick pics and torso shots but no face pics.

'What's our strategy from here?' Mila says.

Kyle has his head in his hands. Pokes his face through. 'I mean, we could contact them here? Pretend to be Josh? But of course they all may know he's gone, even if they didn't do it. It was in the news.'

'And if we contact them as us, the suspicious person will delete their account and we'll have no way to trace them.'

'We could keep going back through the pics and the comments they've left, and their profiles, to search for clues.'

'I guess that's something for now, while we think about it,' Mila says, deflated. Her mind goes to the remaining vodka, wedged into the mini fridge. Thinks about Anya's glittery lips and her number sitting in Mila's phone. 'Where else did Josh go? Like in the daytime – what did he do?'

Kyle looks at her blankly. The effort and energy has drained from him.

'I want to go somewhere he went, for no other reason than to be close to him.' Her voice cracks a little. She knows it's partly an effect of the comedown, but the feeling is real within her nonetheless.

'The National Gallery,' Kyle says. 'Remember? There's a photo on the Oglr of one of the paintings – grapes and pomegranate and peaches ...'

'That's right, all that ... *lustful* fruit spilling over a table.'

They both pause, hold the thought of Josh's bright, abundant worldview for a moment.

'I go more for the gloomy paintings,' Mila says. 'Want to take in some German expressionism?'

Kyle stands. 'I ...' She can tell he wants to stay and obsess and search and research, is fighting with himself.

'Just a few hours. You know how things click in the back of your head when you walk away from the problem?'

'That's true.'

Kyle goes to get his bag.

Kyle is staring into fields, at mountains, and the tempestuous waves of Gustave Courbet's *Die Welle*. Funny how Josh was drawn to the fruit and Mila lingers mainly on faces, while he feels an ache at these landscapes: that, if unspoiled, could look the same today as in 1869. Or maybe he is too aligned to the romanticism of *Die Welle* – nature reflecting the turmoils of the human heart. Those frothy waves and the grey sky bearing down. But facing the potential future they all face, would it be so bad to return to such an affinity with nature?

He finds the fruit painting, by Johann Wilhelm Preyer. It makes him hungry. He wants it to provide a clue. He remembers he has to tell Mila about the bartender at Mesmer, how they have to go back to the club on the night Tania is working. Staring at the juicy peach flesh, he feels exhausted.

He calls Mila over and tells her, still staring ahead, hoping to see something he may not have. His eyes blur with the effort.

'I thought we had our plan, to search through the Oglr people's profiles and find out more about them before approaching them,' Mila says, 'because approaching them may scare them off.' She sounds exasperated.

This is all not enough, he thinks. We are lost.

'You just want a day off,' Kyle says, and then regrets it.

She walks away from him a bit. 'Maybe we should have a little break from each other,' she says in a flat voice. 'Do our own thing.'

'Yeah, maybe,' he says, but there's a twisting inside his chest.

'Just don't message them yet,' she says. 'We need to put more thought into it. I'll catch you later.' She walks off into another room of the gallery.

Kyle stands there for a while, staring after her. Why does she get to decide what to do? And how can she stand waiting?

He's the one with the access. He can do what he wants. Josh was *his* best friend. He knew him longer. He loved him.

He looks back at the painting. The curled twigs, the golden fruit, the overripe spilling.

He finds another painting by Preyer. A hasty arrangement of flowers in a rusty jug. Dewy and bug-laden, with some mess about. A discarded brassy ring with a burgundy stone. He raises his phone and takes a quick photograph.

He sends it to each of the three Oglr users Josh was last in contact with: _Moon_, C@llMeByYr and Soldeer7.

His hands shake. He exits the gallery, and while briskly walking across Museum Island to the Pergamon, he raises his phone to his ear again. He calls the police and leaves another message.

In the museum's cool interior, his breaths come short and sharp. He looks at the Pergamon bodies twisted in marble, ancient: Apollo, Zeus, Athena … His friend's body frozen in its beauty on a digital cloud. Not one that will last as long as this. How can Kyle commit him to time? To sculpt him, to paint him? He has none of those skills. Other people only knew Josh in fragments. Except maybe Mila, he will admit, despite the brevity – and circumstances – of their relationship. Is it only this knowledge of Josh that connects Kyle and Mila? Or is their burgeoning friendship genuine? He sits on a bench and decides to go no further into the museum. These gods in marble are enough.

He checks Oglr. No replies. He scrolls through their accounts – mainly the queer movie posters because it wouldn't be good to look at nudes in public. Though he is surrounded by sculpted breasts, buttocks. He needs his laptop so he can open a few tabs, look for those usernames on other social media sites, keep some columns in a notebook. Maybe the links will start to show.

His neck is tight and he is breathless.

May as well cover your hotel room in newspaper articles and photos connected by different-coloured strings, he thinks. But the self-deprecating thought does not override the obsessive, tunnelling one.

He will go back. Laptop. Notebook. Tabs. Columns.

There is no point in the art. It is not helping him figure out anything.

Mila has to sit down, take some Panadol, maybe a Valium. The gallery room whomps with colour and light. She stares at Caspar David Friedrich's *Abtei im Eichwald*, the darkest focal point.

As she stares at the picture – the ruined wall, lonely fingers of trees reaching – it's as though she becomes aware of each stroke of paint. The painting takes up all of her vision. And then she detects movement. The sky in the painting lightens, swirls. The bare branches move softly as though stirred by a breeze.

She blinks, and the painting recedes, stills.

She's never had a visual hallucinatory effect before, on the comedown.

A woman moves closer to the painting, blocking it from Mila, says in an American accent to her husband, 'Did you see that?'

'What?' He is engrossed in the war scene that dominates the far wall.

'It …' She moves closer again. '… looked like it was stirring.' She reaches a hand towards the painting, transfixed, until the security alarm blares, making her and her husband jump.

'What are you talking about?' he says, impatient.

She shakes her head. 'Never mind. I think I need a nap.'

Mila looks down at the floor, afraid. Can it really have worked? From all those months ago?

She pulls her mobile out of her bag, texts Kyle. *Where are you?*

Pergamon.

Stay there.

She stands and her head spins. She moves from the room, the floor, the gallery, keeping her eyes down. Across Museum Island.

Pausing at a patch of grass, she sits down to catch her breath. She glances up and around – no one watching. She examines the blades of grass, each covered in tiny dewdrops and hooks and microscopic bugs, and holding light and water and colour of a spectrum she's never seen before.

Woah.

She reaches her fingers out to touch a pebble in the grass and it hums, as though with life. She pulls her hand back sharply.

Dare she look at the sky?

She telescopes the sun's corona, can almost hear the crackling fire of its surface. The closer atmosphere, this blanket for life, is not blue but cloudy: light bouncing off billions of small particles.

An ant dies nearby and she smells the sharp moment of it. There is an inarticulable sense as it passes – of a life dissipating back into the greater texture.

Her brain sings in its knowledge.

Her heart pummels with fear.

She concentrates hard to rein it in, to suck the senses back down to the immediate, the human.

She stands, half-jogs into the Pergamon Museum. Kyle is sitting on a bench, stooped over his phone, surrounded by marble. She grabs his shoulder.

'What's wrong?' he says, alarmed.

'I don't think Josh is dead at all.'

Twenty-three years ago

JOHN ANSWERS THE door in his dressing-gown. He'd been dreaming about black holes, and when the knock woke him, for a moment he comprehended – at the edge of the solar system – a light-sucking invisibility, visible.

Rick, his astronaut ex-colleague, is out front, looking scrawny and old and hungover.

'What are you doing here?' John says, exiting the house and closing the door behind him so they won't disturb his daughter.

'Is it still working for you?' Rick says, squinting in desperation.

'Come with me.' John slips on the shoes by the door and leads his old rival by the elbow of his tweed jacket. They cross the dewy grass and enter the dusty shed.

Rick gasps at the rings of saffron and rust lichen, bright in the morning sun. 'You have more?'

John clicks on the radio. The Hawaiian station. He likes the calming flow meshed with the control of the percussive elements – soft, steady: waves, days, sun and moon cycles. He indicates for Rick to sit.

Rick frowns. 'You've had this the whole time?'

'I didn't even know if it had affected you,' John says.

'But you weren't going to share?'

'You didn't either, until you … what, ran out?'

'I never had a supply.' Rick runs his hands through thinning hair. 'I never thought of it. The effects just wore off recently. I can't stand it. I don't know how to read the world anymore. I feel empty.'

John looks down at him, slumped and deflated. Feels sorry for him. 'Take some. I don't care. Just be careful.'

'Are *you* being careful?' Rick asks.

John sighs. 'What do you think?'

Rick flakes off a piece, puts it to his tongue. Closes his eyes. Eventually, he opens them again, says, 'I was sorry to hear about Sally.'

John's heart hits the pit of his stomach. 'Yes, well, you could have rung. Or sent a card.'

'I know.' He opens his eyes. 'Do you feel it, calling you back? The *juice* in the stars?'

John nods. 'But I want to go back to space as much as I want to wrap myself around the very core of the earth.'

He won't admit to the ouija boards and sitting for hours in the corner where Sally had died, trying to locate that slip-through. These powers, these senses, explain so much of existence, but also, tantalisingly, hint at yet more mystery.

'No one will ever understand,' Rick says, scratching at his three-day growth.

John thinks of his daughter, and the 'magic' he's revealed to her: making circles in grass, beckoning a bird to sit on her arm, warming her fingertips in winter. Small tricks, and then one day, when she's an adult and he knows her body will be okay with it, he will share all of it with her. The knowledge. If she wants it.

But this idea that it could also *end.* This is new. Something he hasn't considered.

'I'll go get a container so we can pack some up for you,' John says, and leaves Rick in the shed, munching along to the radio sounds of strings and shells.

Eight months ago

JOSH OPENS HIS eyes slowly, the postcard on his wall of Van Gogh's *Sunflowers* coming into view. He likes to wake up to the shades of yellow – mustard and honey and gold – and the cracks of sun coming in through the venetians. He is lucky to wake up this way, he knows. Naturally. No alarm. He never sees clients in the morning. Or sets breakfast dates. Well, maybe if the film festival is on or something.

He stretches out his long limbs, yawns luxuriously, looks at the dumbbells in the corner. He should work out today. After some eggs. Maybe. Or he could stay in bed reading for a while.

Until he has to go meet Mila, the potential new client off SugarMeetMe. And then a shift at the bar later.

When he hears Kyle's cat mew lightly behind the door, he gives an exaggerated sigh but really he's happy to let him in, see his little face. He gets up and opens the door.

'Hey, Sokka-boi,' he says, bending down to scritch him under the chin.

Kyle's door creaks open and Josh sees him, sleep-lined face, holding his towel up in front of his boxers.

'Dude,' Josh says, looking up at his friend.

'Bro,' says Kyle.

An ironic and affectionate exchange.

Kyle grins and moves past him to the bathroom, and Josh lies back down, letting the cat jump up and doughnut between his legs. He pulls a book from the pile on his messy bedside table. Fernando Pessoa: *Smoke of the light which shines occluded / To such gazing as life allows.* He listens to the water streaming in the shower, the splashes as Kyle's body moves through it. He tries not to think of Kyle in this way, but the truth is he kinda thinks of everybody this way. He'd never show it – Kyle is straight and that's totally fine, that's him. And Josh's feelings are welcome in lots of other places.

He's not sure Kyle knows how great he is, though. He's not good at hearing any kind of compliment.

Josh turns back to Pessoa's poems. Is Portugal a place he could go on his travels?

Kyle walks by Josh's open door, towel tightly wrapped.

'Kyle!' Josh calls.

'Mmm?' Kyle half-blocks his naked chest with the door.

'Let's go to Europe.'

<hr />

Mila thinks about the recent chat she had with Kate as she sits in the cafe, waiting for him. Kate encouraged Mila to be kinder to herself. Told her that the fact she is not where she thought she'd be is not because of some failure on her part. Mila knows, of course, there is a mixture of missteps and circumstances; there is capitalism, there is bad luck. But the loop in her brain – children, no children. And then, as she reads the news: It is better to have not had children. But then always looping back.

After they chatted, Mila sat at home, picked up her phone for the sixth time in an hour, scrolled numbly, curling a strand of oily hair around her finger. There were ads for stress apps, face massagers, suction cups that go on your fingers (she did not know what these were for), weighted blankets. There were photos she had seen before. Had she scrolled that much? There was a fertility ad that she moved quickly past. And then a different ad she paused on:

Mature woman and tired of dating? These sugar babies are waiting for you.

With photos of attractive people of all genders.

She clicked on the link to SugarMeetMe.

She flipped through as much of the website as she was able to without signing up. She felt shame, failure. And then excitement. No one would have to know. She signed up.

And that was how she ended up here in this cafe, waiting for a young man.

Kate had also said, 'I think it is intimacy that is important to you, not just pleasure.'

'Can it not be both?' Mila said.

Intimacy is important to everyone, surely, she thinks. Intimacy is knowing and seeing others, and them seeing you, and touching each other, not always physically, but that adds to it. (There is the intimacy of art, and it knowing you, and that is not always tactile.) Is it sexist to believe a woman wants intimacy more than pleasure? If Mila pays for sex, this could remove the intimacy and therefore allow her to understand pleasure on its own terms. But she probably won't tell Kate about this.

She looks down into her latte – she is early as always – as a fresh wave of shame rolls through her.

'Mila?'

Standing in the open glass door of the cafe is the young man from the photo. He is smiling. She stands and takes his hand, chastely. He smells like cheap deodorant and a hint of weed.

'Have you been waiting long?'

'No! No, I'm always early.'

'Ah, no worries then.' He sits across from her, spreading out, relaxed.

Her own hands hold too much energy. She pushes her hair behind her ear, plays with the handle of the cup. 'Would you like a coffee?'

As she says this he is raising his hand and connecting eyes with the waitperson. 'Hey, Skye, can I grab a flat white?'

Mila sees some unspoken messages move between him and Skye. Intimacy.

How does this conversation start?

'Thanks for getting in touch with me,' he says. 'I always like to meet casually first – just make sure you're comfortable.'

'That's good of you.'

He waves it away. 'Have you ever hired a sex worker before?' Mila resists the urge to *shush* him. The cafe is full of retirees and mums. Maybe this is part of a test of her comfort.

'I haven't. I never knew I would.'

'What made you go to the website?'

She allows herself to look at him more. Blue eyes, flick of dark hair on the forehead, vein running down the biceps. Very young.

'Curiosity?' She laughs.

'Desire?' he says, not breaking eye contact.

She nods. 'Um, I guess, something of an experiment in allowing myself to want ... to feel good.'

He nods. His coffee arrives, and they each sip their drinks.

He digs around in his back jeans pocket and pulls out a slip of paper. 'These are my rates.' He slides it across the table. 'And you're supposed to book me through the system so they get a cut,

but I can take cash, too. I'm actually totally free this afternoon.'
He smiles again. Small teeth, one incisor endearingly snaggled.

Her fingertips spark with adrenaline. She drums the table, catches herself, stops. Jiggles her knee. Her next PT session isn't until 6 p.m. She unfolds the piece of paper. He costs as much as she will earn from that job. Her rent is almost due. Her phone bill is overdue. Her body sags a little over the paper.

But she doesn't want worry; she wants pleasure.

'Um, yes. Okay. Where do we go?'

⁓

She is mostly quiet, after they have sex. He doesn't know yet how to make her more comfortable, how to help her open up. This time, at least, she no longer crossed her arm across her breasts, and she told him more of what she likes. Touched the top of his head when he was between her legs and asked if he could go slower to start with. She tastes amazing, sweet like overripe nectarines. He has a few ideas about what to try with her, once she is more relaxed with him.

She has paid for more time and he stretches out in her bed, in her dark grey sheets. Her room is tidy but not entirely clean, dust gathering on shelves and picture frames. The pictures are generic – IKEA Impressionist-like smudged colours. But then she opens the cupboard to get out her robe, and he sees a poster of Jane Fonda from one of her 1980s exercise videos Blu-Tacked on the inside. Wonders if this is more of an insight into her.

'Love Jane Fonda,' he says.

'Oh same.' She pulls on the short, silky robe. 'Are you hot?'

He smiles coquettishly.

She laughs and puts on the standing fan in the corner.

'She's such a hero,' he says. 'A glamorous humanitarian.'

'She does so much political work,' Mila says. 'But I think it took her a while to come to feminism – just the era she grew up in and the influences in her life.'

'Oh yeah?'

Mila's face is flushed red. 'Anyway, it's just from some interviews I watched. I don't know enough about it.'

He often finds, when he's with his sugar mamas, that they shut themselves down like this. Thinking that he probably knows more than they do or that he doesn't want to hear how they feel about whatever topic it is.

'Tell me more,' he says, leaning into the pillows.

She sits back in the bed. 'I don't know. I guess I find her attractive as well, but I get confused about that.'

He tilts his head, shows he's listening.

'Like, I read something once about how there are more bisexual women than men because women are sort of trained in seeing the world through the male gaze. And I … Well, since I first liked girls I already felt a bit creepy, like I was leering or whatever, in high school, and then I just ended up mostly with men anyway.' Her hands tug at the sheets. 'I want to be a good feminist.' She scrunches her face up, seemingly unsure of what she's said. 'I have no idea why I'm telling you this!' She gives a bark of a laugh.

'Because you knew I'd understand your feelings,' he says. 'Queer people have a weird way of recognising each other like that.'

He puts his hand over her hand. She is frozen now, staring into the distance. He aches for her, though he knows this hesitancy is not at all uncommon, even in this day and age. There are myriad reasons people hold back parts of themselves, and despite how far various movements have come, cisheteronormative, patriarchal capitalism is a dominant and pervasive force. It's not just that – there's a real feeling now, he knows, that if you choose to be 'out' or call yourself by a particular label, even within your own communities it can be difficult if you are more fluid, if you change from year to year or even one day to the next. He knows it all too well.

'So you …' she says.

'Am into every kind of consenting adult there is.' He smiles. Her face looks wobbly – oops, sometimes he forgets everyone is not his best friend, as open as him. 'But about you,' he says. 'You're allowed to feel whatever you feel, you don't have to think about where it comes from. When did you first have a crush on a girl?'

'Around thirteen, I guess.'

He nods. 'Well, if you ever want to talk about it, I can be that person.'

'Thank you,' she says. But she pulls her hand away from his, twists on the bed. 'Want a coffee?'

'Sure.'

She leaves the room. He feels bad if he's pushed her. She is so together and strong in so many ways – she'd previously opened up about some of the things she'd been through recently. Her parents having been in danger, and then ill. The break-up with a man she thought she'd spend her life with. How, after he finally agreed to try for children, their intimacy broke down and, after a further year of her still hoping, he said he didn't want them anymore. Josh shouldn't make her feel she's *missing* anything or not good enough as she is. But then he also knows, from his own experiences, from his mates' experiences, how destructive shame can be. How it can occupy a huge chunk of your mind, and colour your thoughts and feelings about yourself, about your life, without you even knowing that's what's going on.

But he won't force the issue. He also knows well that, because of how deep and insidious the shame can be, a person has to face it at a time when they are ready. He is so lucky, with his open and supportive mum. And yet, he's still working up to telling her and his sisters about the sex work. He will soon.

But he is here to make Mila feel good, not be her therapist.

He realises he does want to be friends with her, though. An occupational hazard, for him. In fact, he's got a good idea about something they could do together, outside of this arrangement.

In her bedroom, Mila sits in the chair by the window, sipping tea and watching Josh sleep in the crumpled sheets. She has been trying to keep it to weekly, to save up for him. And then in the moment to linger, to savour. There is nothing wrong with delayed gratification. Maybe it is a kind of resistance to this instant-fix, deliver-to-your door culture? She can tell herself that, but really, she can't afford him any more regularly.

She can't really afford him at all. But *this* is worth it. These extra moments and dollars to have him here, post-coital. To allow the pleasure in her body to linger in his presence. But it's not too intimate, is it?

It got a bit too familiar last week when they talked about sexuality. Thoughts about that have annoyingly been kicking around in her mind. First, there was a stupid kind of jealousy over Josh professing his desire for others; she guesses she successfully blocked this until then.

Over the past week she started to wonder, though, if it was not only jealousy, but also envy: that at his age, he could be entirely, unashamedly himself.

In the past year she's started following a lot of openly bisexual people on Twitter. Her profile: impersonal, a picture of a feminine bicep with a dumbbell as opposed to a headshot. In the beginning she was following other PTs and Pilates instructors, with some idea she would use it for work, but the queer women – cis and trans – and nonbinary people have been the ones she mainly hovers over. She scrolls these accounts but holds back on pressing the heart on their bold selfies: beards and pink eyeshadow, tattoos, spilling flesh, choker necklaces. She doesn't really post.

Lawyer, nerd, bi, she/her
Cat parent, queer, they/them
Pansexual masc space unicorn

Mila's always watched queer-themed films, TV shows – *The L Word, Mulholland Drive, Bound, Gia* – but privately, secretly. It was too overwhelming when, for example, a boyfriend or date would watch Angelina Jolie undressing Elizabeth Mitchell and say, 'That's hot.' The thick sucking black hole in her gut that would open up at those two words.

Because it *was* hot, because she wanted it, because he was allowed to say those words and own them and somehow she could not.

The closest she came to admitting it was to say, 'I don't like labels much,' and blush. Even in all those years with Scott, she admired actresses openly on TV, and he knew about her past crushes and kisses and was completely accepting, but there didn't seem to be any point having a conversation beyond that; they were monogamous.

She and Kate had actually become close as teenagers when they kissed in the back of a car with a bunch of older guys looking on. But while Mila kept holding Kate's hand after that, Kate pulled hers away. When they were older and going to clubs, Kate was sweet and often told Mila if a girl was checking her out. But Mila was usually too shy to approach, and she'd end up kissing some sweaty bloke who sidled up beside her at 3 a.m.

She has only had sex with a woman with a man present, in her twenties. Almost accidental, but burned on her memory. Two friends of a friend, all three of them strangers to each other who got talking at a party. Mila was drunk enough to go with the suggestion, to let herself. In the bed, she only wanted to explore the woman. The man suddenly was all neediness and hair. And yet she sucked his cock while the woman sat on his face. When Mila went down on the woman it was with him watching, wanking. It was the woman who pushed her off to climb back on the man. At some point the man took a photo of Mila and the woman touching each other. She felt joy at seeing herself in the photo: she was young and sexy, and life was full of possibility. The next day all she felt was fear and shame.

She has never been in love with a woman, though she has had deep, lingering crushes that petered out when nothing happened. When she did nothing about them. Mostly they happened when she was already seeing a man. When she was seeing Scott she pushed them down deep.

She just doesn't think she can call herself anything.

Not queer. Not a mother. Not a devoted friend. Not even, now, a lover. Because she is paying for it. How do people like Josh slip into their identities? Choose them, live them boldly? He seems so happy, so at home with himself, she thinks, as she watches the rise and fall of his sleeping chest.

Perhaps that is part of the appeal, why she wants to be around him so much. That he might lead her – not with any additional labour on his part, but by being himself – to her own opening.

Josh and Mila turn down a laneway, Liverpool Street, off Bourke. Brick, bins and a colourful spray-painted mural of a subtropical forest ringed by fire, and an adjoining city half underwater. As they walk towards the secret entrance, Mila emits a giggle. Josh looks at her. He's glad she's as amused by the adventure as he is. This is the first time she's participated in a medical trial. He's done this a bunch – had needles stuck in his arms, been interviewed about his health and habits, even donated sperm to a genetic study. All for a bit of cash. The trials and studies are usually through the various universities around Melbourne, but this one is private: an organisation called Cladion, a subsidiary of Foster-Edwards – a multinational run by the generally forward-thinking Australian billionaire Lisa Edwards. He was invited over email. It'll pay much more than the university trials, and it has certain prerequisites.

In Mila's kitchen last month, as she handed him a cup of coffee, he read out the questions to her. 'Have you ever seen a ghost?'

She looked down into her strong French-pressed cup. 'Um … I thought I saw ghosts as a child.'

She went to explain more, undo the embarrassment, but he said, 'Good!' and clutched her arm, agitating the coffee. She sat it down. 'Here,' he said, handing her the phone so she could read the rest. 'Let's both make some money.'

Now, they reach a large metal door in the brick wall. It looks like the door to any laneway nightclub, closed in daytime, but Josh knows to flip open the cover of a keypad, check the code on his phone, and tap it in. He glances up and sees a camera as the metal door buzzes. He yanks it open. Inside, a dark stairwell. Josh pulls the heavy door closed, shrugs at Mila, then walks up, making a lot of noise on the wooden steps, which dip with maybe a century of footfall.

Mila hesitates behind him. 'What am I doing?'

'C'mon, let it all go,' he says.

He knows she's thinking again about how she should be responsible and just take more shifts at the gym to slowly eke her way out of debt. She has opened up to him a lot more in the past weeks. About most things.

She shakes her head, sighing, but with good humour, and follows him up.

At the top of the stairs under dim light is a plain and battered wooden desk, a person behind it with a shaved head and leopard spots tattooed up one side of their face. 'Hi,' the receptionist says cheerfully. There's no signage.

Josh twists his hands behind his back. He says, 'We are here to connect.' That's what the correspondence told him to say, but he's embarrassed by the underground cult-like nature of the passphrase.

He sees Mila in the corner of his eye – her earnest face. He knows that a laugh is bubbling inside her, which makes him want to giggle too.

The receptionist says, 'The high priestess can facilitate that.' Then stands, smiles, shakes their hands. 'My name is Daisy. And you?'

'This is Mila,' says Josh, 'and I'm Josh.'

'And what pronouns do you use?' Daisy asks.

Josh points himself out as a 'he' and Mila as a 'she' and then asks Daisy in return.

'They/them, thanks.' Daisy smiles. 'Please follow me.' A hidden panel on the wall lights up blue at Daisy's touch. The wall parts, and an intense clean light floods the darkness.

That evening Mila and Josh are still together. She can afford it now, with the money on the prepaid card that was pressed into her palm as they left the bright inner realm of the building. She sits on him, holds him inside her as she moves. He moans, closes his eyes. She no longer covers her breasts with her arm, or pushes them into attractive shapes; she lets them swing as she closes her eyes too, seeks the core of herself.

Afterwards, as she traces his bicep, forearm, down to the thin, silver-look bracelet they were made to put on today, which will track them for six months, he asks, 'Do you feel any different?'

Yes, immediately, she does. But from the money – the too-easy money has filled her with a sensation of freedom, joyousness. She says, 'No, I don't think so.'

'Neither,' he says, one hand on his post-coital cock, comfortable and contemplative.

'But I do feel different since meeting you,' she says. Then wonders if she should have held back.

He rolls onto his side, faces her. 'I'm glad.'

The way he has allowed her to be in touch with her eroticism, her hunger – it's filling the dark places within her.

Even with Scott, her best friend, her partner, her long-term lover, she'd sometimes hid the hunger. If she bit his lip in the kiss, if she stared too longingly from the bed while he got dressed, if she said 'are you in the mood?' (the frustration having risen to spilling) he would usually not be, or not be anymore. But if she waited in a way that didn't look like she was waiting, if she stood up in front of him while wearing something that clung to her arse, if she had on a grey singlet with nipples poking through (she began to learn the tricks), then he might start the action. And she might pretend to be surprised, and let him take the first hungry kiss, and let him grasp first for the crotch, and let him push her gently down onto the bed or say 'let's go to the bedroom' and then it would happen. And then it wouldn't just be him sighing and saying, 'I can take care of you, if you like?' Which she often accepted, but it was a sad fuck when she knew he wasn't into it. And when they were supposedly trying for a baby, it wasn't enough. What was he thinking about, when he was down there? Was he playing a song in his head? She still couldn't listen to Nirvana or Pearl Jam without a sense of twisted longing – holding his hand, pheromonal cloud, smile of a friend: separate, blood beating. She was never able to *be* the songs. She didn't stick like a tune inside his head, even after ten years.

And she found it was always this way, with the men she was with. Having to pretend not to want it, having to let them seduce. Becoming small and curled on the bed while they encompassed her. Sometimes not being able to breathe properly because her lungs were crushed. And not being able to tell them that, because finally she was having sex, and if she told them she wanted it differently they might lose their hard-on.

Until Josh. At first she often made him take her just the way she'd always been taken. In fact it did turn her on, perhaps because she'd been conditioned to it. But slowly, she found ways to articulate the things she sometimes watched in porn on her phone. She tried slowness with him. She told him she wanted him to go down on her and then fuck her and then go down on her again to make her come, and then only after that to come himself. She told him she wanted to undress before him and that she wanted him to watch her, and stroke himself; she wanted to feel she was the most delicious vision, filling the eyes and heart and cock. And because she chose to be looked at, and he complied, she then started to look at herself more – in shop windows, in the mirror in the hall. She took selfies. Blew herself a kiss.

And she looked at him as well. She looked and she looked, and she kissed him before he kissed her, and she clutched, and she was openly hungry, and that was exhilarating.

Afterwards, waves of shame rolled through her body. It was hard. She knew what it was. But knowing didn't stop it. She tried to ignore it. Get up. Go do a Pilates class. Sweat it out. Do some work – get lost in directing, organising, concerns, other people.

'It was bloody strange, that substance,' Mila says, returning to the day's event.

'It was.'

'Tasted disgusting.'

'Tasted alive.'

'Well,' she says, 'it kind of was, from the way they explained it. It's an organism.'

'Mm.' Josh seems to contemplate this. 'I don't know why I don't feel more worried?'

'Maybe it *is* affecting you,' she says playfully. Really, she thinks it is a crock. Has to be. Something desperate and New Agey. Clearly underground and possibly illegal, run by an eccentric billionaire, the one they had to refer to as the high priestess, even though they knew it was Lisa Edwards. What kind of egotistical, God-complex BS is that? This is how the world is increasingly run: cashed-up idealists who are in too much of a rush to properly consider any long-term projects, wanting to be heroes of the people in the moment, be the first and best.

But the experiment will fail. How can it not? The questions they asked Mila before administering the thick, blood-orange substance were laughable; it was only the seriousness of the environment that kept her from rolling her eyes constantly. She and Josh were taken into separate rooms, more corporate in style than clinical. She sat across from a woman, Meg, dressed in a suit, no tie, with the plastic vial of gunk sitting in front of her. She was business-friendly, had clearly learned how to use the correct body language to show openness, encouragement. She smiled and said she had a little further screening to do.

Mila noticed on the wall above her a framed portrait of an astronaut – smiling, American jaw. Had she read somewhere that Lisa Edwards' father went into space?

Meg asked Mila if she had any psychic ability, even if it was regular experiences of déjà vu. She asked if her body synced with the tides. She asked if she'd ever felt an inkling of psychokinetic power, or energy: the ability to shift or transmute objects with her mind. She asked if she could control her body's organs or processes. She asked if she'd ever felt there was something just beyond her reach that could be accessible, that could be real.

Mila was honest about being sceptical of other realms and crystal energy. But … she thought she should tell Meg about Tim, the little boy ghost who used to appear at the end of her bed when she was around two and three, and those other experiences she put down to childhood brain farts. And the dreams could be relevant, too: the dreams in which she was infused, god-like, with orgasmic endorphins and light. She'd never told a soul about them before – they seemed too close to some individualistic idea of 'potential' and 'manifesting power'. But they had always felt *significant*. She intuited that these were the kinds of moments the interviewer was seeking, and Mila would get her money if she was open about them.

The money was the potential. Helping her crawl from her pit of failure and debt and starchy, empty-bellied, empty-roomed silence.

She must have passed, because Meg slid the substance towards her and explained that it was a type of lichen – *Xanthoria*, or sunburst lichen – propagated from a sample that had been cosmically irradiated. The original had been ingested and, reportedly – Meg was careful to say this – had produced a range of effects, enhancing the subject.

'Irradiated?' Mila asked.

'The original sample was exposed to radiation in space, but the levels are low enough now to be safe, don't worry.' She smiled.

'What happened to the original subject?'

'He was able to pass on aspects of his knowledge but not all of it, hence the trial.'

Mila nodded. She could feel that laugh bubbling up. This was absolutely absurd. 'So … space fungus that will give me magical powers.'

'Um.' Meg shook her head, clearly annoyed. 'Lichen is only partly fungal – it contains filaments existing symbiotically with algae. It's a complex life form. And … we don't see the results as magical powers. That's a crude way of thinking about it. We hypothesise that *Xanthoria* enhances the normal range of human perception and ability —'

'Then why the high priestess?'

Meg gave a wry smile. 'Ms Edwards enjoys thinking about the feminine lineage of enhanced ability – yes, witchcraft, covens … and so on.' Meg indicated to the vial in front of Mila. 'All you have to do is drink that and come back for check-ups.'

Mila unscrewed the cap – gave it a sniff. Bland. She lifted it to her mouth and drank down the thick, mealy liquid. 'Ugh.'

'Good,' said Meg, standing. 'Daisy will give you your first payment on the way out.'

Mila looks at Josh now on her old sheets, thinks about him lying on silk. She smiles. She can buy that now. Maybe she'll keep adding to the 'dream homes' Pinterest board that she started when she was with Scott – images of cosy, light-filled bedrooms; desk nooks; abundant plants. She'll keep it private. She isn't sure how people don't get embarrassed sharing their desires openly like that.

'So, six months of check-ups,' she says.

He nods. 'Tell me first, if you notice any changes?'

'I will. It's not like we can talk to anyone else about it.'

'True,' he says. He frowns.

'Are you okay?'

'Yeah.' He sighs. 'It's just Kyle, my housemate. He's a good mate. It'll be hard not to tell him.'

She strokes his cheek sympathetically. She doesn't feel the need to share this with anyone. Her dad and Kate might be the only people who'll notice if she seems a bit different. She's been avoiding Kate, and feeling bad about it, but she just doesn't know how to explain Josh. Despite Kate's lifestyle she isn't conservative in attitude, but still, Mila thinks that having a sex-worker lover and undergoing some oddball experiment will convince Kate of a widening distance between them. Worse, maybe she'll grasp on to it as entertainment, a break from her suburban monotony. No, Mila needs space to allow this to unfold in whatever way it will.

'Kyle, I can read your thoughts,' Josh says through the peephole from lounge room to kitchen in their apartment. Kyle is stir-frying some tofu and veg, and he peers from the pan to Josh with a look of unbridled hope. 'Not *literally*,' Josh says. 'Oh my god, did you think …?'

'No, lol, of course not.'

But Josh thinks he's blushing a little.

'I mean like I know you're craving a steak or some sausages right now,' Josh says, 'and you don't always have to eat what I eat! I can cook, you know.'

Kyle gives him his pained mum look.

'I can!' Josh says.

'Wedges are not a meal.'

Josh loves stirring him up. He would feel guilty about Kyle cooking so much if he truly thought Kyle hated it, but he gets light in his eyes when he talks about how it gives him a sense of purpose and control, and breaks up the day and night.

'Did you pack yet?' Kyle asks.

'I've got days to do that. I'd rather hang with you.'

'You're going to regret saying that by like the second hostel room we have to share.'

'Nah.'

'We'll see.'

'Anyway, I've got a few weeks to myself first, so I'll miss you!'

Kyle turns off the stove, takes the lid off the rice cooker and starts to scoop the meal into bowls. 'You'll miss lots of people, no doubt,' he says quietly.

Has Josh been intense? Maybe he should have some weed, chill a bit. He has been on edge all day, furry around the edges from those dreams. An echoey old rendition of 'Lili Marleen' over some memory from childhood, glimpses of his dead father, and all of it washed in that *Xanthoria* orange.

He takes the bowl from Kyle. 'Thank you.'

'No wuckers.'

He grabs the remote. 'What are we going to? *Hannibal*? *Fargo*? *Queer Eye*?'

'Didn't you download *The Twilight Zone*?'

'Oh, fuck yeah.' He navigates through the icons. Kyle set it all up so they have the TV on smart mode for streaming apps, plus Chromecast (mainly for YouTube), plus a connection to their computer network so they can play downloaded files – he is basically a genius.

Josh starts the show and tries not to look too much at Kyle in his comfy flannel PJ pants on the other couch. The thing is, Josh both loves this cosy situation and can't wait to travel. He's really fucking lucky. He knows that. He also feels on the edge of something.

Is it to do with the lichen? The six months is up, the subtle silver-coated bracelet has been removed, he's been cleared and so has Mila and fuck-all happened, but … he thinks about it all the time. Like the substance is someone he met or someone he anticipates meeting. It's too strange to articulate to Mila or Kyle; it's too weird to even think about. He pushes it from his mind and watches Rod Serling, with cigarette perched coolly in his beautiful hands, speak about the eerie portal they are about to enter.

⁓

It is the last time. For now. For a few months while he goes overseas. Mila wants so much in these moments that she can't speak. Her throat and mouth are crowded with want. But he knows her so well now. Her body. Her patterns. Her rise and rise and fall. She knows herself better now too, because of him.

He needs to give that gift to others. They need him. The way she has needed him. She must not be wrenching, jealous. These feelings, truthfully, *are* subdued more than ever, for her, or they were up until the leaving. She has suggested a whole day. A movie, maybe; she likes to hear his opinions. He is always generous, open, thinks about the motivations behind people and art, the intentions. This is a salve. It is not the way people always are – especially online, where she has many of her daily social interactions.

So a movie, and then bed for the rest of the day, perhaps. She has a gift for him: a small wooden stud for his newly pierced ear.

She gives it to him over a glass of wine after the movie. The leaving is an event; they can drink in the daytime.

'This is beautiful, Mila,' he says. 'You really didn't have to.'

'I want you to know how much our time together has helped me.' She plays with the rim of her wineglass.

'And this isn't the end of it,' he says. 'I've just been hanging out to do a big trip for so long.'

She nods. He has talked about it a lot: seeing the art and architecture, walking in Marlene Dietrich's Weimar Berlin footsteps, soaking in the Budapest baths … He hadn't been able to plan the trip in earnest until the bracelets came off, the experiment clearly having been a dud. For them, and probably for everyone involved. Though they could have been part of a placebo group – they'll never know.

They laugh about it often. It comes up again now. 'I mean,' he says, 'were we supposed to suddenly be able to walk on water?'

'Or read someone's mind?' she asks.

'Trippy as.' He shakes his head.

'It was, and for that much cash.'

'Madness.'

It's all madness – this sublimely unstructured new phase. Her lack of future-planning and regimentation. The control will come back now, though, when he's gone. Won't it? She shouldn't let it. She is new. She is a phoenix. She may not be a mother, a spouse or home-owner or successful businessperson, but she *is* a lover. It's an identity she can own, even just inside herself.

'Let's go,' she says, the eros kindled in her.

She wants to take him back to her place and make love to him one more time. Not as a way to hold, but as a way to let go.

It is three weeks into the trip, and Josh has loved every moment – of cramped rooms and loud train carriages, long beery dusks, instant connections, echoey galleries and smaller offbeat exhibitions, Bohemian witch queens, plays in other languages where he can only watch the body for clues, silly pop nightclubs and serious underground ones – but now he's counting down the days until he gets to share it with someone close. Another week and he'll be flying to London to meet up with Kyle, and they'll continue the adventure together.

This morning he is having a lie-in, alone in the four-bed dorm, scrolling through the invites and trying to decide what kind of mood he's in, trying to remember to reply to them all and not be rude. He's feeling different, as though he's still a bit high. He squints at the phone, and it's like if he concentrates, he can see the mechanics behind the shell. *Huh.*

He puts it down, tries to home in on what is different in his body. He puts his hand to his chest and … it's strange … he can feel his heart beating but he also *is* his heart beating, and he is liquid and fat and, burrowing down, is a bundle of divisions and connections he has no name for. And it's not like he can *see* it or touch it or … it's like he can simply comprehend it, like a sixth sense.

Wow, what the fuck did I take last night? And where do I get more?

He opens his eyes again, finds he can consciously shift his focus out of his body and into the air. And the same thing – the structures are less complex but there is water in the air, and air in the paint on the walls, and there is the *distance* between where the light lands and his eyeballs.

He looks at the book on his bedside table, *The Sea, The Sea,* and he can note the air that sits between its pages.

Hm.

He throws on some clothes and goes down to the lobby of the hostel.

'Hey Josh,' the manager says, a bald guy who always wears a hoodie no matter how hot it is. 'Where you off to?'

'Not sure yet, mate, have a good one!' He waves as he pushes through the door.

He tries to bring it all in, to just be a human body walking down a street. The glorious sunshine seems to shine through him, though, illuminating his minuscule moving parts, showing how he's connected to its waves, to the air, to the veins in the leaves of the trees; and he feels that if he concentrates enough he could close his eyes and scroll back time on this very street. He can hear the Wall coming down, the triumphant calls and the music; he can hear the bombs; he can hear marching. His phone buzzes and he looks at it, narrows his focus. Another nude from that woman on Oglr – maybe this is the distraction he needs. If it doesn't calm down then he'll call Kyle. It's like 10 p.m. in Australia now; he can call him in the morning.

Josh has met the woman, Luna, in person – that's how she came to follow him on Oglr. With Belle and some of the others from the hostel a couple of nights ago. She's been low-key reaching out to him since. He calls her mobile. 'You wanna meet up?'

'Sure,' she says. Posh accent. Over from London.

'Where are you?'

She gives him the location of her Airbnb in Kreuzberg. He puts her on speaker and opens his map. 'I can walk,' he says. 'Be halfa.'

'Pardon?'

'Half an hour.' He laughs.

'All right.' she says. She sounds nervous.

He walks – concentrating on step, step, step. The history of the pavement coming up through the arches of his feet. The white moon in the bright sky. The hearts beating around him.

He remembers something he heard about taking drugs, that sometimes it's like a zipper opening and that if you keep trying to pull up the zipper you'll have a terrible trip but if you just let the zipper open and accept whatever spills out you will have a good time. And thinking about it this way, he is able to let go of holding together the division of where the edges of himself meet the world. He incorporates the newness of this expansive sensation. He is buoyant and happy.

It is Mila he should contact, really. Because it was too many hours ago that he took anything for this to still be part of some trip. He knows that. He's just not really sure he can let the thought in. *Let the zipper fly open.*

It was supposed to have worked months ago. Why now?

Luna is waiting out the front of the block of flats when he gets there. 'What do you want to do?' she asks.

He can't help letting out an elated laugh. 'To be honest, I'd like to fly right now.'

She looks puzzled.

'Never mind, let's go to the park.'

They walk in the direction of Tiergarten. He grabs her hand.

'Do I have to pay for this?' she says casually – he told her about his work when they met.

'No. We met socially. I'm sorry if I didn't make that clear before now.'

'That's okay,' she says.

But there's something else going on with her. He can sense the sparking nerves, the fast blood. 'Is everything okay with you?'

He drops her hand, in case she's uneasy because he's moved in too fast, intimidated her.

'Yes, why?' she asks.

'You seem a little nervy.'

'Do I?'

He presses his front teeth to his lower lip. 'I'm good at reading people.'

'I just think you're quite lovely, is all.' She continues walking, looks away from him.

They reach the park, and the trees are so beautiful it's like the green has entered his mouth like a fat frog, but cream-sweet like the milk he once drank from his mother. He veers off the path and stops in front of an old oak, sensing its multiple rings and the amount of CO_2 it has sucked from the air in all that time.

'What ...' Luna says. He sees her vaguely out of the corner of his eye.

He snaps back to her. 'What?' he echoes.

'It was like the tree was bending to you.'

He teeters. 'Was it?'

She nods.

'Let's sit for a moment,' he says. This is too much to take in.

Luna glances around her, like she's checking who is watching. She scratches her ear. 'Let's go somewhere more private.'

'I'm a bit wibbly wobbly,' he says in a pretend British accent.

She tilts her head at him, laughs. The thing is, he suddenly doesn't want to follow her anywhere that is less out in the open. Her heart rate has skyrocketed now – she's desperate, for some reason. But so many other signals are coming at him, too. He finds it hard to feel worried, though on some level he understands he should be. There's just the thick, immediate *presence* of everything.

He allows her to take his hand and lead him, as he gawps at every blade of grass and bird and reed and every *grain* of mud, to a darker, dense copse of trees.

'You can rest here,' she says. 'You seem a bit faint.'

'Thank you. But you …'

And then four men are coming in through the gaps in the trees, dressed casually like they're just out for a stroll – one with a bike helmet slung over his elbow.

'Who …?'

Luna jabs Josh's arm with something, and it immediately dulls all the new sensations, smooths out his brow, slurs the words in his head.

He hears Luna distantly say, 'You two stay behind. We'll pretend we're his mates and he's a bit out of it. Where's the car?'

'West.'

'Good.'

Whatever they've given him is a slug through his blood. His arms are around their shoulders. He feels Luna dig for his phone in his pocket. He can't seem to speak. The fear is there, but distant. The idea he must get away. Must contact Mila and Kyle.

And he remembers, somewhere in the slow brain as he is being dragged along, his eyes rolling back and no longer lit up with joy, that this may be his fault. He's never been good at keeping secrets.

Was it the hostel manager he was talking to a day or so before Luna arrived? He was totally drunk. The manager had brought up magic, seemed pretty passionate about it. Josh was just trying to connect, as he always does. Relate. He was on the other side of the world from the experiment. And it hadn't worked anyway, so he thought, What's the harm?

Now

'**D**on't come any closer,' Mila says to Kyle as he stands in the doorway.

'I got chamomile tea.'

'I can smell your genes,' she says. 'Like a mix between ... mulch and the chemicals used to develop photographs.'

Kyle clutches the box of tea bags, wondering if he should stay or go.

'It's your ancestors squashed down inside your DNA.'

Goosebumps rise on Kyle's skin. She glances at him from under her wild hair, which seems to have grown an inch overnight. He moves in just enough to set the tea bags down on the bench.

'I took two Valium – that wasn't gonna cut it,' she says, pointing at the tea.

'I'm sorry.'

'Did you know your people come from all around the world?'

'I do ... But I've never felt fully connected —'

'You *are*. You're connected to all of it. East–West.' She shakes her head at him, eyes wide. 'I can *sense* the moon, the tides ... as just one element in the *macro* mix. Then there's everything in here.' She gestures to the walls containing them.

He tries only to look at her with sympathy. He's still in disbelief. Like maybe he's flipped his lid once and for all and is strapped to a gurney somewhere and this is all playing out on his eyelids like in a *Twilight Zone* episode he's definitely seen – about some pilot who thinks he's still in the war?

But Kyle saw Mila turn the lights on without touching them and, like, he always gets annoyed in movies when people take too long to believe in something supernatural. Well, now he's thinking of *The X-Files*, which is such an *iconic* show but god he really doesn't know why it took Scully so long to believe Mulder. After all she'd seen? Kyle needs to not completely freak out on Mila and to convince himself pretty quickly that he can play a role. Because otherwise, like the sceptical characters in those movies and shows, he will somehow put her in danger – or himself, or both of them. This is real life; there isn't any need for the stalling tension of the 'oh my god, I can't believe it' character dynamic. If he chooses to go along with it, he can get straight to the 'what do we do?' part. Right?

And Josh could be alive, after all – and more than! Well, Kyle may need a Valium, too.

A sidebar, he thinks, is that he was never destined to be Batman. He suspected as much. Someone has to be Robin. And in a way he already has been – the shorter, cardigan-clad companion to the tall, bright and queer superhero Josh.

Kyle pulls a chair over by the door, sits as far from Mila as possible in the hope she can't smell his cytoplasm. Checklists are forming inside his head. His hand twitches for a pen or laptop: research anything he can find about the company that did the experiment; look up these specific symptoms; find lore that could help her learn to control it – to hide it, too. And how will he build his own strength and skills? Shit. Like, she's in danger. If they have taken Josh, faked his death, they could take her, too. Kyle needs to learn kung fu.

'We have to leave this room soon,' she says. 'If we don't act normal, they will know.'

He nods. 'So we think someone took Josh – because they realised he had these ... abilities. And faked his suicide so no one would try to look for him?'

'Exactly.' Mila starts to roll down the blind next to her. 'How can we look for him while avoiding them taking me off the face of the earth? To find him may mean to confront them.'

Kyle is racking his brain, over-aware of its inadequacy despite the ancestors populating his nuclei. 'Uh, what about social media?'

'How so?' she says.

'We go to an airport, check in on Facey saying we're flying to the next stop on our Euro tour, add something about feeling resigned and sad – because if anyone has been trailing us they'll know we've been looking into what happened to Josh – and then get on a plane to where we really want to go. It'll throw them off for twenty-four hours or so, surely.'

'I never check in on Facebook,' Mila says. 'So it will look odd if I do.'

'I do. I know that makes me, like, fifty, but it's more so I can look back and there's a record of places I've been. I'll do it.'

'We can't buy the tickets online.'

'True, and what about ...?' Thoughts occur to him about microphones, cameras.

'I've checked the room,' she says, and her pupils go large as she scans the room. So, okay, Superman, not Batman, he thinks.

'Wait a minute, can you ...?'

'See through your pants?' She gives a cheeky grin, but her pupils resume their usual size. 'I won't abuse it.'

He tries not to move to cover anything.

She says, 'I should have just enough money on my prepaid travel card, which shouldn't be traceable, to get to a new destination.'

'Yes, but where?'

She lies down on the pillows, stares up at the blank white ceiling. 'It started in Melbourne, so might that be where operations continue?'

We can't know for sure, he thinks. 'Your powers don't —'

She gives him a frustrated look. 'I don't know what the fuck they do.' She rolls over in the bed, facing the window. 'Don't have a wet dream about me being Captain Marvel or something.'

'I won't.' He'll try to give her whatever space she needs, not control this. 'Well, let's not rush a decision, then.' Also because if she doesn't know what she's capable of … He imagines planes exploding, the force of the moon sucking them out of the atmosphere.

'Those people could be hurting him,' she says, still turned away. 'A monkey in a cage.'

It's true. And they could have been for all this time.

He and Mila have to make a decision, but they also have to be safe, stay out of harm's way. If only they knew for sure one way or another that they were being followed. And if only they knew for sure where Josh was. This Cladion mob could have other branches. Be spread out all around the world, like its parent company. And surely no one but Cladion is monitoring the participants of its secret trial?

Luna brings Josh tea as she does every morning – the jasmine scent laced with something. The gauzy white curtains blow into the room. The barred window looks out only to half a metre of air and a brick wall; not even the size of an alleyway, just an awkward squash of buildings somewhere in London. Multistoreyed terrace to terrace. Still, he likes the window open so he might glimpse the gestures of the planets. But his ability is limited here, subdued. Luna, who believes she is a magician, would be furious to know he can sense no link between her and the powerful forces beyond the window.

She sits on his bedside. He looks at her openly, always openly, hoping these captors will remember their humanity.

'Does Berlin have another source of the lichen?' she asks. 'A further strain?'

He stays silent.

'Is she really looking to find out what happened to you or does she know you're activated? Do you have a magic way of communicating with her?'

'No,' he says firmly. He needs to keep Mila safe. 'She would have no idea. I don't know why she's looking into my disappearance, okay? Probably just for some sort of closure.'

Luna's sweat smells like patchouli, powder. 'Do you have a secret way of telling her how to become activated?'

Has Mila also peaked? The way he did? He'll have to see if there's some way of reaching tendrils out. Later, when he's alone.

'It only worked for me.'

'But how? What is the secret?'

'I've told you everything about every moment leading up to me taking the *Xanthoria*, and every second after it. Maybe some people are just predisposed.'

She shakes her head. 'That can't be right.'

'Can I have some lunch?' he says, curling his legs up under himself.

She looks torn. 'I'll ask the chief. Give us the secret, and you'll be treated like a king.'

'I don't have any secret.'

'Well, then we might have to take her, too.'

'To what end?' he says, panicked. 'She knows nothing, and she's not … magical.' He echoes their terminology.

'Is she not?'

The group learned of Kyle's planned trip from Josh's phone, and one of their insiders in Berlin told them when Mila arrived and started sniffing about – the hostel manager, he presumes. They know from Josh's earlier messages to Mila that she did the trial, too.

The tea on his bedside begins to boil in the mug. Luna watches it.

'You're angry,' she says.

He doesn't reply.

'We won't move until we know, but we *will* figure it out.' She means they won't catch Mila until they know she has peaked. And what about Kyle? Will they wait until Mila is alone, or will they just find some way to make both of them disappear? 'Have a sip of that,' she says, nodding at the tea, 'while it's nice and hot.' She smirks. 'And then I'll take you down.'

Luna leads the way downstairs into the ritual chamber. Josh is in a hooded robe, a darker blue than the others. The basement room is lit by candles only; otherwise, thinks Josh, the wallpaper and carpet installed in the '80s might ruin the mood.

Luna kneels at the front of the room, but it is a round-faced man, the chief adept, who begins to lead the ritual from a small stage. The chief speaks, appealing to a confusion of angels and Egyptian gods. He calls on their help to reach an 'inner plane' and then, inevitably, to unlock great wealth, both spiritual and material.

Josh wastes his energy making the candle flames gyrate, spinning smoke into something that looks like a portal. That's the bullshit they expect. The punters 'ooh' and 'aah'. There is no way he will reveal to them the ineffectual nature of these sessions – rituals this group have seemingly performed for a while and have now unimaginatively adapted to real power. Is that not the way it always is, though? Josh thinks of his dalliance with corporate work – how there were always talented people who were squashed into shape instead of truly being able to contribute, to enhance the company's potential. The company would make noises about fostering a neurodiverse workplace but then impose rules about what employees could have on their desks and at what times of the day they could use their headphones. Most insidiously, these companies would make people be open and 'proud' of their 'identities', when those things were often still a discovery, or in flux. Prescriptiveness, parameters masquerading as celebratory openness.

But here, Josh is grateful for the organisation's short-sightedness, because it means they can't truly use him. For the moment, while he works out what to do, how to get away from them, that is good. His new innate senses continue to tell him the trees are important, water is important, earth is important, the greater cosmic forces are important – time and space are inextricably linked. People are, too – the alive, organic bodies and what they contain, each carrying its own history, and histories. Superbly complex. The other 'plane', or whatever word might be most appropriate, is not separate from the organic. It's both inside and around it; it's the history and the future, too. It's matter, consciousness, memory, and an ineffable … illumination. But being shut in, and in darkness, is stifling and prohibitive to his ability to tap it, to connect with all this, with the … He doesn't really know what to call it yet. Words like 'energies' and 'forces' seem corrupted by enterprises like the one that is holding him captive. Or those words sound like something that would come out of the mouth of a hippie boomer stoner.

This is more like an intuition or second sight. But it isn't sight, per se, it's sort of all the senses bundled together, and then some. Like a knowledge that has been lying dormant, until the *Xanthoria* encouraged it out.

The existing senses can also be enhanced at will. And Josh guesses that the extra perceptions, if he ever has time to play with them, could also be explored, exploited. Those elements at the edge of his grasp – the psychokinesis, the perception of time.

After the ritual, as Luna goes to lead him from the room, an old man clutches his arm. Josh knows, even in the dark, that this man is both old and sick. 'Please … can you heal me?' he asks.

Swiftly, Luna emits a blue buzz from the sleeve of her robe – a taser – and the man slumps back in the darkness. Josh's heart beats hard in his chest. The man's desperation and sorrow are confronting, but Josh doesn't know if he can heal people. These 'powers', in fact, may not have any practical use; he might just be a fancy transhuman colour-and-light show. That would be for the best, really, because otherwise it won't just be this group who wants to own him and Mila and anyone else who may have come through the trial, or any subsequent trials. It will be militaries, governments, other ridiculous moneyed organisations, none of them wanting to use him and the others for anything kind.

He is a tool here, but he could be used as a weapon.

He has to find a way out.

Back in the room afterwards, hungry and exhausted by the meagre effort, he conjures an image on his eyelids of Van Gogh's *Sunflowers*. He seeks some channel between him and Mila, between here and Berlin. He seeks her in space: her face, her heart. He thinks of *Star Trek* and beaming up, a process of dematerialisation and rematerialisation.

There is some sense of her, across-ways. Or is he merely tapping into his memories of her? The presence of her within his own self, his own body?

Nonetheless, he beams that yellow-and-orange image through. If she can understand he's alive, she will also comprehend that she too is in danger.

As he's drifting off, his eyelids flash with … What was that? He tucks time back a little.

An image of Kyle's glasses, sitting on an open notebook.

⟶

Mila wants to go back to Tiergarten, the most tree-dense place around. And a walk would seem normal and natural to anyone who might be watching. But she and Kyle can't communicate about the unusual situation while they're outside, just in case.

The hardest thing will be to act like she is not completely overwhelmed – by light, colour, sound, the micro-pressures in the air; by people's blood and organs and the time ticking by inside them with each beat of their hearts.

Though, the experience is very different to the anxiety and the *pressing in* she felt back in Prague. It's almost the opposite: instead of shrinking down she is expanding, stretching out, to encompass it all. This doesn't feel like pressure, it just feels loud, and like she needs a moment to catch up to herself, to her new capacity.

She puts on sunglasses, a hat, white clothes (reflective, she convinces herself). She lathers any exposed skin with sunblock. Kyle does the same because he always does anyway; he burns easily.

They walk, past the spy museum and through Potsdamer Platz. She can almost hear Pink Floyd playing 'The Wall', the music lingering in the air from 1989, over the former no man's land of division, the buildings obliterated after WWII, the 1920s clubs, the older city gate, and bouncing off the red and yellow bricks of the Legoland sign that is above them now.

In the park there are large flat stone paths and wider dirt tracks, wide open grassy spaces, patches of shade and light. Willow trees trailing water from bridges. Birds that chirp and one that sounds like machine-gun fire. With the murmur of nature, the potency of people and human history falls away for Mila. She can feel the hum in her core and through to her fingertips: the sense of harmony, of bee and bird and branch and fox. She can't help exclaiming aloud.

Kyle looks at her sharply.

'It's ... a beautiful day,' she says coyly, hoping her face lets him know there is more going on. She observes that he is a part of it. He is earth and water and air. And he is sublime.

There is so much she could do here, she feels. In the open spaces. There is so much to draw on – like that river of sunlight, or the gummy centres of blades of grass. Even her teeth gak with the potential, and desire. And then as she and Kyle turn down another path she sees that they are on the 'strip' where she scored the drugs.

Something clicks.

Josh was pretty clean when she was seeing him in Melbourne; said he'd been taking a break and wasn't doing anything 'hard' for a while. But when he was in Berlin he was clubbing, and had drugs, as she did. Was this the reason the lichen finally worked? Did a cocaine or MDMA – or a combination – high awaken what the substance had planted?

She laughs.

'What's up?' Kyle says.

'Oh, I was just thinking of something that happened. Never mind.'

'You are radiant, you know?' Kyle says, then clears his throat. 'I mean ...'

He means in the park, she thinks. 'I know what you mean. You are, too. It all is.'

'You're still high,' he says.

'You could say that.'

He is beaming. Back at the hotel, she told him about the sunflowers that had popped up in her mind, how she was sure this was some sign from Josh.

Now, as a thought enters Mila's mind about her parents, her phone buzzes. She takes it out of her pocket and it's her dad. She gestures to Kyle that she's going to sit on a nearby park bench and take the call.

'Dad,' she says to the video screen. She hopes he can see that she is radiant, too.

'Hello darling.'

'How are you and Mum?'

'Oh, okay. Same old. We miss you.'

Normally this would twist her up, even make her react in a kind of cranky, pressured way, but she doesn't have any of those feelings now, in the park. She can see the pure sentiment of what her father has said is just that – that he is not trying to lure her back. That he simply, truly misses her.

'I miss you both so much,' she says.

They make small talk and she hears all about the local gossip and what her aunts and uncles are up to, and she tells her parents about the places she's been. She can see Kyle twitching – but they have their plan and there is nothing more to do before the flight, so she relaxes.

Feeling so good and whole makes her able to ask her dad something. 'Dad, I know this question is a bit out of the blue, but … were you disappointed Scott and I broke up? That I didn't get married and have children, like grandkids for you and Mum.'

'Darling …'

'It's just that you both seemed quite … distant around the whole experience.'

'Did we?'

'A little.'

Her dad sighs. 'I didn't realise you were hanging on to anything like this. I mean, we just struggled to see you so upset. We didn't know the best way to help. We thought it was what *you* wanted. Some space.'

Ha. Mila thought she'd presented a pretty brave face to the world. She even convinced herself she wasn't shattered by the break-up, by the abrupt termination of her idea of what life would look like. What life was even *about*.

'All we've ever wanted is for you to be happy,' her dad continues. 'You know that.'

Mila nods at her dad in pixels, homing in on the love in his voice.

'And it doesn't matter if that's with kids or travelling or having a good work life or being creative … just as long as it feels right to you, chook.'

Mila tears up – her dad hasn't called her chook for at least five years. All this time, she realises, she's been genuinely worried they were disappointed in her. That's why she's struggled to help out any more than she has: not because she doesn't care deeply about them, but because she felt she hadn't turned out to be the daughter they'd imagined. And being around them was a constant reminder of that.

'Thanks, Dad. I'm still finding my way a bit, I think. But you don't have to worry.'

I could be in terrible danger, she thinks. But I am also illuminated.

'And don't you worry about us either,' he says.

'I do. And I'll come help out more when I get back.'

They have to find Josh as soon as possible – for him, but also so she can do this.

'Nope, won't hear of it,' her dad says. 'We've got a good community here, and people are dropping by all the time. But we would love to see you just to see you.'

She smiles. 'Love to see you too.'

'Okay, looks beautiful there, I'll let you go!'

'Okay Dad, love you.'

'Love you too darling.'

She hangs up.

'All good?' asks Kyle. His gaze still darts around, looking out for the both of them. She lets him.

'Yeah,' she says. 'We've got hours. You want to call your folks too?'

Kyle scuffs his foot in the dirt. 'I guess.'

'Would you rather do it from the airport?'

He nods, relieved.

'All right.'

She'll call Kate there. She flicks to the last message from her friend: a picture of Ty with food all over his face and hands. She aches to give the child a cuddle.

One thing at a time.

On the way back to collect their bags, they duck into a mart for a cheap lunch. Mila stares into the open fridges; she could almost talk to the friendly squiggling bacteria in the yoghurt. The lettuce leaves and shredded kale are mustardy wet, in temporary plastic domiciles, before they will become nutrient mulch. It's not sentience, necessarily – well, not in each element in their discrete parts – but as a whole, she discerns an answering comprehension.

She buys a protein bar, dense and powdery. And a little quieter than the fresh food, having been processed.

They collect their bags from behind the reception desk at the hotel, and ask the staff to call a cab. Not using their apps will ensure a greater chance of not being followed.

Mila is desperately keen to get to Josh, but not looking forward to being stuck on a plane for twenty-four hours.

⁓

Josh is slowly gleaning more about the group through their uncareful interactions with each other. The bald, round-faced chief adept sometimes comes into his room and sits on a chair, and Luna sits at the man's feet, at the hem of his ludicrous purple-gold robe, with one hand placed upon his knee. The chief adept doesn't come often, because – Josh realises, having been around this emotion enough – he is envious of Josh. Mainly, he sends Luna to continue to grill Josh about the circumstances surrounding the *Xanthoria* experiment in Melbourne. Did Josh take anything alongside the lichen? What did he do that day? That night? They go over it again and again. Josh is honest about all this because he doesn't think they're asking the right questions.

Then Luna comes to his room, alone, smirking. 'Do you know?' she says.

'Know what?' he says, worried, thinking about the sunflowers. He hasn't been able to connect since.

'Our operative saw her leave a shop and look at the buckets of flowers out the front – and the petals that were not yet open, they bloomed. He said she was stuffing her face and barely seemed to notice.'

Since they know that Josh and Mila slept together on the day they took the substance, he is sure this will convince them even more that the peaking is related to what happened then, rather than any time after. In a way, this is good. But now Mila is in serious danger.

Through the constant questioning, he's realised the chief adept must have tried the *Xanthoria* – perhaps all of them here have. And clearly no one has had any reaction. But for them to know of its potential in the first place, and for the trial to have existed, surely there was someone out there who had, at least once?

He remembers George, the scientist who oversaw his participation, mentioning an 'original subject', but that they – Cladion – hadn't been able to replicate the effects as yet. So it must have been some time ago? And what happened to that subject?

'I didn't know,' Josh says to Luna.

Her long straw-coloured hair is oily at the scalp. She tilts her head. He can never tell whether she believes him, whether she is patient, placid, or a little dopey. All he knows is they won't let him go – they'll keep trying.

Luna sighs now, gets up. 'No lunch today either.' She leaves.

Josh listens to her walk upstairs. He bends his hearing around the walls to follow her, but regrets it when the chief adept speaks to her in a low, lustrous tone. Perhaps they're now fucking while eating the lichen, expecting the effects to come on six months later. He shrinks his hearing back, worried about Luna. She has been in the inner realm of this organisation for many years, he gleans, but still. Attraction to power, devotion to a leader – is that consent? She knows too many of the org's secrets to leave. Certainly, she knows what they are capable of. Or is it her who sat his shoes by the river, wrote the email, masterminded it all? She was the one who left him the newspaper to read about his disappearance, afterwards. Somehow Mila and Kyle saw through the ruse, thank god. But then again, perhaps it would have been better they thought him dead. Getting on with their lives. Except Mila would have peaked anywhere, right? If she did what he thinks she did.

If he gives Luna what he believes is the secret, will she be free and will she set him free?

It's too dangerous — she could give power to all the rich old arseholes who meet underground in this London home.

A few hours later, Luna enters the room and Josh leans back, feigning relaxation, readiness, cooperation. She's changed into a green velvet robe-slash-dress with crystals hanging from her neck and the curved, bejewelled and carved gold cross all the members wear. Her white-blonde hair is clean now, and reaches almost to her waist.

She sits on the chair. 'Hello again.'

'Afternoon.'

She asks him casually if any of the masters are speaking with him.

'What do you mean?'

She tilts her head. 'Some of us can channel people from the past. They speak to us, and through us, their wisdom. We call them ascended masters. Particular magicians will have relationships with particular masters. They see the world as it is because they have lived before and have since achieved great spiritual understanding.' She peers earnestly into his face. 'I was wondering if you had channelled someone yet, a great magus like you.'

'I haven't tried.' Josh is spooked by the idea. 'Do these … masters give predictions, or …?'

'Sometimes. Often they just communicate wisdom that is needed in the moment. Ways of seeing and being.'

'How did you learn to communicate with them?' he asks, flattering her.

Roses rise on her cheeks. 'Through much practice, in my case. Others seem to be born with the skill, or sometimes it comes on quickly, like to an ordinary person just going about their life. It's often a bit scary for the family and friends – we have a couple of people in the organisation like that. Normally there's quite a price for entry, but if someone has special skills – like you, of course – we want to keep them close.'

'You kidnap them, too?'

She purses her lips.

So he isn't the only prisoner. But are the others no longer useful? Why is she coming to him for this? Maybe the org realised his version of this 'channelling' might be more genuine.

'If I am able to do this for you,' he says, 'will you let the others go?'

She blinks. 'You don't understand. Each ascended master is different, and it is the sum of their wisdom that helps us flourish.' She shakes her head, as though Josh is a baby – innocent and unformed.

If he does a convincing job of it, maybe the 'master' from within could predict that they will let the others go …

'I would like to watch a channelling,' he says, 'to understand better how to do it.'

She smiles. 'Good.'

⌒

Forty thousand feet in the air, Kyle is using the plane's wi-fi to give himself a crash course in esotericism, magic, miracles, transhuman tech and substances; and there is nothing, really, to explain this exact situation, though he finds that Cladion has a website and is not backward in coming forward about its goals. The company is researching the intersections between science and traditional occult alchemy, the site says, and it has a humanitarian aim: to share knowledge that will help humanity progress spiritually and scientifically (Yeah, right, thinks Kyle) by 'restoring our connection to both ancestral and cosmic understanding'. Experiments are not mentioned. He wonders why the heck the billionaire Lisa Edwards is behind all of this.

He had a moment, a few years ago, when he was fascinated with billionaires and their visions. Mostly Elon Musk and his Neuralink brain chip, which will apparently cure brain disorders and allow you to download and watch memories like videos. But then there was the whole Musk, Jeff Bezos and Richard Branson space race, and it didn't seem like a race to change the world but to waste billions on a dick-measuring contest. He's since become more sceptical about the power and influence these individuals have, and how much they can truly innovate for humanity when they are too rich to be in touch with what humanity is. He can't help thinking about Mr Burns from *The Simpsons*, surrounded by his 'yes men'.

Kyle hopes using the plane's exorbitantly priced wi-fi and then deleting his history will help to avoid any tracing of his data. He follows one thread and ends up in a deep dive, reading about modern magic and its different schools and aspects, descended from common sources like religions. There are descendants of the Western Mysteries and its esoteric orders of the early twentieth century, and then there are covens of witchcraft; there is ritual magic inspired by ancient systems such as Celtic, Egyptian or Nordic; and then there is a loose paganism that includes earth worship. As far as he can tell, what Mila is experiencing has aspects described in a range of phenomena: the moon-worship of witchcraft, the god-force energy of the Western Mysteries, or similar concepts in various other cultures, such as the Chinese qi (a vital force), the yogic concept of prana from the Hindu tradition, or the French philosophical concept of Élan vital. But it also has something of an infusion of history, which is perhaps related to the ancient ritual magic sources? It could be more like being tapped into something similar to the Jungian collective unconscious. And then a communing with nature suggests a somewhat pagan element ... A more modern term, 'psychokinesis' (coined in 1914) or 'telekinesis', which describes being able to move, transmute, affect objects with the mind, doesn't quite cover all of it.

In short, Kyle is fairly lost. When it is possible, Mila should read all of this to be able to understand and find what works for her. Right now, she is drooling beside him, having heavily sedated herself for the flight in fear of maybe letting off sparks.

The flight attendant rolls down the aisle with breakfast before their layover in Hong Kong, and Kyle asks for a cheeky whisky. He can't join Mila on the Valium, because he has to stay alert for the both of them, but he needs something. The attendant puts the tiny bottle on his breakfast tray next to the foil-covered scrambled eggs and the chemical-scented coffee.

'Do you think she wants anything?' the attendant asks, pointing to Mila.

'I'll keep my yoghurt for her.' Kyle feels very grown up, very responsible. In just one month he has travelled, sleuthed, and begun being a sidekick. He has already been married and divorced. He has handled situations he never thought he'd have to handle. And, he thinks as the whisky nudges his endorphins, he has made a new friend.

He looks at her, cosy under eye mask and mouth covering.

Maybe more than a friend?

No, it is rude of him to think that, now, when she is going through this. And when she and Josh already have a connection.

I would get married again, he thinks. In a heartbeat. Despite last time. Despite it not working out, and the alienation that came with the loss of closeness. But marriage is like another kind of adventure. And he liked the planning of the event, and the planning of a life together, and the rhythm of their days before it started to go south.

Would he have his Robin outfit on under his tux? He sips his whisky, chuckling to himself. Maybe he will do a little sketch in his notebook of it. Add a few muscles. God, one whisky and you're drunk, Kyle.

And don't forget that Josh is alive, thank god, and Josh is who is so special to her. If she's going to end up with anyone …

The plane starts to descend and Mila pushes up her eye mask, runs a hand through her hair. 'Going okay?' she says sleepily.

'Yeah,' he says, smiling at her.

'What? Is it amusing that I have to sedate myself?'

'No,' he says, correcting his expression. Of course she's stressed, worried. But he was just trying to be supportive, sweet to her; couldn't help smiling, really. Maybe at the absurdity of it all, too. 'My head is crammed with esoteric shit,' he says, 'for when you feel up to it.'

'Oh … cheers.' She sighs, stretches a little and looks out at the clouds. 'Wow.' Again, she must be seeing, smelling, feeling something he can't.

'I saved you some yoghurt,' he says.

Now she turns and smiles back at him. He hands it to her, along with the small plastic spoon. 'Thanks,' she says. She stares into it like it's alive.

Trays are collected, and the pilot announces some expected turbulence and for them to put their seatbelts on now. Kyle's heart races; he hates turbulence.

'You okay?' Mila says.

He swallows. 'Will be.'

'About fifty per cent of the passengers got worried then,' she says, eyes unfocused.

'Turbulence reminds us it's unnatural to fly – to be in some metal thing hurtling through the air,' he says, gesticulating nervously.

The plane jolts and rumbles. Kyle gasps. Mila hands the empty yoghurt container back to him. 'Can you hold this, please?' She closes her eyes.

Kyle watches her. 'What are you doing?'

'I just want to feel what is causing it.'

The plane jolts violently up and down, lifting Kyle from his seat. 'Mila …' he whines.

'Hold on.'

And then, through the window, he sees clouds disperse. He feels the plane even out, begin to slide gently through the air again.

She opens her eyes.

He is grasping the armrests, white-knuckled.

'I couldn't test it on the ground, in case we were being watched.' She has a wry look on her face. Her hair is still flat against one side of her head, from sleep. 'I'll take more pills in Hong Kong, don't worry.'

He inhales deeply. Okay, she is basically Jesus, or Moses or whatever. Or Thor, or Aiolos, or Hermes … She is Mila, king and queen of wind, or cloud. Of the elements. She is Captain Planet. Sleepy and cranky and fuelled by strawberry yoghurt, she is a goddess.

They've erected a small stage in the basement for the ceremony. Josh sits, shrouded and secret, at the back of the room. He is to play no role today, Luna said; he is only to observe. He doesn't think he could do much, anyway. Since he learned that other people are being held captive, he has felt weakened further. And since he overheard Luna telling the chief that Mila and Kyle boarded a plane back to Melbourne, he's felt confused, fuzzy. And worried. The geographical distance potentially explains why he hasn't been able to get another message through.

A woman in her forties, dressed in flowing, sheer pastels, and muscular beneath, is led to the stage by two people in the usual robes. They sit her onto a chair. Josh squints and can see the tasers beneath their layers of clothing. But the woman does not protest – used to the rules? Or maybe she actually has a sense of belonging here.

She sits for a long time, in a soft spotlight, then raises her hands palm up and looks to the light, as if pleading. Her mouth begins to move, but she isn't making any sound. And then her lips stop moving, and she peers around the room. People shift when her gaze meets theirs, strong and unwavering.

'I am the master John Wayne,' she says in a deep, gravelly voice. Josh stifles a snort. *John Wayne?*

'I have travelled the plains of desert, and the cardboard Hollywood sets, and I have met many enemies who attempted to destroy my soul, to deprive me of family and love, and to turn me into a purely animal hunter; but these were the lesser plains, for I now have travelled through the vertical, and the expanded, and the interior ...'

She, he, the woman and John Wayne, look into Josh's eyes,

and a shiver runs down his spine. It's true that he can sense less about her while she's in this … trance. But her eyes are alight, and he can hear her brain sparking.

John Wayne goes on to tell them to seek their own expansion, to travel with their bodies, and their hearts and souls, through darkness and into golden light.

The room is dead quiet, stunned and inspired.

Bullshit, Josh thinks.

Yes, he should be able to do this. To pretend to commune, and not only try to convince his captors to let some of these people go, but also use it as a way to get back home, to Mila and Kyle. The org already knows where they've gone and may be planning to go there regardless. He needs to convince them that he has to come along. That way, he can escape – once his powers are enhanced out in the open – and warn Kyle and Mila.

It is freezing cold when Mila and Kyle land back in Melbourne. Sheets of rain hit the plane windows upon landing. It is early and dark. The rooms and corridors of Tullamarine Airport are muted as they head through immigration and customs.

'Did you get any sleep?' Mila asks Kyle, rubbing her temples.

'Not much,' he says.

She did, because she was sedated, but she feels furry. She is tempted to go and stand in the cold rain. Shouldn't these powers make her not need sleep or coffee?

A worrying thought creeps in: What is my body going through to adapt to this?

'Okay, coffee,' she says. 'Then straight to the city. That's the plan, right?'

He yawns, but nods. 'The longer we leave it the worse it could be for him.'

They walk towards the coffee shop in the arrivals hall. Mila can see, in Kyle's creased expression, the shape of his shoulders, his pensive hazel eyes behind glass, that he is overwhelmed and scared. He wants to protect her and his best mate, and yet he and Mila could be walking into an even more dangerous situation.

'You know, I can do this on my own,' she says. 'Now that I'm … enhanced. You're just putting yourself in danger unnecessarily.'

She doesn't want to look at him while he considers his reply. She is next in line and orders their coffees: oat milk latte for him, skinny cap for her.

'Of course I'm coming,' he says.

She is relieved, though she feels bad about it.

Kyle pulls out his phone. 'I cleared all the history and have popped my Aus sim back in – here goes.' He turns it on, then puts it in his pocket as they take their coffees and find a seat, wheeling their bags into a space behind it. Kyle's pocket starts to buzz, and buzz, and buzz. 'Shit,' he says, taking it out.

Mila watches as he touches the screen and scrolls. He looks pained.

'What is it?' she asks.

'It's Jeanie. My ex-wife. She's in hospital, been in an accident …' Tears start to fall, and he squashes his eyes with all of his fingers, lifting his glasses.

'Oh my god, is she going to be okay?' Mila can feel his heart beating, everything flowing through him – the blood and water. She wants to reach inside him and slow everything down. She thinks she can at least make her hands warm, like a heat pack; she stands and puts her warm hands against his cheeks.

He gives a little gasp. Lowers his hands and peers at her. 'I don't know. I have to call.' He shakes as he does.

Mila listens as he talks to his ex-mother-in-law, as he tries to hold himself together. It seems Jeanie is in a bad way – lots of broken bones – but has woken up and is asking for him. He apologises again and again, Adam's apple bobbing beneath his stubble, for having been out of range, until Mila can hear the MIL frustratedly ask him to stop.

'Just get here,' Mila hears. And he looks up at her, and his mouth gapes.

'You can go,' she says. 'I told you, I can go on my own to Cladion.' But there is the returning ache of loneliness. Shouldn't these powers make her a better, more generous person? Maybe it's just the jet lag, the benzo hangover. 'I'll meet you in the city later.'

'Uh,' he says into the phone. 'Of course I will. Of course.' He dips his head apologetically at Mila, his eyes still squeezing out tears. He hangs up. 'Mila,' he says, grasping her wrist. 'Don't go without me.'

'I'll be okay.'

'You need back-up. A lookout. I … it's just that she is still sort of family, you know?'

And I am a sugar mama going to find her lover, Mila thinks. I have no spouse, no friends, no superhero wingman devoted to my cause. She glances at a television screen showing footage of a house collapsing in a flood.

'Mila!' Kyle points at her coffee cup – milky froth is bubbling up inside it, out the sippy part and down onto her fingers.

She didn't feel herself doing it. She drops it, gasping. 'Shit.'

People look at them. She has to be more careful. She grabs a bunch of napkins from the coffee cart, mops up the mess.

Kyle throws back the last of his coffee as Mila puts on her small backpack and clutches her suitcase handle. 'I hope Jeanie's okay,' she says, trying to sound compassionate.

He still has a red patchy face, streaks of wet. She kisses him softly on the cheek, then walks away.

Luna has not left Josh alone to give him a chance to practise. So he will just have to dive in. He asks her if he can open the window; she agrees. She sits quietly, but on the floor near the chair as opposed to on it, as though the chief adept is sitting there. Maybe this is just her respect for magic: sit low, allow it to flow on high. He crosses his legs on the bed, closes his eyes, having no idea how to even begin 'channelling' someone. He wishes he were alone so he could rehearse the words he wants to say aloud – the performance.

A gentle breeze comes in through the window. He tucks his hair behind his ears, concentrates on the back of his eyelids. In his mind, he asks: What do I do? And then, new surroundings begin to materialise. A bar or cafe, with old painted signs above the rows of bottles. The room is empty, with chairs stacked on tables, except for one centre table that a woman sits atop in a tuxedo. She has a perfect face, symmetrical and theatrical. Masculine and feminine. Master Marlene Dietrich.

She gives him that famous smoky, knowing smile.

If he speaks aloud here, will he be speaking in reality? Will Luna hear him?

But Marlene speaks first, in her German accent. 'You must keep them here, keep them content with you. You must not let them have her, too. And then she can do the work that needs to be done.'

Mila is to play some great role, and he is to be the sacrificial lamb?

He then thinks of Kyle, still not daring to say anything aloud. He looks at Marlene's face, and it falls. Is Kyle in danger? She turns away. She transforms, ages, her outfits rotating, until she is an elder Marlene in the most intensely sparkling gown he has ever seen, a huge fur coat sitting off one shoulder and flowing about her heels.

'Performance, glamour, sparkle. You have this in you.' She winks. And then, briefly, her whole being turns yellow-gold, and clay falcons sit upon her wrists. Josh remembers this image: a statue of Libussa he'd looked up at, on the balcony of a building in Prague. The witch queen. Leader of warriors.

The falcons take flight and the bar dissolves in a shimmery crackle. There is the blackness of his eyelids again. He slowly blinks open his eyes. He is grateful the room is shady.

Luna is staring at him. 'It worked, didn't it? I saw your eyeballs moving.'

He nods. 'So I didn't say anything?'

'The master did not speak through you, no. What did they say? Who was it?'

'It was Master Marlene Dietrich. She told me ...' What he thinks is that this was simply his subconscious. He thinks it's likely always that, with these 'masters'. He thinks the woman in the basement was exposed to John Wayne movies in some formative psychoanalytic stage of childhood and they had a profound effect on her, maybe because something happened simultaneously that scarred her subconscious. For Marlene Dietrich to be his – well, he's obsessed with her, has been since he was a kid and first encountered pictures and video of her. And then later when he read about her life he found all these parallels – the bisexuality, writing love notes to a teacher, reading Schiller and Goethe on aesthetics ...

If his subconscious was going to throw up anyone, it was going to be her. And Libussa is a recent fascination in the same vein. An ancient woman, perhaps only a myth, but a powerful one: she presided over an age of Bohemian freedom. He doesn't believe he has encountered a spirit. Yes, these powers make everything 'extra', reveal layers to existence the average person can't comprehend, but he's still doubtful this includes realms of glamorous dead. What she revealed are simply his deepest fears: the organisation finding Mila, and Kyle being in danger. The 'channelling' was just an intense, hyperreal dream.

But he needs to fight those fears. 'She told me you do not need any of the other visionaries, now you have me.'

'Go on,' Luna says.

'And she told me the answer the chief adept seeks can be found at the source. In Melbourne. And I must be present to unlock it.'

Luna looks down, apparently considering his words. He can't see any suspicion on her face, but the chief may be harder to convince.

And then the chief opens the door and walks into the room. He is in his emerald green again, a long vest-cloak with gaudy clashes of red and gold. A singlet beneath. He is both burly and soft, with downward creases where his aged pectorals slice his pits.

Luna spins her head to look at him, remaining on her knees.

'I knew you'd be more comfortable just with her,' he says to Josh, to explain why he'd been lurking and not present.

'What do you think?' Luna asks him.

'I think we must face our destiny.' He says this with a straight face, dark eyebrows bristling over serious, hooded eyes.

Josh holds back the smile threatening at the corners of his mouth.

'But first,' the big man says, 'we would like you to channel her again for the group. Our members will pay handsomely to witness a genuine master.'

'I will, but you gotta let John Wayne and any others go,' says Josh, standing and peering into his eyes.

'Agreed.' With a swish of his emerald cloak, the chief adept leaves the room.

—◦—

Kyle is completely undone. Already feeling a world away from everything that has just happened. Melbourne has a way of doing that, immediately drawing you back into your routines and obligations. His planned departure from that, his planned adventure – where he was going to be immersed in culture and fun and newness, walking around foreign cities – didn't work out. And despite what that means, here he is, walking into the Alfred Hospital to see the woman who was once the love of his life, whom he would apparently still drop everything for.

When he gets to her room she's alone behind her individual blue curtain, small-looking – that achingly familiar heart-face, high forehead, thick dark hair all over the pillow. Those rosewood lips.

'Kyle.' She reaches her arms for him. Into his hair, she whispers, 'When I came to on that cold gravel, I thought of you.'

He cries, though she always got annoyed at how much he cried. He's crying so much he can't speak.

And then she stiffens a little, says 'hello' to someone behind Kyle. Kyle wipes his face on his sleeve, turns around to see a tall blond guy, coffee in one hand, the other reaching towards him. 'You must be Kyle. I'm Sam.'

'Oh …' Kyle sniffs, stands, shakes Sam's hand. It still feels weird to shake hands, especially in a hospital surrounded by germs. Kyle resists the urge to go straight to the sanitiser.

Jeanie speaks. 'Kyle, this is my boyfriend, Sam.'

'Oh, nice to meet you.' Kyle can't quite look the guy in the eye. He can't quite look anywhere because his eyes keep filling up.

'Sit, you two,' Jeanie says. 'How was your trip?' she asks Kyle and takes his hand, squeezing it between hers. Right in front of her boyfriend. Is he really that little of a threat, that she can be openly physically affectionate with him – her ex-husband – and Sam won't bat an eyelid? Seems so.

He sighs. 'It wasn't very much fun, as you can imagine.'

'He was meant to meet up with his mate,' Jeanie explains to Sam, 'but the guy walked into a river just before Kyle was due to go over.'

Sam gives a sharp intake of breath. 'Jeez, that's ... harsh. But you still went?'

'I didn't know what else to do with myself, and ... I thought I could find out a bit more about what happened,' he finds himself admitting.

'And did you?' Sam asks.

Kyle's hand still sits damply between Jeanie's. 'Not really.' He is a terrible liar, always has been. He hopes his face displays disappointment. The guy probably doesn't care anyway, is just making conversation, indulging him, and waiting for him to leave.

And he does have to go. *What do you need me for?* he wants to scream. He has always been there for Jeanie, and always will be. But surely Sam or whoever she is seeing is supposed to take over this role? He knows it's incredible to be so close to someone, even after all they've been through, but sometimes – he feels bad for thinking it – he wonders if she realises that she's been breaking his heart over and over again. Maybe she has no comprehension of this.

He hears someone say 'knock, knock' from behind the curtain, and they all look over and suddenly Mila is there. Peeping her head around, at the end of the bed, still dishevelled and ethereal and hot as hell. She smiles at him, and he extricates his hand from Jeanie's. 'Mila.'

'Who are you?' Jeanie asks.

'I'm Kyle's friend, Mila,' she says. 'How are you feeling?'

Jeanie shoots a look at Kyle, probably wondering what he's doing hanging out with some older babe.

'I'm Sam,' Sam says, standing, when it looks like Jeanie is not going to answer.

Mila hesitates before shaking his hand. 'It was hard to find a park.' Something to explain her lagging behind. Her suitcase must be sitting next to Kyle's just inside the room.

Sam moves one chair over on the bedside, leaving space for Mila to sit beside Kyle. 'We got here as soon as we could,' she says.

Kyle's heart is flooded with gratefulness. She has listened to everything I've ever told her about my marriage, he thinks. Even the words behind the things I said – she heard them too.

'Uh, thanks,' Jeanie says. 'I'm in a lot of pain.'

'That's awful,' Mila says, truthfully. Kyle notices she is trying to work something out. Her facial expressions have become so familiar. She couldn't do the X-ray thing without someone noticing, and she said she can't see so well through skin, but she can also smell and hear and sense things in the body. 'Where is the worst break?' Mila asks, but Kyle sees her hand already hovering above Jeanie's shin.

'My ankle is smashed,' Jeanie says. 'If I wasn't so high on painkillers I'd probably be terrified.'

'Yes,' Mila says, distantly.

Kyle tries to warn Mila with his eyes. Mila places her hand down, gently.

'Your hand is so warm,' Jeanie says.

Kyle is nervous Mila will set the sheets on fire. But she pulls back, gives a weak smile. 'I've always had hot hands.' She clutches them in her lap.

'Anyway,' Kyle says. 'I'm so sorry but we have to go.'

'You just got here,' Jeanie says sadly.

'I know. I'm sorry.' He and Mila stand. 'Nice to meet you, mate,' he says to Sam, in a blokey voice he wasn't aware he had. He leans down and looks Jeanie in her familiar eyes. 'Get better,' he says. She says nothing, frowning, and he gives her a peck on the cheek.

They rush down the hospital corridor, dragging their cases.

In the elevator, he turns to Mila, to thank her. But she looks bereft.

'We're going to find him,' he says instead.

'It's not that,' she says.

'What is it?'

'I can't heal people.' She gives him a lopsided grin.

'Oh ...' He puts an arm around her back. 'Not Jesus then.'

She slaps his arm away playfully. She has told him about her parents: her dad's chronic illness, her mum's mental health issues; their general difficulty and decline after the fires and through the pandemic.

The doors ding open and Kyle walks beside her out to the tram stop near the hospital, bathed in the eerie yellow of the sun filtered through thick winter clouds.

'It was intense in there – with all the sick people,' she says.

'Could you diagnose, even if not heal? Like catch tumours early or whatever?'

'I'm not sure. It's murky, what you get. It's not always shapes; it can be more like motions, processes. I suppose if there was some blockage ...' She seems to brighten a little.

Kyle thinks about the duality of waves and particles in quantum mechanics. He has been looking at all these esoteric sources, but perhaps he needs to think about the possibilities in terms of physics. If she can see, or 'sense', as she explains it, 'motions and processes', perhaps she simply has an enhanced awareness of the quantum.

'Are you much of a science person?' he asks, as they hop onto a tram, windows foggy with breath on the inside. Smell of wet wool. They grab the central pole. Kyle is glad he still carries hand sanitiser in his pocket.

She smiles. 'I should be. My dad's a science teacher, but no. Why?'

'I'm just still thinking of ways we might be able to explain or understand … it.' He looks around the tram. Probably best they drop the conversation for now.

She nods. 'I want to find Josh first. Then I might have the spoons to think about the what and why.'

'Yeah,' he says. 'Fair.'

'But one thing, I can't help but think – I can't heal people,' she whispers, 'but I can move air, maybe fire, water.' She looks at him pointedly.

'Extreme weather events …'

'Even the polar vortex – I don't completely understand it, but I know it's collapsing.'

'Because of climate change,' he says.

'Right.'

He's sure the doubt must be showing on his face. He thinks again about Musk and Bezos. 'Have you read those studies about how power literally changes your brain?'

She frowns at him. 'I do recall something. Leaders can't actually read other people well. What are you saying?'

He doesn't know what he's saying. 'We should be careful.'

'Did they only study men?' She smirks.

'Sorry,' he says.

She shrugs. 'Look, I don't know. It's just that maybe there is something useful in this experience. But I also don't dare to hope.'

'I know what you mean,' he says, trying hard to empathise. He needs to change the subject. 'Hey, thank you so much for showing up at the hospital.' He can feel those stupid tears coming again. He swallows.

'I realised I didn't want to go to Cladion alone,' she says. 'We're a team.'

He can't help grinning at that. But there is still some inadequacy sitting within him, stirred up by Jeanie, and by her new boyfriend. 'Mila, with your ex, with Scott, did you feel it was … equal?'

She looks at the ceiling of the tram, considering. 'In the best days of the relationship, we felt so connected. But I think now it's extremely rare to connect with another person on every level. And so there's always something you might feel you need from them that you're not getting. And these things are, can be,' she looks back at him, 'influenced by social expectations, and gender expectations, or whatever. And, like, what you grew up around and think is pretty normal.' She readjusts her hand in the tram strap. 'But the very things you go through in figuring all this out help you to … realign and connect with new people, or better recognise a connection when it's there.'

'Like you and Josh.'

'And me and you, of course,' she says, nudging him. 'But overcoming the hurt, or sort of discombobulation over what you've lost … It can get in the way of embracing something new. Of even embracing what you might be learning about yourself.'

He nods. 'You've become very sage.'

'Become?'

'Ha, well, sager?'

'I just hope there's a larger meaning to this. Some purpose for good. But maybe,' she says, her voice dropping an octave as she looks back out the window, 'it will end the way everything else does.'

The tram screeches around a corner and up St Kilda Road towards the city.

⁓

As the tram heads towards the Yarra, Mila experiences a strong, heavy sensation that starts in her feet and travels up through her body. It's like the land beneath her has an echo that resonates up as she passes over it. By the time it reaches her head the ages are superimposed, now and *then*, or, as it seems, *always* – she has no words for what she experiences, but it is powerful.

It is people moving high and low with the rise and fall of the river. It is a hand around a bird's egg and another digging yams. It is coming together through dances that go on all night and all through the centuries. There is presence and histories in the rocks and trees and the birds that circle now – layers that are beyond her grasp.

But then she also sees the slashing of trees, the paddocks and buildings and the white figures with guns. She forces herself to stay in it, to witness what she can. To witness it in her body as they pass over this echoing.

It is not just this one place, of course; it is everywhere. But on this axis was where it seemed to overflow into her.

As she starts to come back to the sound of the tram screeching on its tracks, she is not sure of the most appropriate thing to do.

For now, she whispers words to acknowledge the privilege and responsibility of what she has seen, sensed and heard.

They get off the tram at Southern Cross railway station so they can stash their bags. Standing by the lockers, Mila is nervous. It's building in her stomach, wriggling through her to the hairs on her neck, the centre of her palms. Her shoulder blades and neck are tight like a bird's wings pinching back before it takes off. And she is nervous about being nervous. If anger and warmth produce heat, won't this feeling produce something? Lightning from her fingertips? Turn the cold rain outside to ice? She jumps up and down a little and shakes her hands out, trying to shift the adrenaline.

Kyle looks at her. 'In my reading on the plane,' he says, 'some of these ... energies were related to the breath. You could try some breathing exercises, to find more control?'

'Like yogic breathing?' she says.

'Yeah, like into your belly.'

'Or four-fold breath.' That feels right. In, hold, out, hold. Fill, hold, empty, hold. And picture it in the body. (Oh wow, she can.) Expel the negative on the out-breath. Draw in strength on the in-breath.

Slowly, the station noise quietens, and she is more aware of herself than of her surroundings. Without forgetting those surroundings, and the presences within them she has witnessed. But she focuses in on her heart beating, her feet on the ground.

She opens her eyes. 'I guess these ancient practices have stuck around for a reason.'

Kyle looks pleased that he's managed to help. When he smiles his cheeks push up his glasses, and he unconsciously corrects them with his index finger. 'So,' he says practically, extracting his notebook, 'our inadequate plan is ...' He opens the book. 'To show up and ask about Josh.'

'Yes,' Mila says. Keeps taking those deep breaths. 'We don't have time to come up with anything more elaborate. We don't have, you know, weapons or anything.'

'Except ...'

'Yeah, except me.'

'Okay,' Kyle says. 'And I'll just back you up, keep my phone in my hand.'

She can tell he is struggling with the vagueness of the plan, but neither of them has been able to come up with anything better while they think Josh is in danger. To move in swiftly and try to help him, or find out where he is being kept, is all they can do.

'We should at least tell someone where we're going, in case we disappear too,' Kyle says darkly.

'I'll text my friend Kate. We always texted each other before dates, in case the guy was a creep. I'll say something like that. If she doesn't hear from me ...'

He nods.

They jump on another tram to take them up Bourke Street.

By the time they get to the metal door down the alleyway, they are drenched. It's the kind of sideways rain that defeats even large umbrellas. Mila knows the door code, having returned there several times over the six months post-ingestion for her check-ups. She types it into the panel, rain streaming around her umbrella, and the panel beeps back at her. 'Shit, of course it must expire.'

'Do we really just want to blast in there, anyway?' Kyle says, still sounding unsure, or even more so, now they are here. 'I mean, what if we don't find Josh and they capture you.'

'We have to,' Mila says firmly. 'I can't stand the thought of him being locked up or used. Maybe I can offer myself in his place. And you can help get him out of here before it's too late.'

Kyle shakes his head. 'It never goes like that.'

'What do you mean?'

'I mean, in movies. They won't just let him go.'

'Well, I don't know what else to do.' She stares at the door, then bends her sight to see the lock mechanism. She concentrates on the particles of air around it, but just when she's about to manipulate it, it buzzes open. She looks up at the camera, then at Kyle, who nods in understanding.

As Mila cranks open the door, she sees someone clopping down the stairs in Doc Martens: the receptionist, Daisy. Their hair is now blue, still with a shaved patch on one side. 'Mila?' they say brightly. 'Is something the matter?'

Mila shares a look with Kyle. 'We're here for Josh.'

Daisy pauses on the bottom step, then seems to notice Kyle, and frowns. Of course the trial is supposed to be confidential, even if Cladion is open to the public about its aims.

'Does your friend know what we do here?' Daisy asks.

Mila nods. Maybe Cladion hasn't been following her; maybe Lisa Edwards and her team have no idea she has powers now too. Or that she and Kyle have been looking for Josh on the other side of the world. Or maybe it's just that Daisy doesn't know.

'You signed a contract, Mila.'

'Where is Josh?' Mila says, but breathes, trying to keep herself steady, trying not to burn up.

Daisy looks truly confused. 'I don't know. I haven't seen him since you both last came in. Wait ...' Their eyes open wide. 'Does this mean?'

Mila is frustrated, frightened. She fights to keep her impulses down.

'Let me go get Meg and George. Wait here. Please.'

'Tell them to come with Josh, or I'll ...' *No.* Don't reveal anything. 'I'll go to the feds.'

Daisy runs up the stairs. The door lock clicks behind them.

'Four-fold breath,' Kyle whispers. He puts his hand on the small of her back. Like a sailor steadying the mast. It is not enough. She craves skin on skin, his warmth flowing into hers. She reaches back and clasps his hand. She feels his heart skip.

There's mould between the walls, between buildings. It crinkles microscopically.

Daisy clomps back down the stairs. 'Please, come up,' they say.

Mila and Kyle look at each other. They won't find out more down here. Although moving away from the entrance feels risky, they start to climb. At the top of the stairs, the door behind the desk is open, a bright, white light shining in. Mila feels muffled in here, under thick layers of brick and concrete. Is that how they've managed to keep Josh? By neutering his powers until needed for their own gain?

George and Meg, the scientists, walk towards Mila, ignoring Kyle. Meg wears a bright novelty shirt with small Saturns across it. George is in pale blue, with a paisley tie. They have looks of wonder on their faces. 'Mila, has something happened?' George asks. 'Do you feel different?'

'Where is Josh?' she asks again.

They look at each other, puzzled. 'I'm afraid we don't know.'

'I …' She falters. Their bodies do not seem to be on high alert – does that mean they are telling the truth, or that they are psychopaths? 'Can you prove you don't have him?'

'Mila, we don't kidnap people,' Meg says.

'What would you have done if the experiment worked?' Mila asks.

They both look disappointed.

'Well,' says George, 'it was in the fine print … If it does – or, did,' something cryptic in his face here, 'we would have allowed that person to make use of all our facilities to develop their ability. We've designed a whole arena for it.' He sighs. 'And we would have provided counselling and support and also protection.'

'Protection from what?' Kyle asks.

Meg and George now look properly at Kyle.

'This is Kyle and he knows everything and needs to be here,' Mila says firmly.

'Uh, okay,' says George. 'Protection ... from the public, if the participant wished to be open about it. From the inevitable attention of people who may want to use them for ill. We always thought the participants would choose anonymity, not that we would force it upon them.'

'But if they didn't choose anonymity, wouldn't you all be in danger? Anyone interested would also want to know about the *Xanthoria*, about all your research,' Mila says.

'And if that were the case, at that time, we'd simply release it. If everyone has access to it, that will make it less powerful.'

Mila is baffled by this. 'But that's access to the research, not the actual substance. So wouldn't people fight over it? Or is that the real reason there's a billionaire behind this?'

Meg shakes her head. 'No, no. There would have been plenty to go around; it wasn't hard to propagate.'

'It would change the world,' Mila says.

'Only for the better, we believe.' Meg smiles.

'But wait ...' Mila latches on to what Meg just said. '*Would have been plenty?*'

Meg, George and Daisy exchange a sad glance.

'Let us show you,' George says, gesturing to the bright light and the white, concrete and steel of secret labs beyond.

Twenty-one years ago

'DARLING,' RICK SAYS gently to his daughter, leaning over her bed and cupping his hands. She wakes, rubs her sleepy eyes. 'Happy birthday,' he says, and he opens his hands so the light of the minuscule sun he is carrying slowly transfuses the darkness.

She gasps. 'Thanks, Dad.' She sits up, reaching for the sun, and he hands it to her cupped fingers, and then *splat*, he extinguishes it with his mind as her other palm comes down. She laughs. It's a game they play on special mornings.

He opens the blinds to let the outer morning in. 'Thirteen.' He shakes his head. 'Growing up so fast.'

'Da-*ad*,' she says affectionately.

'I made pancakes.'

'Yes!'

They go downstairs where he's more careful, the housekeeper being around. They eat with gusto: toppings of maple syrup, jam, and brown sugar and lemon – Lisa's favourite. She's looking more and more like her mum, which makes his heart ache, makes that cosmos open up inside him. As she's holding the pancake, it's her fingers he notices: short and brown, with nails like half-Saturnian rings.

The butter-gold morning is interrupted by Rick's hired convertible screeching to a halt at the head of the driveway. Again?

John goes out to him. 'What the hell, Rick?'

'It died!' he says, exasperated.

Lisa appears behind John in the doorway. 'Lisa, go back inside.' She obeys and he walks towards the car. 'What do you mean?' he asks Rick.

'The lichen you gave me last year, it died.'

John is puzzled. 'That's odd. It's hardy stuff. Survives on rocks in the arctic, in deserts.'

'I know, but it doesn't like me anymore, or something. I can't figure it out.' Rick paces, pulling at his sleeves. 'You have to tell me what you're doing.'

John doesn't want Lisa to hear this. 'Give me a sec.' He goes back in the house, sits back down across from Lisa, who is eating a jam pancake. 'Rick is my old astronaut bud,' he says. She nods. 'He's upset about something, so I'm just gonna go for a bit of a drive with him. Work it out.' John smiles. 'I'm sorry. I won't be long, birthday girl.' He stands again, kisses the top of her head. 'Esther is here – she'll help you get started on the party decorations.'

'Okay Dad, see you soon.'

He ruffles her hair. Good-natured kid.

He heads back outside. 'Let's go for a drive, talk this through.'

Now

MILA AND KYLE are led into a corridor that runs between a series of LED-downlit glass rooms against raw concrete walls, each cell with different materials in it – rocks and plants, oddities like tiles and bits of rubber – all coated in flaky, red-brown rings. The rooms also appear to host a range of temperatures and conditions: icy, moist, desert-like, smoky.

Mila pauses in front of one where the lichen sits on a flat grey stone: a mucky, faded corona of brown. It's too dark and crusty.

It's wrong.

Daisy walks ahead, cooing and fussing in front of some of the rooms, shaking their head.

Kyle is two steps behind Mila. She has felt his worry intensifying as they've gone deeper into the facility. She puts her hand out, like a guide, gives his arm a squeeze. She wants answers and so she is going to have to trust Cladion, for now.

'About a month ago, the lichen just started to decline,' Meg says, walking in front. 'No matter what we do, we can't seem to stop this. The species is being affected by some unknown environmental factor.'

'It doesn't sort of hibernate in winter or something?' Mila asks.

'It never has before.'

Mila peers in at some lichen covering a partly decomposed shoe. Humans, she thinks. We will try anything.

'May I?' she says, indicating to the glass door.

Meg nods.

Mila enters the humid glass cell. She touches the *Xanthoria*, thinking maybe she will pick up on some sadness or sense of loss. But there is nothing. Just a peeled-paint feel.

She knows that inside her it is alive and thriving.

She walks back out to them. 'Maybe its purpose was to find a host? Maybe once it has been incorporated, the excess dies off.'

George, Meg and Daisy stare at her. Kyle peers into the smoky glass cube.

'That didn't happen before,' George says. Meg gives him a sharp look.

'You really don't have Josh?' she asks.

'We don't.'

'Well, he's missing,' she says. Kyle comes to stand beside her. 'Who else knows about the potential of this stuff?'

'Every participant of the trial, and our research partners in London,' George says.

'And, well,' Meg says. 'We do know of a possible splinter group …'

They are still staring intently, but almost shyly, at Mila. 'Shit, did it … work?' Meg says. 'We were just about ready to pack it in.'

Mila is dismayed by how little Cladion has considered the effects of what they have been playing with.

Kyle presses a hand to her back again. She sighs. Decides.

Closing her eyes, she raises her hands and concentrates on the moisture in the corridor, drawing it from the roof, corners, vents, under the cracks of doors. She then opens her eyes and draws together a small cloud, pushes it to float over the heads of the researchers. It breaks, raining upon them. They gasp, squeal. George and Meg start crying, hug each other.

'It worked!' George cries. 'My god.'

'We have to call Lisa immediately ... Daisy?'

Daisy is already running past Mila towards the door.

Eventually, George and Meg's eyes return to Mila. She is not smiling. Kyle remains close to her.

'You have no idea what you've done,' she says. 'Josh is in danger.'

Their expressions falter.

'You have to help us find him.'

⌒

Josh is not used to lacking touch. He is used to craving it but also used to getting it. He is not under-stimulated, though, despite these walls surrounding him, as he can sort through and wonder at each new sensation that comes over him. But it is different to what has sustained him for years: sex and other kinds of intimacy – eye contact, skin sliding over skin, the heat of the mouth. He does wonder what sex would be like now, in the moments when he is not trying to plan for how to get Mila, Kyle and himself out of this mess when he and this group's leaders get to Melbourne. He wonders if it would be better or worse for his lover, with this power at his disposal. Would it make him more intuitive, more giving? Or would it make him a beast, given over to his own sensation and satisfaction? Would he be channelling from without or within? The harmony of leaves to sunlight, the tides and the moon, or Marlene and John Wayne and his childhood and his ancestors' childhoods and every atom in the blood, the water, the flesh, coming to awareness? Would it possibly be too overwhelming? But he desires it. He desires to touch and to know.

And with Mila – with both of them able to tap into something greater, it could be unforgettable.

He hears the voices of Luna and the chief adept again, through the wall and upstairs. Luna sounds upset, exasperated. 'As I told you, I haven't done anything different, my chief, I swear. We can get more when we go to Melbourne. With the woman there, too, we can get everything we seek at once.'

'You think they'll let us waltz in there and take their stores and Mila, and walk back out?'

'They will want to see Josh. That will get us through the door. And with the two of them, we might finally understand what the common factor was.'

'You should have gotten that out of him by now.'

'He doesn't know. I believe him, he truly doesn't. Maybe it's just that some people —'

'Enough. If it worked for my father, wouldn't I be one of those people? We're missing something.'

'Yes, my chief, you're right.' The sound of her touching him, soothing him. 'I know we'll work it out. If Edwards has figured it out, then we will.'

'I told you I don't want to hear that name.'

'I'm sorry,' Luna says.

Josh hears them murmur sweetly to each other again. Then lips, skin. He bends his hearing back.

He puts the puzzle together: Mila has gone back to Cladion. He doesn't know if that's a good thing or not. Is Cladion keeping her prisoner, too? They don't seem to be associated with this org, which seems to be called Cosmic Dawn, and it sounds like the chief adept doesn't want anything to do with Lisa Edwards. In Melbourne there will be a face-off. A struggle. His and Mila's bodies just pawns, property.

And what about Kyle? Josh desperately hopes he has gone home to their apartment and back to his cat and his neat, sleep-smelling bedroom with his stacks of books and his gaming computer with the fluoro green-lit keyboard. Out of harm's way. Josh will stay with that image of Kyle – sweet Kyle, in his bedroom, away from all this mess. Safe.

Kyle watches Mila in awe as she drills the punching bag so hard it bounces all the way up to the concrete ceiling before she catches it again with her fist. George and Meg watch, too, and Meg scribbles something on her device. The space is a mini arena, with gym equipment, obstacle courses, and odd assortments of items stacked on shelves (such as bricks, dried coral, a piece of petrified wood, jars of coins). There are red mats on the floor, rows of seating across two of the walls, and large pillars dividing the space.

'And how does it feel to do that, Mila?' George asks.

Kyle sees something cross Mila's eyes before she answers; she is still being guarded, not telling them everything. Probably smart, thinks Kyle. He's willing to trust them – they seem decent – but it's not his body going through this. His body is just going through epic jet lag. He tries not to slump over on this rubber mat. He wants to ask if he can go make a coffee in the little kitchen, but everyone is so focused on Mila and he doesn't want to interrupt.

'It feels like a normal workout,' Mila says, 'like, endorphins and being a bit puffed and so on – it's just that I have more brute force and quicker reflexes.'

It's true that she is panting a little, and sweating. Her slim, muscular arms glisten. She's wearing a tank top they gave her with Cladion emblazoned across it.

George asks, 'Do you feel like you're channelling anything to create that strength, or that it's innate?'

Again, that flicker across her eyes. 'Channelling, I guess. But it's in me as well. I honestly don't know how to describe it.'

'Ha.' George looks amused; Meg makes notes again.

'So how is Daisy going with the data?' Mila asks. 'Any clues on the movements of these groups?' There's frustration in her voice.

'They're working on it,' George says dismissively. 'Why don't we go to the next drill?'

'Not until I know where our friend is,' Mila says, standing with gloved fists raised.

George sighs. Meg says, 'We want to find him as much as you do. Of course we do. To think there are two of you who have —'

'Going through the drills will help you if we need to take Josh back by force,' George says.

They are all silent for a moment. Kyle feels useless. He really should be getting on the punching bag, too. He doesn't want Mila to feel she has to do this alone.

'Maybe it would help,' he says, standing up, 'um, if you stop watching Mila like she's a rat in a cage and just let her use the facility on her own?' He is surprised at himself.

Mila looks at him gratefully. She nods. 'That *would* help.'

'But ...' George starts.

'Okay, we'll ... give you some space,' Meg says.

Kyle partly wants to go with them – he has so many questions. But he doesn't want to leave Mila's side. He'll make a list.

Before George and Meg have the chance to leave, the door behind them opens and closes as Daisy comes in, upright with purpose. 'We've got moles on the inside now, with our colleagues and in the splinter group.' They smile. 'If he's with either of them, we'll know soon.'

'Good work,' says Meg.

'Thank you,' Mila says.

'Give me those gloves,' Kyle says to Mila, trying for a jokey tone. He puts them over his hands, pumps his fingers a few times to get used to the feel. 'So you just ...' He throws a punch at the bag, feels a ping in his wrist and a crunch in his shoulder.

Mila grins at him. 'Maybe start out slow,' she says, then turns to Meg and George. 'Can we get some more gloves?' They nod as they turn to leave.

Daisy sits on the mat where Kyle had been, watches him.

He blushes. 'Are you good at this?'

'I'm pretty strong,' they say, smiling.

Mila walks over to the assorted items on the far wall, and Kyle and Daisy watch her. She picks up the piece of petrified wood, which sits next to an old kerosene lamp. 'This has a few stories to tell,' she says, exploring its grooves with her fingers.

'We're going to find him,' Daisy says intently.

Mila puts down the fossil. 'How long until we hear from your moles?'

'Well, they'll report when there's something to report, but since I've only just made contact I'd give them twenty-four hours.'

'I'm tired,' Mila says. Her frown lines are deep. 'Can we leave?'

'You're not prisoners,' Daisy says, standing. They clasp their hands together. 'But you do have to be careful.'

Mila nods, running a finger over the fossil one more time.

Kyle is both relieved and uncertain. He needs rest, and he's desperate to see Sokka, but he definitely doesn't want Mila to be at risk.

Mila decides for him. 'We'll come back in the morning.'

'Good.' Daisy smiles but looks officious at the same time. 'Lisa will be here by then too. She's looking forward to meeting you.'

⌒

Sokka is sitting on the arm of the worn leather couch when Kyle opens the door. His heart leaps. He tries not to cry out with love and pleasure in front of Mila, who follows him into the flat. His kitty! Sokka is a black cat with a white teardrop on his forehead, and he's a little on the overweight side. He's not moving towards Kyle but mewing hello, and when Kyle approaches him he accepts a scratch behind the ear. Kyle struggles not to pick up the cat and squeeze him to his chest, but Sokka is a go-slow cat and he has to respect that. During the lockdowns and after the disintegration of his marriage he had not easily been able to resist this – the warmth of his pet was crucial in keeping him going.

'Oh, he's sweet,' Mila says. 'Does he like strangers?'

'In the usual cat way – you might need to let him come to you, if that's okay.'

Mila nods. 'He's very happy to see you.'

'He loves Laura, the cat-sitter, though.'

'That's good.'

'Wait, when you say he's happy to see me …'

'I mean from his body language.' She smiles.

'So you can't talk to animals?'

'Not off the bat. We'll see what happens, though.' She raises one eyebrow.

They watch Sokka for a while in the silent flat. He texts Laura to let her know he's back.

'God, I'm relieved to be out of there,' Mila says. 'Nice to have some windows.' She drops bags by the door and folds into the couch.

'So you're sort of inhibited in that facility, aren't you?'

'You can tell?'

'Yeah.'

'You're very perceptive,' she says.

Kyle pushes at his glasses.

She says, 'I don't want to let on, you know, that I'm more vulnerable in there … Just in case.'

'Your kryptonite,' he says.

'Yeah.'

He nods. 'I wonder if Josh's captors have figured that out.'

'Probably.' She stares intensely forward. 'So despite our Cladion friends appearing to be helpful about Josh, I think we need to have our own plan, too.' The cat slides from under Kyle's hands and sniffs the air near Mila's head. 'Because they're too obsessed with observing me, observing the effects. I don't think they'll be able to focus on the mission, and on getting Josh back safely. And I want him to be free of that kind of observation.' She strokes the skin around her mouth. Sokka leaps down to the empty cushion beside her, looks up at her hand. Mila absent-mindedly moves it to the cat, scratches him. He instantly flops onto his back, purring.

Kyle feels warm. 'You're right.'

'Notebook?'

'Mmhmm.' Kyle unzips the top of his carry-on bag, extracts the trusty spiral-bound book with the pen clasped over the cover.

'The main thing is that, when we find him, any meeting we engineer will have to happen somewhere kind of open, but not where there are too many observers.'

'Because you'll both need to rely on your power,' Kyle says, 'but not cause a public display.'

'But god, we don't even know …' Mila says, looking wide-eyed at him, 'whether any of his captors have abilities. What if they observed how it came on, for him or me?' She puts her head in her hands.

Kyle wants to reach for her, but isn't sure if it'll interrupt her thoughts. What else could comfort? 'You want a coffee? I have a machine.'

'Oh, yeah, that'd be great,' she says.

'We'll figure it out.'

Sokka purrs loudly, and Mila seems finally to notice she's been patting him. She moves her head towards his, and he gives her nose a little sniff.

Kyle goes into the kitchen, which has a slight smell of something caught in the drain too long, or bin residue. He cracks the window. It's less cold now than it was this morning; it's about sixteen degrees, and the sun is poking through the clouds. But it'll get dark soon. He likes this weather. He'll go up to his room and grab them some cardigans, a blanket.

When he gets back with the hot drinks and knits, Mila looks stressed. She puts down her phone. 'Calls, emails – I can't really handle this. My parents … when will I see them? And there's an email from a journalist that's a bit worrying.' Mila hands him the phone.

The journalist, Saira Foley, has been contacting everyone (she says) who has been through the trial. She went through it herself and was of course bound by the non-disclosure agreement, but since one of the participants has died – by the wording she doesn't know Mila and Josh are connected – she is risking breaking it, suspicious that there could be a link between Josh's death and the substance.

'How did she find out who else did the trial?' Kyle asks.

'I don't know, but that's very worrying. Could there be a leak? And could that same list be why Josh was captured? And maybe … maybe I'm being followed, too.'

'But why would they have waited until Josh was in Berlin?'

'Maybe it wasn't leaked *until* then. Maybe he revealed something to the wrong person, and then they hacked Cladion's system or … I don't know. Either way, I probably shouldn't go home tonight.'

'Of course, you can absolutely stay here.'

She looks at her phone again.

'Just don't write back,' he says.

Mila's phone beeps. She sighs. Sokka has made his way onto her lap now, is sitting comfortably face-forward on her legs.

'He never sits on people,' Kyle says, pointing.

'We're connected,' Mila says wryly.

'Shall I give *him* the notebook?'

'No one could replace you.' Mila holds his gaze. That warmth is in his belly now. She looks back down at her phone, sighs again. 'You know, we have to write to Eloise.'

The warmth turns to ice. Oh yes, there isn't a link between Josh's disappearance and Eloise's brother's death after all. 'Do you think Josh's kidnappers just did some googling and basically got their idea from what happened to Matthew?'

'Horribly, something like that.'

They both take a deep breath.

'If Eloise still feels it wasn't a suicide, maybe it wasn't,' Kyle says.

'For sure, but … I don't think we can do anything to help now.'

Kyle feels awful. Not being able to help in some way is the hardest state for him to accept. Even worse, to deliver news that would make the person feel worse, more hopeless.

'I'll do it,' Mila says. 'I'll just say that we've found out Josh is alive, that he did it to divert us. That he wanted to disappear. That he's troubled. Feels terrible to lie, but …'

'Maybe we can think of a way to help her down the track,' Kyle says.

'Yeah.' Mila nods reassuringly. 'Though I'm not sure deductive reasoning is included in this … extra-perceptiveness.'

'I'm sorry you have to be going through all this,' Kyle says.

She shrugs. 'I'm sorry for you, too.' But though Kyle is deeply worried for Josh, he has realised his more pervasive, general anxiety is not accompanying him as usual. It's like at the start of the pandemic, when he stocked his trolley with chickpeas, lentils, soup and frozen blueberries and was strangely calm while people around him – who'd never experienced anxiety – fell apart.

They are silent for another moment, then Mila glances upstairs. 'Can I … see his room?'

Kyle's gut squirms a little. 'Yeah, no worries,' he tries to say lightly. 'You can probably stay in there. I mean, that's the only other bed. The couch doesn't …'

She looks uncomfortable. 'That might be a bit hard.'

'Well, you can share my bed, of course. I don't think I snore or anything.'

'What if I do?' she says. 'What if I throw off sparks in my sleep?'

Is Kyle … getting turned on? God, now is not the time. But just the thought of her sleeping next to him. That hand, the way she is stroking the cat, both firm and soft. Damnit, think of something else.

'I can sleep on the floor,' he says.

She scoffs. 'Shut up.' She stands. 'I'll just peek in. I won't be long. I miss him.'

'Yeah, me too.'

Sokka leaps up to follow her.

Mila wakes at dawn on Josh's bed, in a foetal position, having no idea she'd fallen asleep. A soft grey light comes in through open blinds. The planets were colourful in her dreams and now sit beyond the atmosphere, like Dorothy's relatives around the bed when she wakes from Oz. A doona has been thrown roughly over her. The window is strung with red paper lanterns. A small shelf above a desk has an array of dog-eared books: poetry, Anaïs Nin, Henry Miller, Ulysses, pretty much every book that had once been banned. There is a smell of Josh in the room: his hair, his oils, his breath. A sense of him much stronger than she would have felt had she not been enhanced. And, in missing him, all the missing comes in again. That familiar feeling – for her parents' health and happiness, for Scott, for Kate and Ty, for the lost life with its sound and presence of children, even for Kyle in the next room. The tragedy of permanent separation, inevitable singularity.

Coffee. Tea. Something is needed. Also, she is ravenous. Her body definitely seems to be burning more calories. She tries to creep downstairs without waking Kyle. They should get to the facility early, but he has time to snooze a bit more. His door is ajar, a dark cat-width opening. Just this picks up her mood, that such people exist who accept the coming and going. She has never been good at it; she's only had temporary release from the needing to hold.

Is this whole exercise an elaborate way for her to possess, rather than rescue, Josh?

Well, do not others get to possess?

She tucks the thought away. It is a pre-coffee thought. She must come back into her body and in possession of herself.

She hopes the powers are not waning already. But then she is surprised at the thought. She doesn't want this … responsibility. Does she?

Her hands shake slightly as she turns on the tap to fill the jug. Even with the powers enhancing her, making her bright and strong, the scars show through.

When Mila and Kyle arrive at Cladion, Daisy takes them straight into the training arena. Leaning against a concrete pillar in the middle, sipping coffee from a KeepCup, is Lisa Edwards. Mila recognises the inventor, investor and billionaire, as anyone in Australia would. She's in chinos and a polo-neck shirt; she has a no-nonsense short bleached haircut – a big woman and, Mila thinks, a big presence. Is it just because she's familiar? She's a little older than Mila, but those expensive face creams do their work. She's disarmingly attractive. Something Mila hadn't realised from photos. Or maybe whatever the organ is that detects pheromones in Mila is also supernormal. She does feel a kind of tickle in the back of her nose.

'That jet lag's a bitch, isn't it?' Lisa says, smiling and shifting off the pillar to come forward.

Mila is a bit tongue-tied. 'Mmm.'

'Great to meet you, I'm Lisa.' She reaches out her fist to bump. Her accent is Australian but with some sharper edges, more global.

Mila knows the tragic story of her parents, her father the American astronaut and her mother the Vietnamese-Australian computer scientist – how both died when Lisa was young. She was then brought up in Queensland by an uncle, her mother's brother, who had a bunch of traditional brick-and-mortar businesses. She had her start-up capital from her inheritance but moved far away from her uncle's traditional businesses into the realm of entrepreneurial tech. In recent years she has been opportunistic among disaster and peril – inventing drone systems and networks for delivery; investing in new content distribution platforms and then sponsoring popular, previously offline venues to enable their businesses to transition and thrive in a new way; helping to implement policy around sustainable energy that elevates the companies she has stakes in. She is generally considered a forward-thinking billionaire, but people Mila follows on social media argue over specific interests (or generally rally against power imbalances and the influence of the 'few' over the many). Mila is not overly educated on the specifics of Lisa's businesses; maybe it is just that Mila has been self-absorbed, only interested when issues affect her personally. Or maybe she has just never felt she has any control over it all anyway, and so didn't think her opinion mattered.

But now.

'I'm Mila.'

'Kyle. Nicetomeetyou.'

Lisa rubs her hands together. 'I'm not going to pretend I'm not excited to see. But I do understand your friend is missing, and that has to be our priority.'

'Thank you,' says Mila, guarded.

'Can I just …' Lisa gestures at the wall of odd objects. Mila follows her over, and Lisa picks up the kerosene lamp. 'When I was a kid I saw my dad turn this on simply by looking at it,' she says. 'I have never, ever gotten the image of his smile out of my head, as my eyes no doubt lit up.'

Mila obliges her, seeking the particles in the wick, the kerosene, the air within the glass. The lamp flickers on and the kerosene gives off its rich smell. Lisa's eyes do light up. Her arm shakes, and she puts the lamp down.

Her eyes are wide when she looks at Mila. 'I knew I hadn't imagined it.'

The lamp flickers out.

'So,' Mila says, 'you knew it was the lichen, but no one else has ...'

'Experienced symbiosis.'

'Experienced symbiosis, until now?'

'As far as we know.' Lisa runs her hand over an old digital alarm clock on the shelf. 'My father and his colleague carried the original samples home from space, but both died in a car crash on my thirteenth birthday. They weren't friends by that stage, so I can only imagine Rick came to see Dad because they were sharing symptoms. But he seemed angry. Dad went with him in the car, I think to get away from the house so I wouldn't hear them argue.' She swallows. 'Dad had shown me a bit of what he could do, and he'd told me it was related to the lichen. He had it absolutely everywhere through his study. I brought it with me to Australia, to my little room above a pub in Queensland, but I didn't try it until I was older. I guess I just understood it was strong stuff. But nothing happened. Over the years, I tried all kinds of ways of getting it to activate, to no avail.' She shakes her head. 'I started to wonder if perhaps certain people were more susceptible to it, and I wasn't one of them. And so the trial was designed to test that out. You and Josh ... Of course, I still wonder if that was the case. We haven't had time to crunch data. But could there be some other factor that brought it on?'

She stares intently at Mila. Then seems to notice she is doing it. She focuses back on the objects on the wall.

'Anyway, plenty of time for that. Rick had a kid – Stephen. Younger than me, but interestingly he has a real fascination for magic.'

'And how does it work?' Kyle says, moving towards them.

'Well,' Lisa says, 'we were hoping to study the trial subjects to figure that out too.'

'Because I read,' says Kyle, pushing his glasses up on his nose, 'that there has been research in human direct sensory perception – that is, perception of the quantum. Photons of light, for example, and, and, the ear ... being more sensitive than previously imagined, and, the olfactory system actually being larger than the nose, like, receptors existing in cells throughout the body ... and of course, this article mentioned that Tibetan and Indian and other Asian cultures have had this knowledge for centuries. I mean, there's that yogic idea of being able to control the organs, so it even goes beyond perception to manipulation. I wonder if it's something like that – that the substance, once activated, enhances the body's ability to understand the quantum?'

Lisa stares at Kyle, nodding. 'You know, I never put it together quite like that before. Kyle, you might come in useful here.'

He blushes.

'Any theories as to why it's now dying off?' Lisa asks, frowning.

They are interrupted by Daisy, who runs through the door with their iPad thrust out. 'We have some reports from our moles.'

'That's great,' Mila says, relieved.

Daisy says, 'Follow me.'

They all exit the arena and head down a hallway towards a bright boardroom.

'Can we turn the lights down at all?' Mila asks, as they enter.

'I'm afraid they're not dimmers,' Daisy says.

'Oh, hold on.' Mila concentrates. The lights mellow down, but one blows, making Daisy, Kyle and Lisa jump. 'Sorry,' she says.

Daisy swallows. 'It's never not going to be cool,' they say. 'I wish it had worked for me.'

Mila wants to get angry – the innocence of that statement. The foolishness. But then, she could also give Daisy the key to peaking. What she thinks is the key, anyway. Lisa's story about her father was certainly compelling and makes Mila feel she has no ownership over this process, but she needs to hold as much as possible close, to protect herself and Kyle, and Josh, until she knows who they can trust and what Lisa's bigger intentions really are.

'I wish it were you rather than me,' Mila says. But that may be a lie. The awareness she has, this affinity, does make her feel more *herself*. More full and alive.

But where she'd felt best was in the park in Berlin. That's where she most felt she could be connected to some fabric, and even be an integral part of it, and that that mattered, and that it could blanket any hole inside her.

'Okay,' says Daisy, turning on the flat screen against the wall in the boardroom and hooking up their tablet. 'Our London colleagues at the university have incorporated several new students, but like us, no new test subjects recently. The students all seem to have come at will – no coercion. And our mole has found no particular threat in the department, or heard any word about someone who has levelled up.'

'I hope the mole can be trusted,' Kyle says.

Daisy nods, but doesn't reply to this. 'Nonetheless, I asked for descriptions of new students and anyone who has come through in recent months.' Daisy brings up the list of descriptions.

Mila scans through them. 'None sound like Josh.'

'Okay,' Daisy says. 'And then there's the splinter group, who call themselves the Cosmic Dawn. The reason we call them a splinter group is because they recruit a lot of the students from our colleague organisation and build their ideas off ours.'

'Badly,' huffs Lisa. 'Remember how I mentioned Stephen?'

'The child of your dad's astronaut colleague?' Mila says.

'Yep. Well, he heads up this group. Between his involvement and the fact they recruit our students, we know they must have something to do with the lichen. Previous moles haven't heard a mention of it, though. The group sells all kinds of BS "remedies" and "spells" and lots of powdered substances out of a little shop at their London HQ, but we've tested them all and found nothing noteworthy.'

'Right,' says Daisy. 'The Cosmic Dawn are what we'd call an ad hoc ritual magic group, and they're a commercial organisation. They have descended from an older, and always patriarchal, group. People can only access their inner circle and attend meetings by paying enormous amounts of money, and otherwise they make a tidy sum by selling rituals, the merch, advice – you name it – not just out of the shop but also online to people around the world. There's a kind of subscription system.'

'I take it you don't approve,' Mila says, noting the distaste on Lisa and Daisy's faces. Mila thinks Lisa must be comfortable holding a lot of contradictions inside her if she can look down on this other group's commercial activities while she sits there with a fat ten figures in her bank account.

Daisy says, 'There has always been secrecy around esoteric knowledge, but that's more about only passing on what you know if you feel someone is ready to hear it and take steps to understanding. It's not intended to be ranked and sold off to the highest bidder. Here – we do really believe that human beings can have great power *and* be ethically conscious of it.'

Mila goes to roll her eyes at Kyle and sees him looking at Daisy with wonder. She catches his eye, and he clears his throat.

'Okay,' Daisy says. 'Cosmic Dawn. The mole has attended several recent meetings. At one he said there was a new person channelling an ascended master, and that their style was very different to that of the others.'

'A man?'

'A young man, yes.'

Mila's heart races.

'Ascended masters,' Kyle says. 'I read about that, too. Who was he channelling?'

'Master Marlene Dietrich.'

Kyle and Mila leap up from their chairs as the lights surge and one of the bulbs explodes. They all cover their faces when the glass goes flying.

'It's him,' Mila says through her hands. 'We have to go to London.'

'Okay,' Daisy says, lowering their arm and squinting up at Mila. 'I'll book the flight. But we need a plan; I'll have to call on some operatives. We should leave first thing in the morning.'

'What about sooner?' Mila asks.

'Look, it doesn't seem like his life is in immediate danger,' Lisa says. 'And our spy can keep watch of the situation. If we don't prepare, there's every chance they'll snatch you too.'

Mila looks at Kyle. He shrugs, clearly as overwhelmed as she is. Do they have any choice but to trust Lisa? Mila doesn't think they can do it alone.

⁓

The next morning they weave through the 8 a.m. suits on Bourke Street, Kyle dragging one small bag behind them. They decided not to pack much, to hope they would be in and out of London, with Josh recovered. They still have no strong plan for how to draw the Cosmic Dawn into the open air, somewhere there won't be many witnesses. He hopes that smart Daisy has been working on it overnight.

Kyle can see the stress is getting to Mila. She is stuttering her words slightly, and her brow is permanently drawn. She wears her all-black outfit: tight jeans, tee, leather jacket and boots. No make-up. His own jeans are feeling a little tight after all this time away from the gym, and his striped shirt feels a bit too jaunty for the seriousness of the situation.

Rounding the corner into Liverpool Street they see a woman lingering near the door. They pull up short and Kyle follows Mila's lead in pretending they took a wrong turn, looking up at the street names and then backing down Bourke. Mila stops in front of the Paperback Bookshop.

'Do you think it's the journo?' Kyle asks.

'Saira Foley? Fuck knows.'

He is going to suggest the four-fold breath but thinks she might slap him.

She gets out her phone. 'I'll call Daisy.' They alerted Kyle and Mila yesterday to the fact that yes, there seems to have been a leak, and that the reporter was sniffing around.

But as Mila draws the phone up to her ear, the woman appears around the corner. 'Mila?'

She hangs up the phone.

'I know you from your photo. Why are you back here?'

'You shouldn't know who I am,' Mila says.

'I have my ways,' the journo says, putting her hands on her hips. She is short and pert.

Kyle notices an escalation of fear and frustration in Mila. His own fingers tingle with it. What can he do?

'Are you going somewhere?' the journo asks. She has a mousy bob and wears a skirt suit with a grey coat.

'Who are you?' asks Kyle, stalling.

'I'm Saira Foley, from *The Nation*,' she says, haughtily, 'and you?' She reaches out her hand to shake his.

'I'm Dean ...'

Mila's eyes flicker.

'Cane – ton,' he finishes. He never has been good at coming up with things on the spot.

'And do you know much about what happens behind that metal door?' Saira asks. She has an intimidating pointiness, he thinks.

'No, what door?' he says. 'I was just, um ...'

Kyle tries not to look down. He can see, from the corner of his eye, dark slivers of ice coming from the pointed toes of Mila's boots.

'We were going to the library,' he says, pathetically, pointing away from Mila to try to draw Saira's gaze.

'With a suitcase?'

'To fill with books. We're doing some research together.'

The darkness spreads to under Saira's short-heeled boots. 'I just want to know —' Turning, she slips on the ice.

Kyle feels bad for her as she goes down, yelping. Mila yanks his arm, and in lightning speed they are in front of the door in the alleyway, and Daisy opens it. She must have seen that Mila called.

Once inside, Kyle and Mila catch their breath.

'Daisy, tell me one thing,' Mila says. 'The experiment was confidential, yes?'

Daisy nods. They all remain standing at the bottom of the stairwell.

'And so that journalist has already broken her contract by emailing us all. But you said that if it had worked – which it has – the affected would be able to choose whether to go public. So that means the contract would be broken by that act, and everyone who signed the identical confidentiality agreement could then talk about the experiment?'

'That's right. The fine print said they should check back in with us and run a series of tests and then if they chose to reveal their experience, all other participants of the experiment would be notified.'

'So as long as she doesn't know that it has *worked*, she can't legally report on it.'

'That's right.'

Mila nods. 'Then she can't ever know.'

Daisy hangs their head a little. 'I did presume that one day it would all be out in the open, and I know George and Meg did, too. Lisa believes it is far more dangerous for this to become commodified, privatised.'

Kyle has a catch in his throat.

Mila stands tall. 'I don't believe Lisa ever properly thought it through. This is not some simple pain-relief drug that could help millions of people, or a vaccine for a rampant virus: this is an entirely life- and world-altering concept. I think Lisa – once we've got Josh back and are through this mess – needs to reconsider her supposedly radical approach.'

Yes, Kyle thinks, what are her real motivations? Lisa probably wants to be the first person to *truly* change the world, not just let a bunch of rich people experience zero gravity for eleven minutes. She wants to go down in history as a genuine innovator, beating her white male billionaire counterparts. But at what cost?

Then Mila gets that look on her face, the one she has when she is bending her senses. 'And I suppose Lisa heard all that.'

Daisy peers up at the door beyond the stairwell.

It slides open and Lisa is silhouetted by the white light.

205

'Wear this,' Luna says to Josh, holding out a navy business suit, crisp white shirt and tie. A pair of brown loafers sit by the door, socks rolled neatly inside.

'For a long-haul flight?' That's going to be bloody uncomfortable, he thinks.

'They give you PJs on the plane. You have to blend in.'

Business class, then, Josh realises.

Luna kneels in her usual place by the chair, as though waiting.

'Now?' he asks.

'The flight is in five hours.'

He begins to remove his clothes. He can feel her watching him. He wonders if she stays because she craves to take back some power. He would give it to her, temporarily, if she wanted. Though it would be dangerous for her if the chief found out. Josh knows he could overcome a horde of greedy 'mages' out in the open, though.

Soon.

But only when he can help Mila as well.

He takes off his underwear and reaches into the drawer for a fresh pair. He detects the changes in Luna: the dilations, the openings, the wetness. He has always thought a slight teasing never hurt anybody – to be in a state of physical anticipation is to be in a state of hope. To fantasise is to be comforted and transported.

He pulls the underwear up slowly, adjusts himself into the right place, glances at her. She looks down, cheeks red. He puts on the suit pants – a luxe material, breathable, not so bad. He adds the rest of the outfit and then slings the tie around his neck and looks at her helplessly.

'Oh,' she says. She stands and reaches out to help knot it, keeping herself back a little.

He steps in closer. Their breaths mingle.

'When we go to Melbourne – back to the source, as you suggest, we must rescue her from Cladion,' Luna says.

'Why does she need rescuing?' he asks.

'I think you know.' Luna's hands are still around his tie. She steps back.

If he plays too coy they may not take him with them, might keep him locked up here and go after Mila separately. He has to make them believe he has become one of them – that their Stockholm syndrome has worked.

'You want me to help rescue her from them?'

'They are dangerous, are they not? Look at what they've done to you. We will help hide you both.'

He tries to seem like he's thinking it over. Eventually, he nods. He can't act too hoodwinked, though – there has to be some balance. 'Once you have what you need from us, Luna, you have to let us go.'

She glances at the ceiling. She whispers, 'We will. I will.' Something has changed in her, he sees. It is power she respects and is drawn to, and she is changing her opinion on who possesses it.

⌒

'High priestess,' Daisy says, with an ironic look on their face as Lisa walks down the stairs.

'Mini me,' Lisa says, fist-bumping Daisy. She locks her eyes on Mila's. 'How did you sleep?'

'Fine,' Mila says, feeling guarded again. Lisa has such an openness about her, a charm, but Mila's been thinking all morning about how she absolutely should not trust the person who got them into this mess in the first place. 'I don't think you should come to London.'

'What?' Daisy sounds worried. 'But you'll need help, back-up?'

'I don't know.' Mila stares at Lisa. Kyle is silent and steady beside her. 'Whether Josh is being held by them, or I'm being closely watched by you, it could be the same. To be exploited.'

Daisy sighs with disappointment.

Lisa looks at Mila levelly. 'I can understand that, Mila. You don't know me from a bar of soap —'

'I know you think everyone should be "enhanced" in this way,' Mila says. Kyle's hand hovers at her back but she gently pushes it away. She needs space. 'I know that Meg and George and Daisy believe your intentions are principled; that you want to make people stronger and more connected. But I also know you're going to find a way to profit from it. My own parents have the smoke density system on their house that you developed after Black Summer. Uh …'

Mila is momentarily distracted by the vibrations of a spider walking in its web in the corner – the web both an extension of its body and a kind of language.

'Mila, okay,' Lisa says, putting her hands up. 'Obviously I have a natural inclination for profit, and I see opportunities here, yes – but I assure you I try to balance that with truly doing what is for the greater good.' She lowers and opens her hands; her brows are raised and brown eyes clear, emphatic.

'But you're just one person,' Mila says. She thinks about those studies Kyle mentioned, about how power causes psychological corruption. 'How do you decide what *good* is? In beating your competitors to market, don't you sometimes suppress ideas that could be even more helpful? Or more affordable?'

Lisa pauses, nods. 'That's a good point, Mila.' She reaches for her arm. 'Why don't we go upstairs and talk more about this?'

'No, I think Kyle and I should go to the airport now.' Mila shares a glance with him. He nods.

Lisa looks pained. Mila feels for her for a moment, thinking of her face lit by the kerosene lamp – knowing her grief is twisted up in all this. But Josh is who is most important.

Daisy jumps in. 'Mila, please let me come, and the few operatives I've trained.'

'You and the operatives can come,' Mila says, 'to help us create whatever distraction we need in drawing the Cosmic Dawn into the open. But I will rescue Josh. And once I do, we'll be free to go wherever we like.'

Daisy looks at Lisa. Mila can tell that Lisa is fighting with something, beyond the link to her father. Curiosity, Mila thinks. Lisa is desperate to see what she has done. To see her own power in action.

'Okay,' Lisa says eventually.

If she tries to follow them to the airport, Mila will have to stop her, and she will regret wanting to see what Mila is capable of.

⌒

It is sunny on the way out to Tullamarine Airport. Mila and Kyle's eyes are shaded by the tinted windows of the large people mover. A couple of rows of strangers sit in front of them: the 'operatives'. They're dressed casually, as though for a trip. Kyle isn't sure whether to make conversation with them. He wonders how someone gets to be a thug-for-hire. Are they ex-military? The kind of private security that works on mines or, worse, detention centres? Or just nightclub bouncers trained up? Might be easier not to know.

Mila is glued to the view. He wants to touch her reassuringly. Doesn't quite know how to, once he's acknowledged the thought.

He flips open his notebook, and Mila glances down, too. He has drawn a diagram: Kensington Gardens in London. The Italian garden, specifically. The pump house will provide cover. The operatives can surround it, subtly steer away tourists.

Mila's phone keeps buzzing. She doesn't look at it, but Kyle sees her frown. He wishes he could take the pressure, the responsibility, away from her.

'Do you need me to help you come up with more excuses?' he asks, nodding at the phone.

She shakes her head.

The car pulls off to the left, to the airport and up to the car park rather than the quick drop-off. They'll have to get themselves sorted, split up appropriately so as not to draw attention. They are all booked in seats that roughly surround Mila's on the plane.

Once they park, Daisy jumps out first. They beckon to the operatives, directing them. Mila exits ahead of Kyle, stretches. Operatives with bags are already walking off towards the international terminal building. Kyle goes to get their bags from the back, wheels Mila's up to her. He's so glad he has a dryer they were both able to use – they basically unpacked and repacked the same clothes from Europe.

Mila is staring at the band of sunlight coming in through the sides of the multi-level car park. Her face is flushed, aglow. 'I could almost float into it.'

This makes Kyle afraid. Mila and Josh dissolving in sunlight.

'But …' She lowers her voice so only Kyle can hear. 'The waves are weaker than they were.'

'What do you mean?'

She glances around. 'I mean that the initial high … has diminished somewhat.'

'Maybe it needs a top-up.'

Mila shrugs.

After talking to the driver, Daisy joins them. 'I haven't heard back from Cosmic Dawn yet about the meeting. Time zones.'

'But the plan is to go straight to the park, yes?' Mila asks. 'When we arrive.'

'As long as they get the message, I expect they'll be there.'

Kyle is still not sure they should be using Mila as bait, but she thinks that's the only way the group will be curious enough to meet with Cladion, the only way they can be convinced to bring Josh with them.

'Okay,' Mila says. 'Let's go.'

They wheel their suitcases across the car park, down an airbridge and into the terminal. The flight to London via Singapore is in three hours.

Mila, Kyle and Daisy sit at a table in the food court. The operatives are spread out across surrounding tables, headphones in, pretending to read, scroll. Kyle flips open his burger container, gives an exaggerated lip-smacking noise that makes Daisy smile. Mila is too nervous; she focuses on steadying her breathing. She has been poking around inside herself. Her DNA. What she finds corresponds to shadows of people, shapes of land, and languages. There is so much history inside her, beyond this lifetime. Inside every person. Even in this lifetime, every moment is potent in its effect – on your environment, on others and on the future, and even in how it reshapes historical perspective. When a lonely forty-year-old woman chose to create a profile on an escort service website, she had no idea that this would lead to such an extraordinary set of circumstances. Every moment is potent. But every effect is uncertain.

And then, sunflowers. Flashing across her vision. She diverts her focus from the inner to the external and immediate. The food court becomes an atrium of light. Noise fades down to one individual heartbeat, a pattern her hippocampus has stored. The familiar smell of a person's hair, about three days after he last washed it. Josh.

Her eyes lift and bend towards him rounding the corner, his eyes lifting also to hers, burning blue beyond a veil of hair that seems to have grown at rapid speed, down past his suit collar.

She must keep control of her senses, not alarm or alert her companions or his. Rapid thinking. How to extract him? How to get away fast, with Kyle too, but not cause a scene? She scans her body quickly, ensures she isn't setting fires with her fingers.

They must have walked ten steps. Josh will be calculating, too.

'I have to go to the toilet,' she says, standing. Kyle's burger is paused near his mouth. She attempts to speak with her eyes to him, but he just looks frazzled and hungry. An operative stands nearby, to trail her. One won't be hard to shake off, but she needs Kyle to come too. She starts to walk towards the bathroom, bouncing her eye off reflective surfaces so she can keep watching Josh. He has four personnel with him, not too bad.

Mila sees them pause, a woman in flowing pastels reading something on her phone: perhaps the message from Daisy about the meeting spot in London. The woman curses, her eyes calculating time, then she reluctantly taps the shoulder of a strong bald man beside her. Mila sees Josh attempt to butt in, reads the word 'toilet' on his lips as well.

The pastel woman looks for the toilets, her gaze turning towards Mila.

The woman tilts her head. Does she recognise Mila, even from the back?

Mila risks a glance back to the table – she needs Kyle.

He stands suddenly, in the middle of the food court, having spotted Josh.

And then, a roaring in Mila's ears, a plane's engine. Josh glares at the large glass wall beyond her, which looks out to the runways. People stand from tables, uncertainly, all around the food court. They follow one another's gazes towards the window. They begin to shout, point and run. Kyle darts his head back and forth – to Josh and Mila. Daisy and the operatives do, too.

The window shatters spectacularly as the nose of a Boeing 737 edges through. People scream. Mila ducks into a crouch, covering her face with her hands. When the glass stops falling, she turns to see the frightened faces of the pilots in the thankfully undamaged cockpit. The plane's engine stops; the plane stops, wedged in the food court window. Cold air flows into the space from outside. Mila feels it around every exposed hair on her body. It runs beneath the soles of her boots.

Across the hall, Josh collapses to the ground. The pastel woman crouches over him as the personnel on either side of him and the bald man run towards Cladion's operatives, tearing off the legs of chairs, smashing and grabbing shards of plant pots. The two sides clash as an alarm sounds and boots are heard coming in from the distance. There is only the smallest sliver of time.

Mila looks up to the cockpit, and the shaken pilots have left. She moves the cold molecules of air beneath and around her shoes to propel her forward in a swifter than normal run, but one that hopefully won't look unusual on any camera. When Kyle goes to follow her, she holds up a hand. It's too dangerous for him; he can't see these patterns in the air and the patches of heat and the smell of anticipatory fear. There are so many signals that she's not sure even she can navigate them.

She has one focus: Josh. Josh. Josh. Who is passed out. Exhausted, it seems, from the action with the plane. She can carry him, but she has to get to him. The operatives are focused on her now. She throws off thwacks, and she slices with quick liquid-muscle movements. She sidesteps, she ducks. She occasionally hits back, catches padding or flesh, and feels wrong for it. She has never worked on her strength for the sake of violence.

One of the Cosmic Dawn operatives falls, a young woman, and Mila is taken aback. Pauses, momentarily. And there's a sharp sting in her bicep. The pastel woman. A needle. Mila whacks it away. Too late. Her vision blurs and her muscles go leaden. She fights it. She clutches the edges of a table. Hears Kyle call mournfully for her from across the space. She blacks out.

Josh can't pull himself out of this warm, cosy unconsciousness. It is the red velvet colour of his childhood lounge room. That Brunswick house overfilled with dusty books and protest placards and cigarette smoke and bottles of cheap tempranillo. One of Mum's 'friends' in the kitchen, making a morning coffee for her. Josh would go and crawl into bed with her, and she'd read to him whatever he wanted. If the guy found it awkward she never stayed with him long. They had to love being around kids – Josh and his sisters, and kids of Mum's large friendship group, who were often camped out there too – or find another lover. Maggie, Josh and Cece were treated as equals, friends, but not so much that they missed out on parental comfort. Josh had a safe, loving childhood with an intelligent, warm and encouraging guide. His greatest privilege in life.

In his mind, now, he sits in that crowded lounge room with a throw knitted by his mum's friend Nita across his knees, immersed in the biography of Marlene Dietrich he has read over and over again. Leaving it lying around all the time when he was fourteen was the first way he came out to his family, to himself. Telling them he related to her, understood her.

'Oh my god, you are *obsessed*,' Cece would tease, firmly in her indie rock phase, always about the new and cool and alive and thinking Josh was such a weirdo for loving his black-and-white images and rusty-sounding recordings.

'Lili Marleen' floats into his head now, a heavy, weighted soundtrack warm as the blanket in the close, book-lined lounge room. But it's a sad song, isn't it? About distance and longing. 'Your sweet face seems … to haunt my dreams.'

Since that young age he knew he'd always sit with these feelings, incorporate them, always be feeling for someone, missing someone, distant from someone, but still, he knew, able to give love to who he was with.

Who is he with now?

He manages to swim up from the warm, red comfort. His body is twisted and cold. He tries not to make a noise. Squeak of wheels beneath him. He seems to be on a baggage trolley, Luna's pashmina draped over him, her jasmine smell potent. They are rushing – he mustn't have been out long. Still in the airport, moving with the crowd away from the food court, the scene of the accident. He peeps out. Security guards in a huddle running past, but too slow to see the fight? Only responding to the strange incident with the plane? Josh had blacked out the security cameras before he drew in the plane, so maybe puzzling about that has also kept them occupied.

Where is Mila? He reaches with his sense out into the air, cold metal cutting into his back, and finds the shape of someone else on another trolley. Inhales her scent. Goddamn fuck, he thinks. This is getting worse. He reaches out further, desperately, for the shape of Kyle. His senses are majorly dulled. He can't find him. *Please be safe.* Hopefully Kyle won't be pulled into giving some eyewitness account. Or Daisy, whom Josh saw in the food court and remembered from the trials. The thugs who were with Mila, Kyle and Daisy – most are out of action. Is that a good or bad thing? Should he be wishing they would follow? He tries to send the sunflowers to Mila, her familiar body curled up so near to him. She is too sedated to respond.

Had Cladion been holding her captive, too? Or had they been helping her and Kyle to find him?

He must think of the immediate. How to get them out of this. And where to go? How to hide?

Angled away from cameras, he is being lifted into the back of an SUV on the topmost level of the car park. He can see shapes, relative to open air, through his eyelids.

The chief adept only speaks to issue instructions. He tells the driver to go to the prearranged place. Josh senses Luna's heartbeat and sweat. Uncertainty.

They roll out onto the freeway towards the city.

Josh plays unconscious, like a spider.

The SUV pulls off the freeway and down. Josh pulls up his mental map – Kings Road, towards the south, the bay.

Kyle can't believe what he is about to do. But he also can't think of any other solution. After he hid under a table as everything unfolded in the food court, after he let Daisy do all the talking to the security guards, he has a lot to make up for. His friends have been trapped for two whole days and he is out in the world, and though they're the ones with the powers it is up to him, now.

As he exits his apartment, he closes the door gently so as not to wake Daisy. He took a huge risk with Daisy. He'd needed someone who'd consumed the *Xanthoria*. And he felt a bit bad about that, about using Daisy, but hey, they agreed because they wanted to know. They promised not to say a word to Lisa until after Kyle had followed his plan all the way through. But Kyle hadn't shared every aspect of it.

He arrives at the warehouse in Port Melbourne in an Uber. Daisy knew where to look because Lisa had called in some favours to track Mila's phone. Cladion are forming their own foolproof plan, apparently, for getting Mila and Josh away from the Cosmic Dawn. Kyle will get to them first. He still doesn't know if Lisa can be trusted.

There's a nasty Antarctic wind coming off the bay. He pushes the knot of his grey scarf in closer under his coat collar. It had been a present from Jeanie, Tassie merino wool. His heart races. He's not sure if he's shivering from cold or adrenaline. He takes a look around the quiet Sunday morning streets and out past whipping palm leaves to the grey-churned water. You could almost believe that the world has not been fundamentally altered, in recent years. During the darkest days of the pandemic, he thought a lot about times of earlier hardship and how people had suffered but also just 'got on' with things. Now he is at the periphery of another world-altering transformation, occurring in the bodies of two people inside. Looking out over the windy bay, you'd never know.

He walks up to the large rectangular structure and the two suited men who stand on either side of the door.

'I have come to give these people the information they seek,' he says. Is that the buzz of a drone he can hear overhead, as well? Probably Cladion's.

'And what is that?' one of the men says, smirking, looking him up and down.

'How to activate the lichen – achieve symbiosis,' he says, using some of the language he's heard the Cladion people use.

The door bursts open, and the woman from the airport stands in front of him. She wears a cream wool dress over light floral leggings with purple suede boots. 'Come in,' she says.

He takes one last look out over the water, then follows her through the door.

Mila has been alert enough and quick enough, this time, to catch the sedative in the layers of tissue and redistribute it into her sweat glands. But she is still exhausted, worn out from even that action. Maybe the smaller acts of power take more effort than she realises, or maybe it is again being indoors, though this is an airy warehouse, not brick or stone. She has definitely noticed some diminishing effect. She is thirsty and craving bread with butter and jam. Comfort food. And coffee, too.

The signals are not strong from Josh. He may be properly sedated over there on the far side of the warehouse floor. If she wasn't so frightened and fed up she would enjoy the smells in here – the barrels of whisky ageing in oak casks, stacked row upon row, all different expressions. It must be the storage warehouse for one of the Melbourne distilleries, and there's a bar and shop over by the door.

She sees the woman, who she now knows is called Luna, walk

quickly over to the warehouse front door and open it. And then she hears Kyle's voice.

What the hell? she thinks.

Has he gone and got himself caught, or come here willingly? She slits her eyes, tries to arc her senses closer to the entrance. He is speaking with Luna, showing her something on his phone. Mila strains to bend her hearing as much as she can. It's muffled, but it sounds like electronic music. Marimba. Tropical melodies.

Kyle says, 'MDMA is what he's talking about. He took it that night. And so did Mila the night before she showed the first signs.'

No, Mila thinks. She squeals and they both look towards her.

Kyle hasn't even secured their release before giving their captors the information. And now – these people will all have powers, along with anyone they choose to give them to, and Lisa's drone sits outside too, and will hear this, and she will have the powers as well. A cult and a billionaire will be the ones that can exploit the lichen.

Kyle, what have you done?

Luna comes up to Mila's cage – a separate, locked area of the warehouse floor for some of the older whiskies – and peers through the bars at her. 'Is it true? Did you have MDMA before you became fully-fledged?'

Mila frowns at Luna, closes her eyes.

'And I have some right here,' Kyle says, walking up behind Luna and holding up what looks like an old film container.

———

Josh, chained by hand and foot to some empty barrel racks, watches Kyle taking a cap first, chasing it down with a sip of single malt. He has only ever seen Kyle take a puff on a joint, giggle and then go to bed. Never any hard drugs. Luna and the chief adept follow.

It'll be a while before it kicks in. Josh puts his head on the rug beneath his body to snooze again, going back into the zone of velvet rich warmth, trying to work up his strength.

When he wakes, there is something wrong. He can't sense the world in micro quite the way he could before.

He remembers overhearing one of the conversations between his captors about the lichen dying off. Could it be dying off within him and Mila, too? Or, does the power have a limited store? An action as large as the one he performed in the airport may have drained much of his reserves, never to be replenished.

He thinks of one of the books that got him through the lockdowns, *The Myth of Sisyphus*, and he tries to go into a state of the absurd, in the Camusian sense – one where you can be happy rolling a boulder up a hill again and again. Here, looking at a friend through bars, can he find something of life even in this moment, a moment where all is upside down and chaos? Kyle *must* have a plan. Josh has to trust his friend.

He moves his consciousness through what now feels like an old body: to the air on the pads of his fingertips, the cold beneath the rug he is laid upon, coming up through his shoulder blades. The warm, wet blood moving through him. The sound of his own heart.

The chatting and giggling has begun.

'I can feel it,' says Luna. Which means she's probably still fifteen minutes off really coming up. 'We need some music.'

The chief adept goes to rummage behind the bar. He finds the amp and connects his phone via bluetooth. He takes a while to decide but then some horrible '90s pop starts synthing out of the speakers.

How incredibly awkward, thinks Josh. The drug will want to break down the power dynamic. And sure enough, they're starting to share happy stories of connections – friends, lovers, family. Luna and the chief keep touching each other, pressing their hands together.

'I just want to touch you for a moment, Kyle, too, if that's okay.' She leans forward and squeezes his hand. 'What a cold hand!'

'Is it?' Kyle says, beaming.

'Be careful,' the chief says. But it's uncertain what he means.

Luna lets go of Kyle's hand and curls back into the burly bald man. 'So this was the key the whole time,' she says.

'It's the only factor coinciding in both cases,' Kyle says.

Josh can't hear the drone anymore. He's not sure if that's just his super-hearing receding, though. Likely the others are back at the lab in the city getting high as fuck, too.

Trust, trust, trust.

'Let's go and talk to your friends,' the chief says, and gestures towards Josh on the floor. The three of them walk over, grinning. Josh now notices how alert the security guards are by the door: hands clasped, shoulders rigid, and moving in ever so slightly to the group.

'Maybe you can loosen this now?' Kyle says to the chief and Luna, crouching down and picking up the chain attached to Josh.

'You're right,' says Luna, crouching beside him. 'Just move this way a bit.' She pushes Kyle hard, and he loses his footing. He's sprawled on the ground as the security guards run in fast. They cable tie his hands around his back on a pole near Josh. He yelps.

Josh has been too slow, too sluggish.

He still trusts that Kyle had a plan but believes it's gone very wrong.

Mila moans with frustration from her cage.

Luna and the chief stand over Kyle. Luna says, 'Did you think we hadn't already tried drugs to activate it?'

'Oh,' Kyle says.

Josh is puzzled. But *isn't* that the trigger?

'Give it some time,' Kyle says, his voice soft.

'Well, we might have more now you're taken care of.' Luna giggles.

The chief's face is its usual stern, but there is some gumminess to it. They really did take the MDMA.

'No,' the chief says to her. 'The winds must blow us elsewhere. If the young man figured out where we are, Edwards will have too.' He jimmies his jaw.

'Oh yes, great one, of course.' Luna and the chief look into each other's eyes. The security guard behind Josh shifts uncomfortably on his feet. Luna looks at the guards. 'Let's think about how to transport them.'

'Will do,' the guard says.

Luna and the chief walk back to the area from which the terrible music plays. They begin to slowly throw items into bags and pockets.

Josh looks to Kyle and Kyle's huge pupils stare back at him. 'Bro,' he says.

'Mate.'

⁓

Mila watches the two security guards walk over, as a remix of Tears for Fears' 'Head Over Heels' starts up through the speakers. One of them is beefy and the other built like a boxer – lean and gristly. The boxer's suit has shiny iron-marks on the cheap material. She was thinking maybe they'd have to fight their way out of here, try to draw on those last reserves of energy, but the cheap suit gives her an idea.

She's silent as they open the cage, pull her arms behind her back and cable tie her.

'What are they paying you?' she whispers. Neither replies. 'We have access to a billionaire and superpowers.'

'You don't seem too super right now,' the boxer says.

She snaps the cable ties, stands with her hands on her hips. The guards look at each other.

'I won't hurt you,' she says.

'You're supposed to be sedated.'

'I stopped it from entering my bloodstream.'

The bigger man clears his throat uncomfortably. Luna, the boss man that she has worked out is Stephen, and others, are still in the bar area.

'Our billionaire will protect you, and pay you, if you help us suppress them and get out.'

She can smell the stale saltiness of the big man's sweat, and the boxer's cheap, sweet deodorant trapped beneath the polyester.

'How do we know we can trust you?' the boxer asks.

Stephen starts walking towards them, and Mila quickly puts her arms behind her back and lolls against the big guard, pretending to be tied and tranquilised. The man catches her, holds her roughly.

'We've got a truck coming,' Stephen says. 'Get them ready by the back door.'

The guard nods. He puts some fresh cable ties on Mila's arms. 'Go get the other two,' he says to the boxer. 'Let's get them down there.'

When they reach the truck-sized garage door at the back of the warehouse, Mila assures the big guard again that Lisa will reward him for helping them escape.

The boxer comes up behind them with Josh and Kyle. Mila nods at them both, wanting to smile, wanting to embrace her friends, but she has to concentrate. The guard's heart rate shoots up. He places two things in Mila's hand: a car key and a card. 'It's a grey Ford Falcon station wagon, parked around the side in the alley. It's my mum's, be careful with it.'

He hits a big green button on the door.

They hear both Luna and the chief from the other side of the warehouse: 'Hey!'

'Truck's not here yet,' the chief calls, starting to jog across the warehouse floor, down a row of barrels.

'Go,' the guard says, as the door has risen enough for them to roll under.

Mila snaps the tie off her wrists, leaps towards Kyle and snaps his, then realises Josh is fairly sedated and does his too.

'Under, under,' she yells, pushing them. 'Thank you,' she says to the guards. She holds up his card, to show she'll be in touch. She slips it in her pocket and rolls under the door like a whisky barrel.

The door starts to close again behind them, and they hear more shouting.

'We have to run,' she says. It's dark and the boys struggle and she half-drags them around to the alley and to the old dinted Falcon. 'Jump in.'

Kyle slides into the back and so Josh flops in the front. Mila starts the engine, turns on the headlights, and shoots down the alleyway and into the night.

Something between a sob and a moan erupts from the back seat. 'Oh god, I'm so sorry.'

Mila can't deal with Kyle and his mistake just yet. Here, finally, is Josh. She glances at him and he smiles at her and they reach out to hold hands. He is still wearing the suit they must have put him in for the plane. His hair is oily and down to his shoulders. Same clear blue eyes.

'It's going to be okay,' he says.

'Pfft,' she says.

'We need to go to the lab,' Kyle says. 'We'll need protection, once they come after us.'

'No way,' Mila says, looking in the rear-view mirror. 'What the hell were you thinking, anyway?'

'I ... thought I had such a solid plan. I thought it would work.'

'To just give them what you thought was the answer? Did you think you could get them high and negotiate for our release?'

'No, no.' He shakes his head emphatically. He chews his lip. 'Daisy helped me to test an idea. Cladion said the lichen had almost fully died off, and Mila, you mentioned how the waves seemed to be getting weaker. I told Daisy my theory that it was fading out in general but that, like, they might have powers otherwise, and so Daisy wanted to try and they got some MDMA and we got high.'

'And nothing happened,' Mila says.

'Yes,' he nods, 'Daisy has no powers. I waited another day to be sure. So I knew it wouldn't work for the Dawn – that either the lichen is fading and can't be activated anymore or that the drugs were never the answer as to how it got activated.'

Josh says, 'And it seems they're not. Luna said they'd already tried it.'

'But it was a huge risk, Kyle,' Mila says, frowning at him through the rear-view mirror.

'I had to do something.'

Mila sighs. 'You could have gotten hurt.'

They are all silent for a moment.

'Where are we going?' Kyle says.

'Somewhere we can find out for sure if these abilities are diminishing.' Mila floors the accelerator, as the first hint of blue peeks over the horizon. She reaches her senses out beyond the car. One drone, high up in the sky. She shifts the air around it, sending it into a tailspin, down towards the bay.

⁓

Mila pulls into the familiar driveway, her two friends snoozing despite the sun now being high. The eucalypts hang low over the car; a few branches can be seen among the long grass in the yard. It's been too long since she's been back to help. Kyle and Josh stir as she turns the tyres from the gravel driveway to concrete carport.

'My parents' place,' she says, smiling at their sleepy faces. Kyle looks pale and parched and Josh rested and refreshed.

Her dad comes out onto the veranda, shielding his eyes trying to see who it is. 'Hi Dad,' Mila says, waving as she gets out of the car.

'Mila! I didn't know you were coming.' He holds the handrail as he edges down the two small steps off the veranda. He's in comfy cargo pants and an old pilled jumper.

She runs to him and wraps him in a giant hug. He smells like childhood. And all her senses pick up again: the line of her genes, the alignment of the earth to the plants. Each singing gum leaf. Although there is a haze around it all, even in this open air.

'Who is it, Michael?' Her mum appears on the veranda.

'It's me, Mum,' Mila calls. And then the other car doors open. 'And my two friends, Kyle and Josh.'

Her mum comes down to her. Mila wraps her in her arms, too. Her mum is usually a little more physically reserved than her father, but she hugs back heartily. 'It's good to see you, darling.' She smells of woodsmoke, paper, a tea towel. Mila can sense all the days she's been gone.

'You're not drinking anymore, Mum,' she says.

Theresa looks startled. 'How did you know?'

Mila shrugs. 'Clear eyes?'

Her mum's face has speckles at the cheekbones, a sag at the jaw. Every frown and smile and secret howl painted on. Mila sees her mother almost as if for the first time. The beeping fax machine tones in the back of her mind. It had been her mum she'd wanted to talk to that night, as a child. Her mum she always wanted to come into her room after she'd had a nightmare, to soothe Mila with her small, soft hands in her hair. A mother's love – too overwhelming, too *wanted* that you convince yourself of the significance of the distances between you. Generational incongruities.

The beeping recedes. Her mother is old, and new. Too beautiful.

'So what are you doing here out of the blue?' Theresa asks. Bluntly, but not upset. She puts her hand on her hip. An old housedress over stockings.

Mila is taking a while to gather all the sensations. She wants to kiss her mum on the top of her fine white hair, though she knows it would startle her. 'Uh, it's a really long story. And don't worry, I'm okay.' She settles for smiling at both her parents reassuringly. 'We'd love coffee. And water.'

Kyle nods weakly. 'Thank you so much.'

'I'll help,' Josh says. 'Theresa,' he holds out his hand. 'And Michael,' he shakes his hand too. 'Thanks for having us.'

'We rarely get to meet Mila's friends these days,' Michael says. 'It's our pleasure.'

Mila's dad puts a hand on her shoulder as they step through the door. 'Chook,' he says warmly. She hugs him sideways.

She thinks about the bullet holes she noticed in the buildings in Europe, the stories in the sedimentary rock deep beneath their feet. The past in the present, even before these powers made it rush up inside her.

Once they've had coffee, water, and picked at some grapes, Mila shows Kyle and Josh a room they can crash in for a nap. They have told her parents only that Josh has been in some trouble, and they've been helping him get out of it, and needed somewhere they could make a plan. Mila borrowed her dad's laptop to message Kate, so she wouldn't be worried about her.

Josh stands at the window in the room, looking out over a wide yard leading down to tall grasses and bush. He understands the bellies of snakes as they slither, the beats of hawks' wings high above. But what matters to him most is the two people in here. In this three-square-metre space they exist, free, or free enough for now, and together.

'You rescued me,' he says to the two of them. He wants to draw them in. He wants to kiss them both.

But Mila is distracted. 'It is fading, isn't it?' she says to Josh.

He nods.

Kyle is reclined on the bed, fighting to stay awake. Mila sits next to him and strokes his hair. 'I'm still mad at you,' she says, but Josh detects no heat in her words. 'So I still can't tell where my mum's family is from exactly. But,' she squints, 'there's something very significant in the map in my mind, a long time spent in a freezing cold place. I think it's what they call epigenetic memory. It's awful.'

'Are you glad you understand something more?' Josh says.

She nods. 'There's so much, though, and all the other threads, all the lines. I feel like some you'd only *detect* precisely if you stood on the spot where your ancestors lived. But this one kind of clangs, in my mum.'

'It's important, then,' Josh says.

She nods again.

'But this is important, too.' He gestures to the space inside the small room.

'Where we are now. Who we are with. Yes.' And then she stands and holds him, finally. It feels like no time has passed, for a moment, the memory of togetherness strong in their bodies. Kyle snuffles next to them. He has fallen asleep.

'We'll use Kyle's phone to call your mum and sisters,' Mila says. They pull apart.

His heart wrenches. 'It's going to be overwhelming to hear the shock in their voices. I think I need just a bit more time to decide how much to tell them.' One of his earliest memories was of his mum receiving the phone call about his dad's accident. They were already divorced, and Josh had barely a memory of his father, but his mother's choked cries could never be wiped from his mind. 'I don't want them to be in danger, either.'

'Yeah, true. I killed that drone, so hopefully we won't be tracked down immediately.'

'And then what?'

She looks pensive, unknowing. 'Did I ever tell you about what happened when Scott and I broke up?'

He touches her hand. 'You wanted a baby.'

She sighs. 'I'm wondering ...' She looks past the wall, to where the morning news plays in the lounge room. 'If there are different ways you can express that ... desire to nurture.'

'You mean how you'll have to help out your parents more?'

She swallows and licks her lips, like she's struggling not to cry.

It's hard to know what to say. He clutches her hand. His only experience has been looking out for friends during tough times; he hasn't given children a thought at all, yet.

'Um,' he says, 'I guess the only thing I know is that, when you're like, looking after other people, you have to know how to fill your own reserves, too.'

She grips his hand harder. 'Yeah. With Scott, I didn't know I needed anything like that. I thought we were all each other needed. How come you know these things, anyway?'

Josh laughs. 'Therapy.'

'Oh.' She smiles. 'This was more of a "get on with it" household. Anyway,' she shifts her foot, 'I'm being self-absorbed.'

'Mila, you just *saved my life*.' He gathers himself, looks her in the eyes. 'Let us help; let other friends help – *tell* them to help; and I'm sure you'll find you can give whatever you need to give. And a baby might still be possible!'

He sees the flare in her: more terror than hope. Or terror in hoping. She shakes her head. 'Things change.'

'Understatement of the year.' He grins. 'Or decade.'

'There's something more I need to find out, before this fades completely,' she says, letting go of his hands, her gaze turning to the window.

He waits.

She lowers her head, sad. 'I already know we can't ... heal people.'

'Yes, I figured that out in London.' He tries to give her his most sympathetic look, rubs her arm.

'But there's something else I wonder. Will you come?'

'Of course.'

⁓

Mila finds the path. It's overgrown but still present. At least she and Josh will be able to detect snakes well before they accidentally step on any. Their shoes crunch on the grass, sticks and undergrowth as they walk down towards the creek. She can already hear the water trickling over rocks, and it moves with the water in her body. It's cool but there's humidity in the air: in her nostrils, ears, on her eyeballs, on her tongue. She's changed into a pair of her mum's tights and a jumper. Josh is in a pair of her dad's trackies and a long-sleeved shirt; they swim on him, but he looks cosy and cute. He's tied his grown hair back in a low ponytail, and he still wears the wooden stud she gave him.

Mila leads the way. They don't talk. There is enough to share in the air between them.

The trees are thick around the creek, and Mila finds the stepping stones where they can cross over. Small birds flit in the shade. They emerge from the dense trees to some bush on the other side, then follow a paddock on a rolling hill and duck under a fence to meet up again with the creek. The sun warms their backs; the dirt beneath the grass smells of excrement and death, which ultimately speaks of nutrients.

Eventually, they come to a denser forest: green shoots at the roots of blackened tree trunks.

'This is where the fires came to,' Mila says, turning to look at Josh.

'So close,' he says.

She nods.

She stares at the trees. She's scared. Scared it won't work, scared it will – just as they are losing their abilities.

Josh steps forward at the same time as her. 'This one.'

They each hold their hands to the blackened trunk. Sensations come to Mila: yellow-red hot. She counters them with cool blue. She picks up the moisture in the air. She channels it. But the tree merely gets a bit wet across its scars. They pull away.

'Hm,' Mila says.

'We can't heal, or reverse what's been done,' Josh says. He puts a hand to his chin, thinking. 'But we can ...' She watches him as he closes his eyes again. She feels him sucking moisture from the air, as it rushes by her pores, her hair follicles. And he moves his hands up and she follows with her gaze to the top of the tree. A small cloud. It breaks, and the new leaves are weighted with this hasty rain. Water slides in rivulets down the trunk. He puts his arms by his sides, smiles.

But she can't meet his grin. 'With only two of us ...' She is thinking of the collapsing polar vortex, the methane releasing from the arctic permafrost.

'Yeah.' His shoulders slump. His face is drawn even after that small effort.

'Better go get you a cup of tea,' she says, and reaches out her hand for his.

'I can think of something more restorative,' he says, and gently pulls her arm towards him. The birds and the water and rustling leaves and the bugs are loud around them. Faint sound of a helicopter. 'What do you think?'

She looks into his familiar eyes. His symmetry; his open want. She kisses him, deeply. Their arms snake around each other's bodies. The tree watches.

But then, as Josh is removing her shirt, Kyle's face comes into her head. There's a flush of softness in her, full-bodied.

Josh notices her hesitate. She doesn't know how to explain.

'I don't know if Kyle and I developed ... I mean, we never did anything, but ...'

He hugs her close, kisses her on the cheek in a more friendly way.

She holds back tears. She wishes she could return to those first times they were together – when fucking was almost a new experience. When she was shifting from one state of being to another. Well, maybe that's happening again, in a different way. And this hug. It's a strong and genuine hug. Bracing.

'We better work that out before we do anything,' Josh says. He pulls back.

'I'll always love you,' she says, surprising herself.

'I love you too,' he says easily.

⁓

Kyle wakes up, mid-afternoon. He gets out of bed and pulls on his jeans and shirt – smelling of frangipani and still warm from the dryer. He stretches and walks into the hallway. He can hear voices in the lounge room.

When he enters, he finds Michael and Theresa on one lounge, and Lisa Edwards, Meg, George and Daisy on the other. Daisy gives him an apologetic look. Mila and Josh are not in the room.

'Ah, Kyle,' Lisa says. 'Good to see you.'

He peers out the window to see a helicopter in the valley. How did he miss the sound of that? He doesn't want to alarm Mila's parents. 'And you,' he says casually.

Michael gives him a puzzled look. 'Ms Edwards here says she's been looking for Mila? She has something for her?'

Kyle is trying to remember the details of the lie they'd spun before. He's a bit fuzzy. Best not to say much.

'We can give it to her,' he says.

'We can wait,' Lisa says. She takes a sip from a cup of tea.

Michael starts to cough. Wet, sick coughs. Theresa says, 'Excuse us,' and helps him up. She moves him out of the room as he continues to hack up his lungs.

Lisa puts down her tea and stands. 'We only want to help,' she says to Kyle.

'It's true, Kyle,' Daisy says.

And then the front door opens, and Mila and Josh enter.

'Well, I guess this was inevitable,' Mila says. She turns her head towards the muffled sound of her dad coughing. 'How'd you find us so fast?'

'Emergency contact, from when you did the trial,' says Daisy.

'Oh.'

Kyle watches Mila's mind tick over.

They hear her dad coughing wetly again. It flips Kyle's heart inside out.

Mila walks towards Lisa. 'What if we refuse?'

Lisa stands from the couch. 'We'll pay you, both of you, and Kyle can have a job too, if he wants.' She doesn't look like the in-control, confident billionaire from TV.

'I don't want money,' Mila says. 'But I'll come with you, if you promise never to undercut any technology that could help people like my dad again, even if it's from a rival company.'

'Any tech that will help a respiratory illness?' Lisa asks.

'Any tech, or advance, that will help with *any* illness or condition. If you don't get there first, you will not offer to market some subpar alternative at a low price so that it floods the market. Never again.'

Lisa looks at her levelly. And then meets both Josh's and Kyle's eyes. 'I promise. I promise to support the advancement of technology to help people and withhold any cheaper, subpar product that is inadequate. Daisy, we'll need to draw up some kind of contract.'

'On it,' Daisy says, making a note.

'In exchange,' Lisa says, 'Mila, you – and Josh, if you agree – will allow us to do tests on you for an agreed period of time.'

Mila holds out her hand and Lisa shakes it.

'I'll just say goodbye,' Mila says.

Kyle watches her as she goes down the hall. Her dad's coughing has quietened down slowly. She is so strong, he thinks. Superpowered or not. She probably could have asked Lisa for anything. He remembers how Mila was worried about money in Europe, how she revealed that she'd wanted a child, how she didn't find her work perfectly fulfilling. Does she now feel she has everything she needs, now Josh is back in her life? Kyle understands that, in a way. Josh is his light, too. Well, both of them are, really.

And he has no role here anymore. He should probably just head home.

But on the way back through to the front door, Mila seeks his face. She has dried tears on her cheeks. She hooks her arm in his. 'Come on,' she says.

In the helicopter Mila tries to pull herself together. She doesn't understand the intensity of her reaction to the confirmation of the powers getting weaker. And of their general uselessness, in a practical sense. That she has no possibility of using them for good. It feels like grief, that old black hole. At first she hadn't wanted this, this enhancement – this secret, this responsibility. She should be relieved.

But now the dark night air, the bare trees white under the helicopter light, and the beating hearts of her friends are all becoming separate from her again. She wonders if it's similar to a secret kind of loss some people might experience after giving birth. That physical separation. For a brief time, she'd had tendrils, like her arteries extended beyond her skin. She saw and was heat and light. She heard the sounds beneath silence. She tasted distances. She shifted elementary particles with her mind. She was aware of the edges of herself as a puzzle piece that slotted seamlessly into a vast universe. She became less alone, and yet felt more understanding and accepting of the inevitable isolation of each body, each mind, on earth.

She thinks of Scott, too. Because this whole experience has, finally, helped her work through the pain and disappointment of their break-up – in that it forced her to realise there *was* pain to work through. And the lichen's expansion then allowed a softening within herself towards others, but a strengthening, too: an acknowledgement that every person is caught up in the chaotic propulsion of life. What this also means, she realises, is that every moment makes something new possible.

She tries to come out of her head, and to the hand in her hand – Josh's. And the hand on her shoulder – Kyle's. She can't look into their eyes, but she gives them each a squeeze back, letting them know she has returned, as the helicopter dips down over Melbourne.

They file into a car and take the short drive to the lab.

Mila does not want to be here, to deal with Lisa Edwards. She wants to go home, or go to Kyle and Josh's place, and debrief, and feel cosy and safe and … well, come down. Watch *The Simpsons* or something.

They enter the training arena. 'We have to tell you something,' Mila says.

'We already know it's not the MDMA,' Meg says.

'Huh,' Josh says.

'Vodka first.' Lisa heads to the kitchen in the corner of the training area, with its fridge full of protein shake ingredients and bliss balls. She comes out with a bottle of Ketel One and a stack of smoothie cups. 'This is all we have,' she says with a shrug. She gives everyone a cup and pours them out. 'To knowing our limits.'

Mila looks her in the eye. 'You did the drugs?'

Lisa shrugs. 'Willing to try anything.'

Josh parks himself on a training mat, sips from his cup. He speaks up to them. 'We genuinely don't know why it worked for us. And —'

'I know what you're going to say,' Lisa says.

'You do?' Mila says.

Lisa nods. 'It's like my dad's friend, Rick. For some reason, it wears off.'

And so Mila and Josh and Kyle raise their cups and clink them dully and drink down some vodka.

Meg pauses with her cup in front of her lip. 'Wait, what?'

'Sorry for the bad news, Meg,' Josh says.

'Let's go check on the *Xanthoria*,' Lisa says, walking to the door. They walk out of the arena, down a corridor and into the greenhouse area where the lichen is kept in the glass cells. Meg and George mumble questions behind them.

'Don't get me wrong,' Lisa says as she opens the door, 'I enjoyed getting high just to check. But my father wasn't much into dance parties, so I'm not sure it was a part of his life.' She stops in front of the brown *Xanthoria* covering a slab of concrete. 'And I have also been wilfully ignoring the idea that if it's been steadily dying off, its manifestation might die off too.'

Around them are the small glass rooms of depleted, flaky circles of lichen.

Mila holds the cup out for more vodka. She's still containing that sadness. Being in this space makes it worse.

Mila says, 'Kyle figured it out. He's been around me the whole time and he clicked that I'd mentioned a diminishing effect. It's still there, but it's fading.' Her voice chokes a little. 'And my parents' house – it gave us somewhere we could properly check.'

'I thought you would be happy with that,' Lisa says. 'Happier than me, anyway. I never got the chance to feel what it was like.' She sips from her smoothie cup.

Meg stares into the rooms, contemplating. 'Well, fuck.'

'It's complicated,' Mila says.

'And you?' Lisa asks Josh.

'Yeah, I'll miss it,' he says. 'But then I never got to truly … expand into it, either. I was being held captive almost the whole time.'

'We didn't know, you know?' Meg says. 'We didn't know it had worked. That you two were out there …' She gestures at the lichen as though out there were in here.

'It doesn't matter anymore,' Josh says, putting a hand on Meg's arm. Mila smiles at his compassion and forgiveness; she's glad he seems to be the same old Josh, though she knows he must be experiencing a similar grief to hers.

'We do need to hide out here for a bit,' says Mila. 'The Dawn might still come for us.'

Lisa nods. 'Yes, we owe you. And I can handle Stephen now, don't worry. I didn't move in earlier because I didn't want to endanger you.'

'You wanted to get high first,' Kyle says, frowning.

'Only so we could match their strength if it worked,' Lisa says.

They walk among the glass lichen houses for a moment, in what Mila thinks is a kind of goodbye.

She enters one of the enclosures. It smells damp like a cellar, like the shower in a mouldy share house she once lived in. She thinks about the night her *Xanthoria* abilities came on for her. About Kyle, nervous and out of place. The girl she danced with. The open air area on the roof where she came up. The sweat on her body. She gets a song in her head. Deep house beat. Tropical melody. She nods along to it. There's a surge through her body, a golden flow. She feels the sparks at her fingertips again, momentarily. She instinctively reaches out and peels back a section of lichen and tucks it in an upper jacket pocket, near her heart.

The music, and the feeling, recedes again. She turns around and is glad to see only Josh had been looking at her. She gives a secret smile.

Three months later

MILA ARRIVES HOME to her apartment after her fourth
client of the day – she's been packing them in, to
recoup income – and she's tired, but she's excited, too.
The boys (as she thinks of Kyle and Josh) are coming over tonight
to hang out before they all go together to her parents' place for the
weekend. Kate is coming, too – bringing little Ty. Mila talked to
her parents this morning, and they were looking forward to seeing
them all.

Mila realised recently that she can be sad about her parents not
being well but she can also just do this. Just show up regularly and
talk with them and have a glass of wine and a laugh and muck in a
bit, and this lifts them, distracts them. It's finally sunk in that she
can ask for help, from the boys, from Kate. That she doesn't have
to be alone. And that is a power she didn't realise she had, because
she'd been holding on to loss and had been somewhat clueless
about the wealth of reciprocal love on offer.

As she gets to her front door she sees someone waiting outside.
It's the journalist from the alley: Saira Foley.

'What are you doing here?' Mila says.

'Mila, please, I need you to go on the record. You know what
I wrote is true.'

Mila has seen the article. She knows it's true, or at least, parts of it. But it's been dismissed, of course, as far-fetched and fanciful. Saira hasn't been able to get it published anywhere mainstream, so it's been buried in a back corner of the internet. Mila feels sorry for her, but she has other people to protect, so she can't say anything.

'I need you to leave,' Mila says, pausing with her key in the door.

'Cosmic Dawn, in London, you know, they told me a lot about Cladion. But what were the effects of the experiment? I know there's more to it. They hinted at … abilities?'

'Why don't you go write about climate change or social inequality? Why do you care so much about this, anyway?'

Saira frowns. 'I do care about that stuff, you know. If companies are experimenting on people with new substances it could affect the world in all kinds of ways …'

Mila purses her lips. Saira is annoying, sure, but Mila has had the same exact thoughts. Why hadn't there been more regulation? How often do these kinds of experiments happen? How much power do billionaires have? Still, she can't tell her. But these are all things she has to consider herself, given her role and responsibility going forward.

'I'm really sorry,' she says, hoping she sounds genuine. She opens and closes the door.

The boys will be here in an hour.

She will make them dinner, hear about their work, Kyle's cat, what they've been reading and watching. She'll get the inside goss on Cladion now that Kyle is working there as a sustainability consultant. They'll go over everything from this year, as they always do, before they have to push it down again to be around people who can't know the details. They'll drink a little, flirt with each other. She and Josh haven't gone back to bed together yet; she knows they're all wondering what relationships are possible between and among them without anyone getting hurt. Josh and Kyle have been friends with each other longer than she's known either of them. She's surprised that she's kind of happy with however it plays out. Josh would always have other lovers. Kyle would be, as he has been through all of this, a steady mast in a storm. Her Robin. And she's feeling more comfortable in the understanding that she might also have more to explore about her own sexuality.

What she has with them is intimacy, and she wonders if Kate was right about her all that time ago, before she went to meet Josh. That it is intimacy that is important to her. When a drink helps her open up; when she feels her parent respond to what she has said; and the deep satisfaction of eye contact, skin contact with a lover or friend. Even when she walked into that church in Berlin – it was not a transcendent awe that she felt, it was a hushed feeling of *closeness* to something beyond herself. Maybe, for her, the sublime and the intimate are the same.

The only reason to continue to pursue the lichen's power is its ability to enhance this intimacy with the world.

She puts her groceries on the bench and goes straight into the bathroom.

'How are you today?' she says to the two circles of *Xanthoria* flourishing atop a large craggy stone that sits in the bath. By the bath is a speaker emitting a deep, low beat, sometimes a tropical melody. The lichen has turned from brown flakes into tiny sunshine orange cups that point in the direction of the speaker.

There's a knock on the door and Mila turns up the song before going to let in Kyle and Josh.

Acknowledgements

I acknowledge the Boonwurrung/Bunurong and Wurundjeri Woi Wurrung peoples of the Kulin Nation, and those of the Gumbaynggirr Nation, as the Traditional Owners and Custodians of the lands on which this book was written.

I must acknowledge the great influence of my dad, Phil, who sadly died while I was writing this book. I was able to spend time with him in his final months, weeks and days, and it was certainly one of the hardest but also one of the richest, most intimate and special times of my life. I am so lucky to have been close to my dad, and to have a dad who was open, honest, encouraging, funny, proud, and hugely affectionate. On one ride in the ambulance with him down the mountain to the hospital in those last months I could hear him in the back of the ambulance spruiking my previous novel to the young ambo. He thought any time was the right time to be proud of his kids. I miss him every day and I'm grateful for the years I had with him and his influence in my life.

My other family members, my mum, Karen, and my sister, Sonja, are parts of my soul. They have been there through the whole process of writing this novel, the difficult events of the past few years, and of course have made me the person I am today.

Sonja, thank you too for being one of my early readers, and some-one who has always helped me be more open to the world. Thanks also to you and Caity for the fun we've had and great projects we've worked on together. To Ez, Jess, Hailey and Sophie, I'm so grateful to have you in my life.

My partner, Christopher, has held me together in more ways than I could ever express. Chris, thank you for being such a sharp early reader, for helping me stay strong, making me laugh, and for taking every step of this journey with me. I became more myself when we fell in love. I'm so excited about our future.

Donna, you care about the beauty of words, stories, and their ability to explore and express experience. You push me, and you also nurture me, and I am grateful. Josephine, my respect and love for you are both enormous and I'm so lucky that you read my work and that we share so much. Gerard, you are so generous and your insight is always spot on, and I treasure the complexity, richness and affection of our history and friendship. Emma, your feedback buoyed me and helped me to know I could keep going. You're a beautiful friend and I'm grateful for our conversations. LJ, while you weren't an early reader of this one, the work we've done together and the deep conversations about writing we've had have inspired me so much in the past few years, thank you. Daisy in this book is a tribute to Alison Evans' novel *Ida*. Alison, I'm so lucky to know you and to have worked with you; you are golden.

To Kate Goldsworthy, one of the best editors in Australian publishing, and a superior human being – thank you for your patience, your diligence, your understanding, and the memes.

To Martin Shaw, my agent and friend, you are such a genuine person and also a rare, uncorrupted force in the book industry. Thanks for enjoying and supporting the stories I'm driven to write.

To Barry Scott, at Transit Lounge, what an enormous privilege it is to be on your list, after having enjoyed the books you've published for so long. Thank you for understanding this book and publishing it.

To Josh Durham, for another ridiculously cool cover. You're the best in the biz.

I have been fortunate enough to visit the wonderful cities in this book, and much of what's in here comes from memory, journals and impressions, but I would also like to acknowledge the following books as inspiration while writing or beforehand: *Magic Prague* by Angelo Maria Ripellino, *The Golden Maze* by Richard Fidler, *Persuasions of the Witch's Craft: Ritual Magic in Contemporary England* by T.M. Luhrmann, *The Berlin Wall* by Frederick Taylor, *Berlin Stories* by Christopher Isherwood, *Journey by Moonlight* by Antal Szerb, *Dietrich: A Biography* by Ean Wood, and work by Fernando Pessoa, Iris Murdoch, Elena Ferrante, my lifelong inspiration Franz Kafka, and others mentioned within. There are also many lowbrow inspirations, and I thank the storytellers whose magical works had me spellbound (mostly through streaming services) through the hard times.

I would also like to acknowledge Climate Reality. I'm grateful to have done the Climate Reality leadership training during Melbourne's last long lockdown in 2021. This training helped me overcome some of my shyness in educating myself and becoming more active on the climate issue. Since then, I've started working with groups in the book industry on how the industry can become more sustainable. I will keep my website updated with links for those interested: literaryminded.com.au.

Praise for *A Superior Spectre*

Shorlisted: MUD Literary Prize for a literary debut novel

Shortlisted: Australian Book Industry Award,
Best Adult Book from a Small Press

Shortlisted: Aurealis Award for Best Science Fiction Novel

Shortlisted: Readings Prize for New Australian Fiction

Shortlisted: Saltire Society Literary Awards First Book Award

'A book you'll read in a thrilling rush and then think about
for months' – Emily Maguire

'This is one of those rare books that penetrates deep into the
reader's most secret self. Read it and hold it close.'
– *The Saturday Paper*

'[A] hugely impressive debut novel: imaginative and original,
erotic and a little bit magical.' – *The Herald Scotland*

'This exquisite novel invites the reader to face the ghosts
that haunt the dark corridors of the mind.'
– Justine Hyde, *Kill Your Darlings*

'Unique, rich and incredibly sensual… Clever, convincing
and unputdownable…' – Karen Brooks

'If you care about the future of Australian fiction,
look no further.' – Readings

'Weighty themes of lust, shame and the power of the male gaze
are beautifully balanced by a moving narrative…'
– *The Daily Mail* (UK)

'*A Superior Spectre* [provides] an opportunity to acknowledge what reading does to us and for us.' – Craig Hildebrand

'Put simply, this book is superb.' – Helen Valentina

'A wild and risky novel, artfully darting between two people separated by centuries and connected by ... you'll see.'
– Steven Amsterdam

'A beautiful and troubling novel that subtly explores how the past haunts the present.' – Ceridwen Dovey

'This is a book about the blurring of lines: of social and class-based gendered demarcations; of the base expression of the flesh and of the higher aspirations of the mind; of sci-fi and reality.'
– *Sydney Morning Herald/The Age*

'In this meta-possession, we are all complicit.' – *The Australian*

'Meyer's full-length debut is a brilliant, deeply unsettling work with the unapologetically feminist rage, passion and awareness of books such as *The Natural Way of Things* or Margaret Atwood's seminal *The Handmaid's Tale*. Meyer is bold and unafraid in her words, immersing the reader in a vividly imagined and realised world that meets questions of bodily autonomy, madness and disgust head on.' – *Books+Publishing*

'Skillfully manages to weave historical drama and dystopian fiction together ... a work of ambition ... clever, intelligent and engrossing.' – *Image Magazine*

Angela Meyer (she/her) is an award-winning writer and editor. Her debut novel, *A Superior Spectre* (Ventura/Saraband), was shortlisted for an Aurealis Award, the MUD Literary Prize, an Australian Book Industry Award, the Readings Prize for New Australian Writing and a Saltire Literary Society Award (Scotland). She is also the author of a novella, *Joan Smokes*, which won the inaugural Mslexia Novella Award (UK), and a book of flash fiction, *Captives*. Her work has been widely published in magazines, journals and newspapers, including *Island*, *The Big Issue*, *Best Australian Stories* and *Kill Your Darlings*. She has worked in bookstores, as a book reviewer, in a whisky bar, as a commissioning editor and publisher, a teacher of writing and publishing, and a freelance editor and consultant. She grew up in Northern NSW and lives in Melbourne, Australia.

literaryminded.com.au / @literaryminded